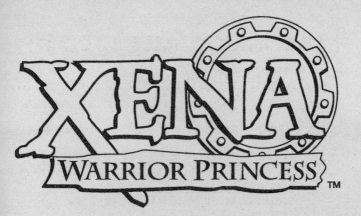

THE HUNTRESS
AND THE
SPHINX

Ru Emerson

BOULEVARD BOOKS, NEW YORK

XENA: WARRIOR PRINCESS: THE HUNTRESS AND THE SPHINX

A novel by Ru Emerson. Based on the Universal television series XENA: WARRIOR PRINCESS, created by John Schulian and Robert Tapert.

A Boulevard Book / published by arrangement with
MCA Publishing Rights, a division of MCA, Inc.

PRINTING HISTORY
Boulevard edition / January 1997

The Putnam Berkley World Wide Web site address is
http://www.berkley.com/berkley

Make sure to check out *PB Plug*, the science fiction/fantasy newsletter, at
http://www.pbplug.com

ISBN: 1-57297-215-7

BOULEVARD
Boulevard Books are published by The Berkley Publishing Group,
200 Madison Avenue, New York, New York 10016.
BOULEVARD and its logo are trademarks
belonging to Berkley Publishing Corporation.

PRINTED IN THE UNITED STATES OF AMERICA

10 9 8 7 6 5 4 3 2 1

For Doug (of course)
For anyone who finds himself or herself in Nausicaa—
or Atalanta.
Or Homer.
It's a long journey.

Acknowledgments

First, I'd like to thank Renaissance Pictures in association with MCA TV for coming up with a show like *Xena: Warrior Princess*. I've been waiting all my television-watching years for a show like this (especially after the Emma Peel-era *Avengers* was canceled).

Second, the riddles in this novel were submitted by a number of fellow fans of the show. I would personally like to thank the winners of the Sphinx riddle contest:

Stephanie Reader
Emily Cross
Kristen Tuey
Kevin Wald
(whose Trojan War riddle ends the battle)

Your riddles gave me not only text and words to add bulk to the novel, but also, in all cases, an idea, a point, something to think about that sent the book in directions even I didn't expect. Again, thank you.

The AOL and extended network of fans of the show are more generous to a writer of prose than I ever dared expect. I'm honored to be part of you.

Finally, thanks to Xena herself. As a kid who grew up in a world where June Cleaver was the female exemplar, a kid whose role model was her Errol Flynn look-alike dad—I am the amalgam both produced. What can I say? It's great!

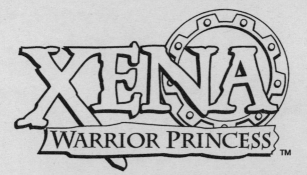

THE HUNTRESS
AND THE
SPHINX

1

"Gab-*Gabrielle!*" Xena's ferocious bellow cut the air of a narrow dirt street lined with trees, small houses, smaller businesses. People stared: too many of them. Athens had grown in the past year. Gabrielle, already halfway across the dusty, broad square, turned and blinked at her mounted companion as if uncertain who she was. Xena cast her gaze briefly skyward and tried to keep rising irritation from her voice. Not very successfully. "Gabrielle, we're lost."

Gabrielle laughed and shook her head so hard that her hair—pulled back in a severe, sensible blonde plait that went well with her simple Amazon boots, brown skirt, and short bodice—flopped wildly across her shoulders. She shoved it aside impatiently. The laugh had been edgy; the smile that replaced it was tight, and her eyes were stormy. "We are *not* lost! I—look, Athens is surrounded by sea on three sides, how lost can you get? And—" She turned, waved her staff at the sparsely leafed trees lining the dusty avenue. "See the length of those shadows! It's getting late, we'll miss the—miss the—" She shook her head again, cast up her eyes, and plunged off down the boulevard.

1

Xena swore between clenched teeth. "Lot of inhabited, hilly *land* between us and the goddess-blasted sea." She stood tall in the saddle and looked all around her: A baker's. A potter's. Someone who dried herbs and sold them in tiny, fancy, beribboned (and doubtless expensive) bundles. Two bored-looking young girls sat behind a trestle table piled high with the decorative bundles, rings of dried flowers crowning their hair. Three houses had been built since the last time she'd come this way—including one with a small fountain set inside the portico.

Ostentatious display of wealth, and plenty of pointless bits of material possessions on which to spend it. "Good thing we left Lemnos with Queen Persephone," Xena mumbled, a grin quirking the corners of her mouth. The little cook would be enraged by the gulfs she'd already seen this morning between the haves and the have-nots.

"Ah." Her eyes fixed on the street's eyesore, an old-fashioned, full-service stable—probably a good one when this part of Athens was new. Now it seemed to be nothing more than two elderly buildings, roughly connected by a thatched roof over a dirt walkway, around which the rapidly encroaching city had swollen. A year from now, it would likely be gone—she couldn't imagine the seller of herb bundles or the owner of that fancy little fountain appreciating the aroma of horse with their afternoon wine.

A squat, dirty boy limped out of the shadows, leading a wet, tired-looking horse. Xena slid from the saddle and tugged at Argo's bridle. He ambled along behind her, then gently veered toward the long, moss-covered stone trough that jutted into the street.

At least one of us is calm, Xena thought wryly as she patted her four-legged companion. There wasn't anything as maddening as an obviously lost person who wouldn't take the moment required to simply stop and ask directions, thereby saving hours or days of pointless wandering. *The only thing more maddening to Gabrielle: me finding someone besides her to ask.*

The boy leading the horse gave no sign he'd seen her— deaf or gods-touched, perhaps. But as she cleared her throat, an extremely grubby, middle-aged man clad in disreputable leathers came up the walkway. He blinked as his eyes took in all of her: long, well-muscled legs and arms, fighting leathers, and a variety of weaponry, her figure enhanced rather than hidden by the cut of her garb. ''Ah—'' He swallowed, then licked his lips as she stepped toward him. ''Ah, your horse needs tending?''

''No, thank you. I need directions.''

''Oh. Lost, eh?''

Her mouth twisted, and her expression was sardonic. ''If I weren't lost, would I need directions? Women's foot races—where?''

''Races—uh, mmm. Well, of course, I can get you there from here, no one better than old Argo.'' She blinked; he glanced at her and grinned broadly, exposing surprisingly neat teeth. ''Means gold, y'know. My poor pop thought his boy'd benefit from such a name—poor old fool. Now, let's see—'' *One of those,* she thought sourly. *Talk your leg off.* But they'd still get where they were going faster, in the long run. Barely. ''Now, well, of course, you must know Olympics aren't happening for—''

''No. *Women's* races, I said,'' she put in sharply. She turned to keep an eye on Gabrielle, who was well down the narrow dirt avenue. The man's eyes followed her gaze; he laughed shortly and without much humor.

''You don't want to let her get far down there,'' he observed, his voice and words suddenly crisp and to the point. ''Bad area, especially since so many men've come home from the war for that hussy Helen.'' Something about her

3

sudden stillness warned him: he gave her another flash of disconcertingly even, white teeth. ''Your little girl's going the wrong direction, anyway.''

He turned, then pointed the other way. ''Go there, a matter of—oh, fifteen cross streets, 'til there's an olive missing all the branches on the street side. King's guard thought 'em a nuisance, all the traffic these days. At the olive tree, take yourself a south. Go another four cross streets, where Tom the Tinsmith has a stall, ugliest building and the largest wife you'll ever see.''

That would take some, Xena thought, an amused grin quirking the corners of her mouth. *After all, I've met Isyphus.* She brought her attention back to the little stable hand. Argo, oddly enough. Her own Argo had slaked his thirst and was lipping the brass on her near shoulder—after the salt, seemingly. ''Now, make an east at Tom's, and go 'til you hit the water,'' the man went on earnestly. ''Ah, that's a matter of, say, two big squares, a statue of Athena, a fountain to the war dead from back when Sparta and Athens went at it—hideous thing it is, too, flowers and harps and . . . Anyway, you'll know it! Then go south once more, through the wine merchants' market; it's just past that. Watch your purse in the wine merchants' market; there are cutpurses everywhere and not half enough guards to stop 'em.''

''I'm not too worried.''

He grinned and laughed heartily, blasting her with breath that was mostly garlic, and a little bad mead. ''You don't look it. You proof to quick fingers as well as swords? Just a warning.'' He looked beyond her. ''Better go after the little girl, she'll get away from you.''

''Good point.'' Gabrielle apparently hadn't yet realized she was alone down there. And the little man had said it wasn't a good area. *Typical.* Xena tossed him a copper and

4

a grin of thanks as she leaped onto Argo's back, turned the horse, and urged him forward.

Gabrielle glanced over her shoulder; there was no sign of Xena anywhere. "*Now* where did she—Well, she'll just have to catch up," she muttered under her breath. "We've already missed the early prelims, I know we have. But—"

"Awww, isn't that *cute!*" A gravelly male voice off to her right rang out. Someone else laughed unpleasantly, and an inebriated-sounding woman tittered. Gabrielle tightened her grip on the staff and spun around. The neighborhood had deteriorated since she'd last paid much attention to the buildings around her, going rapidly downhill from new stucco and fine carvings, or neatly smoothed stone, to ugly little shacks of warped and rotting wood, and teetering piles of stone obviously dragged from ancient ruins. Just in front of her, the building was made of woven sticks and, by the smell of things, it was the kind of tavern where the strength of the drink counted for more than the taste. The sour odor of bad wine mixed with that of unwashed men, an un-cleaned pig sty or sheep pen, something rotting nearby—and wine that had come back up again—nearly cost her her own breakfast.

It took her a moment to make out the two men lounging at a table well within the shadow of the overhanging roof, and the skinny, wild-haired woman leaning over the shoulder of a third man not far away.

Great. Comedians. All they need is the masks with the big goofy smiles, and a ridiculous play about frogs—or maybe mosquitos. Men like that—men who drawled insults at women—deserved a lesson in manners. *I can ignore them, but if I do, they think they got away with something. Then they get worse. . . .* Manners—right. But she could al-most hear Xena overriding such a thought. *Yeah, Gabrielle, three of 'em you can see, goddess knows how many others inside the inn. Ignore them*, she decided, but she could feel the heat of anger in her face as she turned away.

"Woooooo. *Really* cute," the second man responded; his words were slurred; drunk already or drunk still. Probably couldn't even get to his feet. So, no threat—well, not much. It wouldn't look at all heroic, but she could no doubt outrun anything in that tavern.

She kept walking, her jaw set. "Hey, darlin', where you goin' so fast?" the first man yelled after her in his grating voice. She took two more paces, then spun around as heavy steps pounded up behind her. The staff was already up and out. The lout grinned, revealing bad teeth, then spread his hands wide as if to indicate he was no threat, unarmed. "Asked you a question, ya know. Don't like rude women. Too good for the rest of us, are you?"

"Just going," Gabrielle said evenly, a nervous little smile spoiling the chill effect she wanted. She shifted her grip slightly on the staff, then began moving the ends in small circles, preliminary to a strike. He eyed her in disbelief, glanced at the staff with sudden caution, and took a short pace back. "You got any problem with that?" she added sharply.

"My friend said he don't like rude women," came a deep voice at her left shoulder—this one not inebriated at all. Gabrielle jumped, then risked a quick glance that way as she sidestepped to bring the owner of this new voice into view without losing sight of her first problem. This one had the look of a mean drunk—a *big* mean drunk, she thought as her eyes went up . . . and up. Worse yet, if he'd swallowed enough bad wine to slow him down, it didn't show. "*I* don't like Amazons," he added shortly, and swiped at her staff with an enormous hand. He was slower than he thought, fortunately; she had the weapon out of his reach

6

without much trouble. "Hey, Agridon," he shouted tauntingly toward the ramshackle tavern, "you're drunk! What'dya think you're gonna do with this bit of yellow-haired fluff?" Gabrielle bit back a nasty comment as a third man staggered into view.

"Awww," he mumbled. "She *is* cute. Here, shweetie, gi' Agri—Agi—give us a smooch, eh?" He lurched between his friends, arms spread wide and lips puckered. The end of the staff caught him under the chin with a sharp click, his eyes rolled back, and he went down in a boneless heap. She took another step back, sent her eyes toward the brute at her left, then the gravelly-voiced man, who was staring glassy-eyed at his unconscious companion. *Less problem than the monster,* she decided, and aimed a jab at his stomach. But he was already backing away, hands high.

"C'mon, Hadros," he mumbled, "help me with Agridon, will you?" The enormous Hadros shook himself, then glared down at Gabrielle and the staff that was once again weaving a controlled pattern just short of his elbow. *Oops. Not going for it,* she thought, and lowered into a ready crouch, but all at once he backed off with exaggerated caution. The gravelly-voiced man moved in a sideways half-circle, well away from her, grunting as he bent down to grab the moaning Agridon by his collar. Hadros snagged Agridon's nearer arm and yanked. Agridon began yelling wordlessly as they bumped him across the dusty street; his cries could be heard long after they had vanished in the gloom of the tavern.

As she watched them go, Gabrielle managed a smug smile in spite of trembling knees, then squared her shoulders and brought her chin up. *Well! Guess I do okay by myself!*

"You'd do better if you kept an eye on what's behind you once in a while," came a low, hard voice at her ear.

She yelped and spun around. Xena stood right behind her, arms folded, her lips twisted in an expression of extreme irritation. Gabrielle swore an oath that raised her companion's eyebrows, then slammed the end of her staff into the road; dust billowed around her feet.

"Don't tell me, let me guess—they saw *you* and that's why they backed off, right?" The warrior shrugged broadly. "You have any idea how—how maddening that is?"

"You have any idea how maddening it is for me to lose sight of you and then find you in the middle of a mess like this could've become? Come on," she added flatly, "you're the one who's in a hurry, and this is the wrong direction." She gave a tug on Argo's rein and headed back toward the square. Gabrielle's shoulders slumped, and she sighed heavily. With one smoldering glance toward the interior of the now silent and deserted-looking tavern, she turned and caught up with her companion.

Silence for a long moment. They reached the square, turned and walked past the stable, then down the street, which gradually widened. Gabrielle sighed again, cleared her throat, and eyed the warrior nervously. "Look, I'm sorry!" She didn't sound it; Xena gave her a quick glance and laid a hand on her shoulder, silencing her.

"Don't be sorry, that's not useful. Especially not if you get hurt or killed. Just be more careful, and a little more aware of what's around you. *All* around you. All right?"

"All right." Xena wasn't really mad at her, then; more likely worried and sharp-sounding because of it. *Sometime,* Gabrielle told herself flatly, *you really will make her that angry, and what then?* Xena wouldn't just leave her behind. Gabrielle swallowed against a very dry throat. She didn't think Xena would do that. It took her two tries to get the words out. "Honestly, I do try—"

Xena glanced in her direction, then turned her attention back to the increasingly busy street and the people pushing past them. Her face was still expressionless, but her voice wasn't as clipped-sounding. "I know you do."

"It's just—no one takes me seriously! They call me 'little girl' and—and 'cute.' " Her nose wrinkled with distaste. "They *laugh* at me! And it just—I just—"

"I take you seriously, Gabrielle." Xena glanced at her. "But remember what I told you: sometimes it's handy not being seen for what you really are. Especially against odds like you were facing there: three men, one of them that big. You catch them off balance, just the way you did, it makes the odds more in your favor. Only one thing you do differently: next time, don't forget someone could sneak up behind you."

"Like you did. Sure." She sighed quietly. "It's nice of you not to remind me I shouldn't have gone down there at all. I was just—just—"

"I know you were," Xena said evenly. She glanced across Argo's shoulder, then gave her companion a smile. "Gabrielle, I know this means a lot to you. But you can't save time by wasting it."

Gabrielle brightened. "That sounds almost like a riddle! Now, wait, let me think . . ."

"*No* riddles," Xena said firmly, but her lips twitched with amusement. Gabrielle had taken to riddles as hard as any other of her sudden passions—even more so, probably, since this passion was literate. A bard thing.

The girl was smiling, her arms spread wide. "Aw, Xena! Just because you couldn't guess any of mine!"

"I can't guess the answers to anybody's riddles," Xena replied. "I don't like them; I never liked riddles. I have better things to do with my time."

"Well, but—you could get them, I know you could, if

9

you'd just pay attention and then think about them before you come up with an answer. They're really a lot of fun.''

"For you. Save them for someone who likes them," Xena said very firmly. And before Gabrielle could add anything else, she indicated a small building with her chin; a hideous clatter of metal and hammering came from the interior, and just outside, on a shaded bench, sat a mountain of a woman carefully stringing tin pots and cups on a length of rope. "We turn here—that way."

"Gosh," Gabrielle said very quietly after they'd left the tinsmith's behind. "Did you *see* her? She'd make Isyphus look small!"

"Mmmm." In the first large square, a soldier in the king's colors was chasing two beggars away from the statue of Athena. Gabrielle was quiet, visibly trying to keep an eye on everything around them. Xena cast her a sidelong glance as they left the square, and lengthened her stride. The girl was almost vibrating with her need to be *there*. Right *now*. "We're close," she said as they came into the second square. The old stableman was right about the fountain; it was grotesque, the statues not even close to proper human proportions.

"I can smell the sea," Gabrielle said suddenly. She gave the memorial a startled look and snorted. "That's—who'd waste stone on a thing like *that*?"

"Statue to the war dead," Xena said. "*They* probably don't care what it looks like."

"No, probably not." Gabrielle was walking on tiptoe once again, craning her neck in a vain attempt to see over the crowd around her. "If we go straight out to the water, we can probably see the—"

"No shortcuts, no changes. I have directions. Turn south here." Silence. "See the awnings down there? That's the wine merchants' market; races are just on the other side."

10

She shaded her eyes with one arm, glancing skyward. "We won't have missed much, maybe the first run for the young girls. Atalanta wouldn't waste her time on that one even if she were young enough to qualify for it." Despite her best efforts to remain outwardly neutral for Gabrielle's sake, she could hear the sour note in her voice. Gabrielle cast her a quick look. "Almost there," Xena said, and smiled.

"Oh—" There was a question in the girl's voice, which she abruptly seemed to think better of. "Oh, right. Great!" They eased into the shadow beneath the main awning that marked the entry to the market. Gabrielle, who was looking around with a good deal of interest, suddenly stopped dead and stared. "Oh, would you *look* at those cups? I never saw a glaze like that in all my—!"

"Gabrielle, what would you do with a nest of wine cups? Pay attention to what's around us. The stableman said this place is full of cutpurses. In fact, why don't you give me your purse?"

Gabrielle blinked, then stepped away from the counter with one last yearning look at the sky-blue glaze. "Why don't I—oh, no! Not a chance! Last time I did that, you went after some guy who was thumping on his kid, and I didn't have money to buy food or anything. I didn't even get anything to eat until nearly sunset! I could've starved!"

The warrior laughed shortly; her eyes were amused. "I did that to you, didn't I? I'd forgotten. Well, then, why don't you put it where someone isn't going to get it without you knowing about it?" She drew her own small pouch from its usual strap and shoved it under her sword belt, just below her ribs. Snug fit—it wasn't going anywhere. Gabrielle opened the neat little coin bag that had been a parting gift from Queen Penelope, checked its contents carefully, then snugged the strings and shoved it down the front of her top.

Xena chuckled; Gabrielle eyed her sidelong, then laughed as she moved her shoulders to settle the bag. She winced, used her hand to settle it a little better. "Yeah. None of the tales go into how uncomfortable this is, do they?"

"None I've heard."

"Well, I'll know if someone tries to take it."

"I hope so." Xena drew her purse out once more, flattened it better, and shoved it down next to the chakram. Very tight fit.

"That's pretty fat," Gabrielle remarked in sudden surprise. "When did you pick up so much coin?"

"Not so loud," Xena murmured, and gestured sharply at the bustling crowd around them: mostly men, a few women, plenty of servants. King's guard everywhere, but from the sounds far down the aisle, someone had just lost an earring to a thief. Gabrielle frowned.

"Just pay attention. And don't draw attention to yourself in a place like this. In answer to your question, it was a gift from Queen Penelope; I couldn't find a way to say no without hurting her feelings." She grinned at her companion. "Shoulda let you talk, huh?"

To her surprise, Gabrielle suddenly looked solemn and shook her head. "No. Because she could afford a gesture like that, and because it made her feel good to do something for you."

Xena cast her eyes up, very briefly, then went back to her study of the people around them. "For us. You did a little to help ease matters back on Ithaca, you know."

"Well—sure. But nothing like you did."

"She said it was for us both. So you wouldn't have to sleep on stones, wrapped in a threadbare cloak."

"And I haven't, have I? That really was nice of her. But

it bothers you, doesn't it? Like—she'd tried to pay you for what you did? Gave you a reward?''

Xena considered this, then shrugged. ''Mmmm—maybe.''

''Well, then, think of it this way: if some other brute shows up on Ithaca, then there's that much less of Odysseus'—ah—'' she glanced around, the corners of her mouth quirking, ''his *you*-know-what for them to take.''

''Hmmm. Hadn't thought of it that way,'' Xena admitted.

''Besides, you know you won't hoard it to yourself,'' Gabrielle reminded her. ''In fact, that last village—Khyilos?—I wouldn't be surprised if something got left there.'' Her eyebrows went up. Xena shrugged.

''You saw what the need was.''

''You're a good steward for it, then. I wager she knew how you'd use it—and not just to get me used to more soft living.''

''Possibly. Keep your eyes open,'' Xena added sharply, and set a hand over her dagger as a commotion erupted ahead of them. A wave of people fanned out, running toward them. ''Hang onto the stirrup tight,'' she snapped, ''so you don't get dragged away in this mob.''

A boy's golden curls shone in a patch of sunlight, moving at high speed against the main direction of the crowd, two tall, horse-tailed bronze helms right behind him. Laughter followed the guards: apparently the boy was someone known to the market, and he was once again making away with some prize right under the guards' noses. Xena stretched as tall as she could, watching the movement, one hand on the dagger nearer her purse, the other holding Argo firmly to the spot.

He *was* a boy, just beginning to shade into manhood,

though he probably still spoke in a boy's high-pitched tones. The golden curls were lovely, as was the sun-bronzed skin of his arms and face. Tattered rags barely concealed his body—he was painfully thin. *A wonder he can run so fast,* Xena thought angrily. *He doesn't look like he's had a proper meal in all his life.* The boy was heading straight for her; eyes of an impossibly deep blue gazed straight into hers for a brief moment before he turned to glance across his shoulder. The guards were much nearer than they had been. Xena gestured with her head—*That way!* The boy nodded very briefly and skittered around Argo and Gabrielle, sending the latter whirling like an eddy in his wake. Xena shoved her shoulder and her weight into Argo, who stepped toward his right, blocking the guards.

"You, woman! Move the horse! Now!"

She ducked her head in assent, mostly to hide the smile, as she dragged at the rein and let the guards slip past them. "Gabrielle?" Uproar all around them; possibly the girl couldn't hear her. But she was no longer clinging to the other side of Argo's bridle—not anywhere close, Xena realized as she ducked her head under the horse's golden neck. "Gabrielle?" There—an unmistakable golden head, several paces back. Shoved there by the crowd, apparently. "Gabrielle!" She pitched her voice to be heard and to quiet the babble all around them. She got momentary silence, then Gabrielle's astonished voice.

"Did you *see* him? He looked like—like the paintings of Helios back on Ithaca! Ohhhh!"

And then another voice, warmly and resonantly masculine. "Gabrielle? Beloved Calliope, it couldn't possibly be anyone else! Gabrielle!" Xena turned as a small, slender man pressed through the milling crowd. Dark blond curls bounced as he hugged the girl tightly.

"Homer!" Gabrielle's voice soared high with delight. "I can't believe it, Homer! What are you doing here?"

The young would-be bard wrapped one arm around her shoulders and drew her close. "I can't believe it, either! I figured you two would be gone from Athens for years! What are you doing here?"

"The races. Women's races."

"Didn't know you ran, Gabrielle—or is it Xena who's running?" A dimple bracketed the near corner of his mouth. "Oh," he added cheerfully, "didn't see anyone with you at first, Gabrielle. You are—? Of course you are," he added with a heart-melting smile in the warrior's direction. "Hello, Xena. I've heard a lot about you."

"Yes," Xena replied dryly. "So Gabrielle's told me. Always nice to meet someone she speaks so highly of."

"Races," Gabrielle said firmly, and tugged at his arm. "Can you walk with us a little way? I don't want to be any later than we can help. And no, we aren't running, either of us. That is—it's Atalanta. But Homer—or are you still going by Orion?"

"I'm sticking with Homer. You were saying?"

Xena cast her eyes up and kept one ear on the pleasant babble between the two as she fought them a way through the milling crowd. If anything, there were more people here than there had been when they entered the awning-covered aisles. A brief glint of sun off distant water gave her direction. Gabrielle kept one hand wrapped around one of Argo's straps and the other around one of Homer's hands.

"Saying? Oh, yeah. I didn't think you would be allowed out like this. I mean, just wandering around the market. Isn't the Academy supposed to be tougher on first-year people than that?"

He laughed self-consciously. "Well, I passed first levels—"

"Already? That's terrific!"

"Well, maybe it is. I have to admit I borrowed a couple of your tales, altered with a male hero—sorry—for oral finals, and that's probably what put me over the top."

"Ohhh," Gabrielle replied, laughing. "Probably not—or more likely, it was the way you told them."

"Thanks. Anyway, once you pass first levels, they let you outside the main gates to tell tales for coins. Then if you get lucky, they let you come down to the market and pick up new tales to cast into verse. You're supposed to bring back three every day you're out, but no one holds us to that. Sometimes, one can get away with telling his own tales for the people out here. Of course," he added rather shyly, "if you don't tell them well enough, the crowd lets you know. Not so much here, they don't. But most of us avoid the produce market." Gabrielle laughed at once and clapped her hands together. It took Xena the least moment longer: *Produce market: overly ripe fruit and lettuces. Right.* "Anyway," Homer went on cheerfully, "two of the older students are leaving, so we're having a party tonight. I have permission to buy the wine cups and jugs. In other words, I have permission to waste the better part of a day coming up with a pottery design that will suit those being honored. You're just as well off not being at the Academy, Gabrielle. You can't believe the amount of time that gets wasted on such trivialities." Xena could hear him fumbling at something; a bit of unglazed crockery scraped across another, setting her teeth on edge. "Like it?"

"That's a nice shade of blue," Gabrielle replied doubtfully. *Garish, she means,* Xena decided, and bit back a grin. "But—ah—d'you really think it needs *all* those dryads? And Bacchus and Silenus *and* . . ."

"You don't think it's too complicated a pattern, do

you?'' Homer asked anxiously as her voice faded away. ''I think this is what I really should get, because for his final ode, Demarus did the epic of the cherubs and the grape harvest and the great thunderstorm. And the instructor, Betiven, did the music—really wonderful stuff. I hope you get to hear him someday—the poor man's utterly deaf, can't hear his pieces outside his own skull. Well, anyway, Agrilion has such a thing about dryads, swears he saw one in his father's woods when he was small, still thinks he can find her and convince her to love him, if his poetry is pure enough. I just got the one small cup so I can check it against other things before I make a final decision; that way I don't have to carry an entire basket of crockery with me.''

Gabrielle laughed. ''Well, if that's your reasoning, I think the pattern is perfect. I wish I could've heard Demarus and the music. And I'd wager Agrilion can win his dryad if he really wants her.''

''You know,'' Homer began warmly, ''you're such a— a *nice* person, Gabrielle.'' He caught his breath sharply, and Xena stopped to stare at him; he was gazing down at Gabrielle, his hazel eyes wide and his mouth hanging open. ''Wait a moment, you said—you *did*! You said Atalanta? Dear Athena, you did say that, didn't you?'' Xena cast her eyes heavenward—or at least toward a grubby strip of once-white awning figured in blue and gold keywork. Behind her, the horse came placidly following, and, because she was still holding onto the strap, Gabrielle. And so did Homer, who at the moment was firmly attached to Gabrielle.

Crowd swirled around them, and somewhere off to Xena's left a woman yelped indignantly, ''Just take your hands *off* that, young man! I'm old enough to be your mother!'' A shift; people moved out and away as a tousled

17

head of golden curls seemed to float through a sea of bodies, then sharply changed course as someone else—a man this time—swore: "That's *my* purse, you!" On her other side, she could hear Gabrielle and Homer talking earnestly, oblivious to their surroundings.

"Of course I said Atalanta—I've heard about her forever, you know," Gabrielle replied breathlessly. "And I've always been so—so amazed by what they say about her. But I never had the chance to meet her." *Lucky you*, Xena thought sourly. "And so," Gabrielle went on, "when I heard that she'd be here for the races, I said we just *had* to come, and we did."

"Atalanta," Homer breathed reverently. "All the tales I've heard of her since coming to the Academy—say, you wouldn't mind if I came along with you, would you? I mean, no one at the Academy has *ever* managed to even get close to Atalanta, let alone talk to her so we can cast her story into the epics. After all, she's supposed to be goddess-blessed. I mean, all those stories about how her father set her out in the fields to die after she was born because maybe he wanted a son instead, except there's the story about maybe her mother having laid with Ares, and—"

Gabrielle put in hurriedly, "You know, if you *think* about it, you might realize why the lady doesn't talk to any of you Academy types. Would you want some overeager bard shoving his nose in *your* sister's face and asking whether her mother was unfaithful to her father?"

"Huh? Oh . . . ." Homer was quiet for several moments. "Oh. Right. Never thought of it that way before." He cleared his throat. "Well, I promise I won't ask any questions of that kind today, if you'll let me come with you. You don't mind? Honestly?"

"Well, of course not," Gabrielle began quickly. She

seemed to consider this a moment, then added warily, "Xena? Ah—you wouldn't really mind, would you? I mean, if—"

"Not at all," Xena put in smoothly. "Someone for Gabrielle to talk to about all this." That earned her a long, uncertain look from Gabrielle. *She's literary,* Xena reminded herself. *Looks for meanings where there aren't necessarily any. I meant just that: she and Homer can talk about how wonderful Atalanta is. I won't have to contribute a thing to the discussion.* "Look," she added and pointed across Argo's neck. "There's the water, and there's the racecourse."

"It is?" Gabrielle craned her neck, then fell back and said gloomily, "Guess I'll have to take your word for it, all I can see is *bodies.*"

Homer laughed quietly and said, "Well, I can make out the water, and a lot more people down on the hard sand than you usually see this time of day. You know, that reminds me of a riddle—"

"Hey! You like riddles?"

"You can't avoid them at the Academy just now; they're all the rage. But, yes, I do like them. Have you heard the one—" Xena shook her head as his voice dropped a little. More riddles. At least they wouldn't be directed at her.

The crowd was thicker near this western edge of the market, and passage was slower. Stealthy fingers made contact with her thigh; she snatched at them, dragging hand, arm, and astonished owner off his feet. A grubby boy who couldn't have had ten summers under his tattered tunic stared at her with very round, would-be innocent eyes. "If you want to keep these," she said in a clipped, low voice as she squeezed his digits, "keep them off *me.*"

"But—but I didn't—"

19

"You did. Don't do it again, or the fingers are mine. Got it?"

"Ah, ah, ah—got it," the suddenly pale little thief stuttered.

"Good. Pass the word. Me and the two on the other side of the horse, hands off. You do it right, I'll reward you with two coppers at the end of the races out there."

"You—you would?"

"Swear. I don't break my word; see that you don't break yours." She let go of his arm as he nodded vigorously, watched as he shoved his way through the crowd, then turned her attention to the crowd around them. No one seemed to have paid any attention to the little byplay between her and the boy, least of all her two companions.

"Oh!" Gabrielle held up an arm to shield her eyes against the midmorning sun as they came into the open once more. "That's *bright*! I'll wager all the best places on the other side of the course are taken."

"Well, not necessarily," Homer said. He was craning his neck now, staring over the people around them. "It's women's races, after all; they won't have the kind of crowds the men do, or the Olympics."

"Yeah," Gabrielle said sourly. "Oh, well, I guess that's good for us. Can you see a way to get closer to the water?"

"I think maybe I can just—" Whatever else he said went unheard as a new fuss broke out behind them, deep within the wine merchants' market, while before them a horde of very young girls shrieked and squealed as another race began.

"Oh!" Gabrielle sounded wildly distressed; she let go Argo to begin working her way forward. Homer eased ahead of her and took hold of her arm. Xena bit back a grin and followed them. All at once there was room to move, a cool salt breeze blowing over them, hard sand underfoot, and little girls everywhere. "Oh," Gabrielle said again, less enthusiastically this time. "It's just the second run for the child-class girls. No rush—we're early."

"I think—" Homer began. Another shrill outcry silenced him as ten or more young girls in long, loose tunics sprinted barefoot down the hard-packed sand; the cries and cheers followed them to the turning point, some distance away. "I *think*," he said a little louder, as the nearby cries were replaced by excited chatter, "that I can see a place over there, on the other side. Around the end of the course—up here, it isn't that far."

"Let's go," Gabrielle said. She glanced at Xena, who shrugged.

"Fine with me. Better than staring into the sun all afternoon."

Gabrielle's nose wrinkled. "Look, this is me; we're honest with each other, right? So you really don't have to say you're liking what—I mean—"

The warrior smiled, and her eyes were briefly warm. "Gabrielle, it's fine. Everything is. I said I owed you this to make up for that boat ride to Ithaca, and I meant just that. I wouldn't have said yes if I'd meant yes for you, no for me. Besides, I like watching the young women run."

She turned slightly away from her young companion and shrugged faintly. "I could have done that—once. Never mind, it's not important," she added quickly as a line appeared between Gabrielle's brows. "Go ahead. I'll follow you."

The tide was almost all the way in; foamy water slid up behind them as Homer found the opening he'd seen from the other side. He gave the women an apologetic glance. "Um—it's wet. No wonder we've got it to ourselves. If you'd rather, I can look for another place." But Gabrielle shook her head vigorously, braced herself against him, and began stripping off her boots.

"Oh, wonderful! Much better than I could have hoped," she said and sighed happily as cool water rolled across her feet. "Sure you didn't arrange this?"

He laughed. "I'm willing to claim credit. That reminds me, however." He thought a moment, then went into declamatory voice. "I move great shapes but have no shape, I fall from great height but do not bruise, I give life and take it."

Gabrielle laughed and nudged him with her elbow. "Ohhhhh, sure, ask me an *easy* one! Water, of course." Homer laughed with her, looking a little embarrassed.

"Well, it was off the top of my head, and because of the tide, of course. Give me a chance, Gabrielle. I have some you'll never solve."

She planted both fists on her hips and eyed him impudently. "Oh—and is that possibly a challenge? D'you even dare? Because there isn't anyone alive—besides a god or goddess, of *course*," she said dryly, casually flipping her fingers to avert any possible divine anger, "who can outriddle me!"

"I shall take that as a challenge," Homer said loftily, but a moment later the two dissolved in laughter.

Xena's mouth quirked. "Water, of course," she mumbled to herself sourly. *Riddles*. The answers were so simple! Perfectly easy—when you already had the answer. She dismissed the thought; it took a certain talent to make them up, or guess them, obviously. Just not her sort of talent.

Penelope had needed Xena's particular skills—she'd needed a fighter who could level the playing field back on Ithaca, someone who could create an army made up of fog, one woman warrior, Odysseus' young son, and a handful of servants, herders, and farmers. And a rear guard of one determined Gabrielle and a fighting staff to stand between the queen and certain death if the army failed. Well, it had worked, hadn't it? The odd little army had severely beaten Draco's hundred or more armed and well-trained brutes.

Circe, on the other hand, had needed someone to empathize with her and snare her with words—though Gabrielle certainly was much more these days than a soft little villager with a fast mouth. *So? I'm no longer a mere brute with a sword*, Xena reminded herself with a grim smile.

Things tended to balance out, in the long run. The warrior cast a quick glance at the laughing and cheerfully squabbling pair at her right, then leaned out to gaze down the course; the girls had turned at the far end and were headed back. One or two of them were potentially splendid athletes—if their parents could only be convinced that such talent at athletics wouldn't mark a daughter as odd. *Still— there are worse things than being odd*. Not that most parents—including her own—would believe that. No safety in being different.

Not far from her position a handful of white-clad girls wildly waving red ribbons began to shout, "Nau-si-caa! Nau-si-caa!" They shrieked with delight as the runners came closer.

"I have a better one for you," Gabrielle said, then broke

off. "Do you see what I see down there? The two lead runners—look!"

Homer looked, and so did Xena. The girls took up their chant once more as two girls flashed by, a length of rope stretched taut between them. The girl closer to them was red-faced, gasping, and staggering, but Gabrielle clearly heard her shout, "All right, Nausicaa! Twenty paces straight, sand's hard and you're clear, *go*!" The other girl dropped her end of the rope and actually picked up the pace as the first dropped to the sand and rolled off the course. She was still gasping as she sat back up to peer anxiously toward the finish line. "Nausicaa—yes!" she shouted breathily, then fell back flat with a groan as the rest of the girls ran by.

Gabrielle knelt next to the sprawled-out girl, who was trying to catch her breath. "Hey, are you all right?"

"Me? Sure." Pale red hair framed a tanned, narrow, and very cheerful face; reddish freckles dotted a snubbed nose and sprayed across her cheeks. She was still gasping for air. "That kind of pace is absolutely beyond me, especially on sand! Now, I just—I can run," the girl went on ruefully, "just not like *she* can. But she can't do it by herself because—"

"I was going to ask you about the rope," Gabrielle said as the other tried to slow her breathing—without much success. "Oh. I'm Gabrielle, by the way."

"Mitradia. Glad to meet you. It's the only way she can stay on the course. Nausicaa's blind."

"Blind—really!"

"Yeah," Mitradia said proudly. "It's pretty amazing, isn't it? Nausicaa's been blind from the moment she was born. One of the girls' mothers last year lodged a protest after her precious baby lost the race, said she was faking. She's not. But just because her eyes don't work doesn't mean her legs can't,'' she added indignantly.

"You don't have to convince *me*,'' Gabrielle said warmly. "I was impressed even before you told me she couldn't see. She's good.''

Mitradia sighed and let Gabrielle help her up. "I'm sorry if I sounded angry. I wasn't mad at you. I just have to defend her so much—well, anyway, she *is* good. Unfortunately, she's also a princess, so this year is probably her last for this kind of thing. Only someone like Atalanta gets away with running past her—well, her you-know-whats.'' She drew one deep breath, let it out in a gust, and turned to peer toward the finish line, where a high-pitched argument had erupted. "Thanks. I'd better get down there. Sounds like the usual trouble.''

"Mind if I—if we—come with you?'' Gabrielle asked. "This is Homer, by the way; he's a bard.'' She glanced toward Xena, who smiled faintly and waved at her.

"Go ahead, Gabrielle. I'll be here.''

"A bard—really!'' Mitradia brushed sand from her arms and surreptitiously tugged her tunic straight.

Homer's color was high. "Well, I'm at the Academy. *Almost* a bard, if I keep up my studies.''

Mitradia combed her fingers through the short, curly strands sticking to her damp face. "Oh, but—my uncle says you have to be very good just to be accepted there.''

"You sure do.'' Gabrielle nudged Homer and minutely shook her head. "And he really is a very good bard. Goodness,'' she added mildly, "what's all the fuss up there?''

Mitradia sighed heavily. "It's Nausicaa, of course.''

"She's *blind*!'' a girl's voice rose shrilly. "Isn't there a law? I mean, I could have made the final race except for her! I mean, you can't *run* if you can't see, can you? And that other girl—where'd she go, the one who was pulling her? How come *they* get to help each other and we—?'' A deep male voice cut across hers, but the noise all around them made it impossible to understand what he might be saying. Mitradia glanced at her companions.

"Would you like to meet her? Nausicaa, I mean, not the Piglet."

Homer's eyebrows went up. "Piglet?"

"What we call her," the girl replied with a sudden urchinlike grin. "She squeals a lot. I'll be right back." She plunged into the crowd. The shrill voice cut through the babble around them again and was interrupted once more by the male voice.

"I don't believe it, she didn't even finish? Ohhhhhh! Mother!" The girl's voice rose to an even sharper pitch. "Mother, I told you I needed a short chiton to run in, not this awful thing that tangles around my knees. *Now* look what's happened . . . !" Her voice mercifully faded as a deep-voiced, dark-clad woman began leading her away, uttering clucking little noises she must have meant to be soothing. The Piglet didn't sound—or look—particularly soothed.

"A blind runner," Gabrielle murmured. "You know, someone really ought to do something with that."

"Hmmm. Maybe," Homer allowed. "Songs about women runners aren't very popular, though—unless it's Atalanta. Now," he added thoughtfully, "a blind princess . . . hmmm."

"Somehow I'm reminded . . . did Circe find you?"

He grinned. "Did she! You never saw so much chaos as when she walked into the Academy and announced who she was! It was nice of you to suggest that to her."

"Well, it just seemed like a good idea at the time," Gabrielle said. Off to the side and just behind them, another race started; she whirled around to peer through the crowd, then shrugged and turned back. "More little girls. No, it

28

wasn't just nice of me; it was important. Circe needed to get away from Ithaca and put all that behind her. And besides, I just knew you ought to hear her story." She glanced at him sidelong. "You did get to hear it, didn't you?"

"Unlike everyone else, who just heard about her island and her life there—and about Odysseus and his men—I was given a private hearing of the entire tale."

"Oh?" Gabrielle's cheekbones were suddenly pink. "Everything?"

"She said it was. What you told her about Calypso and everything that happened after she came to the mainland. How you talked her out of keeping a herd of pigs on the king's lands." Momentary silence. "She really thinks a lot of you, Gabrielle."

"Oh." Gabrielle smiled. "That's nice. Now I'm *really* glad I didn't try to trick her. So, where is she?"

"Gone home." He shrugged. "Said Athens was too big and crowded; it made her nervous. But Apnis went with her—you may not remember him; he was almost ready to graduate when you and I tested. Anyway, he was smitten with her from the first moment he set eyes on her." He laughed. "Actually, he was well-nigh unbearable. Imagine a bard in *that* kind of love."

Gabrielle made a wry face and grinned at him. "Rather not, thank you!"

"Well, she wasn't looking for male company—despite your suggestions to her about forgetting Odysseus and all that. But Apnis was there every time she turned around, bringing her fruit and flowers, things like that. And after he sang forty lines, extempore, on the beauty of her hair, I think she was well on the way to being smitten with him."

"Oh, that's really nice," Gabrielle said softly. She glanced back toward the starting line and touched his arm. "Look, here they come."

Nausicaa was taller than her friend and reed-slender; red strands shone in her brown hair, which had been pulled away from her face and secured with a simple leather thong. Her tunic was now snugged to her body with a plain blue sash that nearly matched the deeper blue of her eyes. Her feet were bare. Not at all what Gabrielle would have expected of a princess—or what she might have expected of a blind princess. Other than the motionless stare, Nausicaa showed no signs whatever of having been kept from the normal life of a child in a coastal village. *Her father must be a genuinely intelligent man—or whoever's raising the girl is.* At first, she was quiet and shy, but that faded quickly as Gabrielle complimented her on the race she'd just won, then introduced Homer. Nausicaa gently laid her hands first on Gabrielle's, then Homer's, face.

"Oh," she murmured. "Mitts, I didn't know there *were* any young bards, did you? Sorry, sir," she added with a shy smile. "I mean—one knows bards come from somewhere, but my father's court singer is elderly enough to be my great-grandsire and he's been with us forever; his playing's dreadful and he can't recall half the verses to his songs anymore, but my father's tone-deaf and doesn't notice." Mitradia giggled.

"Well," Gabrielle put in cheerfully, "if you ever change your mind about being a wandering bard, Homer . . ."

"But wandering bards are best, aren't they?" Nausicaa asked. "After all, they hear more new tales, but even if the tales aren't totally new, most of them are new to the people they visit."

"Homer's working on a *very* new tale," Gabrielle said. "About Odysseus and the—"

"Odysseus!" Nausicaa's fingers tightened on his arm. "You know tales of the Great Trickster? My father and he fought together when they were both quite young. I've always adored hearing his stories. But he vanished after the battle for Troy, didn't he?''

"Nausicaa," Mitradia put in, ''we'd better get back to the course. Old Stymphe's looking for us. That's her nurse, I mean, her maid,'' she added. ''And we run again pretty soon.'' She smiled. ''You can't get her started on the old Trickster, but you didn't know that, after all. *I* think she's in love with him.'' Nausicaa uttered a very unprincess-like snort, but her cheeks were quite pink.

''I'd just—well, I'd just like to meet him someday, that's all. I'm glad we got to talk, Gabrielle. Homer. Goodbye!'' She held out both hands to them, then let Mitradia take her elbow and lead her away.

''We'll watch you run!'' Gabrielle called after them. Mitradia turned and grinned, then rolled her eyes, apparently attempting to mime exhaustion. Gabrielle watched them go. ''She's sweet—they both are, aren't they? I hope she gets her wish someday.''

''Stranger things have happened,'' Homer said.

The tide had slipped a few paces, and Xena now sat cross-legged on hard-packed sand, her back against Argo's leg, the horse occasionally nuzzling her hair. She glanced up as Gabrielle's shadow crossed her, smiled, and turned back to her study of the crowd, which was restlessly waiting for yet another clutch of girl runners to make the turn. ''Anything exciting?'' she murmured.

''Not really,'' Gabrielle allowed. She stepped back quickly as the main pack of runners shot by, throwing sand everywhere.

''I heard this is the last of the young ones until the next level—semifinals, I think.'' Xena waved a vague hand.

''Oh. Oh!'' Gabrielle stood on tiptoe, one hand on Homer's shoulder for balance as she gazed eagerly around them.

"Oh, dear goddess, that—that's her!" she squeaked. "I mean—it has to be, right?" She pointed; Homer sighted along her finger and shrugged. Xena sighed faintly, rose in one lithe movement, and looked.

"That's her," she said; her voice was expressionless as she sat again. Homer glanced at her, a faint line between his brows, but Gabrielle was too excited to notice anything except the tall, lean, pale-haired young woman striding across the sand.

"Oh. She really *is* golden, isn't she?" Gabrielle breathed. "Just like they say in the tales about her!" *Most of which she paid for herself*, Xena thought sourly. It wouldn't be fair to shatter Gabrielle's pleasure. And she'd never come across the huntress in such a public setting; maybe for once Atalanta would live up to her legend.

And she had to admit the huntress really was a golden, and notable, presence on the Athenian shoreline. Atalanta wore a pale yellow chiton—an extremely short chiton that barely covered a finger's worth of her legs and was cinched smoothly to her small waist with golden cords. The silken fabric fluttered softly against tanned bare arms and throat. She'd pulled her dark blonde hair back into a simple coil, from which little curling tendrils escaped around a slender, delicately featured face. "How does she *do* that with all that hair, and keep it up like that?" Gabrielle added in a vexed undertone.

"Magic, maybe," Homer replied cheerfully. He eyed Atalanta as she strode around the outer edges of the crowd to await the start of the women's preliminary race, then glanced down at Gabrielle. "I like your hair loose, even though that plait probably is more practical."

She smiled. "It's a lie—but a nice one. Thank you. Um—do you suppose she'd mind if I just—I mean, do you think if I—?"

Xena was on her feet again, gazing expressionlessly at the tall, leggy runner who was trying to appear cool and unconcerned—and not doing a very good job of it. *Odd that a race like this would matter so much to her,* Xena thought. Atalanta already had a reputation, and a legend built around her, so she had nothing to lose here, really. Her prowess as a sprinter was admittedly deserved—it wasn't likely she'd make a fool of herself, even running in this tournament against the best young women in this part of Greece.

Atalanta's surprisingly large, deep-brown eyes darted around the crowd, nervously moving from one person to another; her fingers absently pinched the edge of the chiton, wrinkling the fabric. She was shifting back and forth as if uncertain where to go; finally she glanced at the sun, shrugged, and started down the shoreline. Xena touched Gabrielle's arm. "Don't think you'll have to decide about going to meet her, Gabrielle. She's coming this way."

Gabrielle made a strangled little noise, as if she were about to faint. Apparently the huntress's gaze had touched on Xena—of course, the warrior was probably one of the most visible people on this stretch of beach, even without Argo at her elbow. *Why she'd actually seek me out, though . . .*

Gabrielle smoothed her skirt with anxious fingers. "Homer, do I look okay? I mean—not that she'll even—'' Gabrielle stuttered. She fell silent as Atalanta strode toward them and stopped just short of Xena, her head tipped to one side, her eyes narrowed. Gabrielle was too nervous to notice; she was trying to get her voice to work properly. The young athlete turned to give her a remote, questioning look.

Gabrielle smiled. "Ah—hi!" she said brightly. "You must be Atalanta. I'm—well, it's an honor to meet you. I've been following your races for years, and—''

"How nice for you," Atalanta murmured. Her eyes shifted back to Xena. Xena's mouth twitched; her eyes moved, indicating Gabrielle. "Oh," Atalanta said in at least partial understanding. *My friend. Be nice to her—or else.* It wasn't exactly the message Xena intended to convey, but it would certainly do. "Well, then. I'm glad to meet you— anyone who's been a mainstay of my efforts, of course. And you are—?"

"Are—? Oh. I'm Gabrielle. And this is Homer—he's a bard." Atalanta's dark eyes fixed briefly on Homer, took in his disapproving expression. She gave him a teeth-only smile.

"How nice. Well, I have to get ready for the race. Wouldn't want to disappoint anyone, would we? Xena," she said in a silken voice, "so very nice to see you again."

Xena's smile was equally wide and stayed well short of her eyes. "Pleasure's all mine, Atalanta. Just like last time."

Gabrielle picked up on the chill in the conversation this time; her smile became a nervous one and she tugged at Homer's arm. "Well, honestly," she said in a would-be cheerful voice that sounded strained, "it's an honor to meet you. Homer, don't you think we ought to find someplace down by the turning point to watch her first race, like you just suggested?" It sounded like something she was making up as she went; Homer stared at her rather wildly. Gabrielle grimaced at him, sent her eyes toward the two women, then winked broadly. Homer frowned, then his face cleared and he nodded as he finally caught her meaning. She let out a held breath and brought up a cheerful grin as he cleared his throat.

"Well, I just thought it would be a better place to see more of the race. Xena, we'll be back before the final race—unless you—"

"I'll stay here," the warrior replied; a brief smile softened the words. "Go ahead, Gabrielle. Don't forget to eat something."

"Right." Gabrielle's smile was nearer normal this time. "It's not that I'd forget, it's just that—I still have my purse, don't—oh!" She turned pink as she remembered where she'd shoved the purse earlier. "I'll remember. I'm glad I'll get to see you run finally," she added as she glanced up at Atalanta. The huntress had taken the moment to step away from Xena and compose her face; she gave Gabrielle her hand and a charming smile.

"I'll do my best to make it worth your while. And yours, Bard," she added sweetly.

Homer blinked. "Ah—ah—ah—thank you. So, Gabrielle," he went on with a heroic effort, "did you hear the one about why the hen crossed the cart track?"

"Across it or along?" Gabrielle demanded at once, but as they left, she glanced over her shoulder and her eyes were worried.

Xena nodded briefly and made a small gesture to indicate everything was all right. Her young companion relaxed all at once; her shoulders eased, and she smiled happily before turning back to argue with Homer as they splashed toward the halfway mark in the women's races. The warrior brought her eyes back to Atalanta then; hawklike, icy eyes bored into very wide brown ones.

"My, what a cute little bit of fluff," Atalanta murmured. "Too bad she's so chattery. Protégée or what?"

"Speaking of protégés," Xena purred, "where's your usual—ah—you call them bards these days, don't you?" Atalanta's smile froze; her eyes were suddenly all pupil. "As to Gabrielle, I don't see that's your business," she went on flatly. "She's a friend—or family, take your choice. Either way, she's off limits to your kind of unpleasant lip. So's the boy—but you're supposed to be so intelligent,'' she added as Atalanta scowled at her. "Keep in mind he's a bard. Even a blind Cyclops knows it isn't wise to annoy a bard.''

Some distance down the sand, Gabrielle sighed. "She really *is* beautiful, isn't she?''

"To look at, anyway,'' Homer replied sourly. Gabrielle slowed and looked up at him, puzzled. "She's also arrogant and rude,'' he added.

"Oh—that.'' Gabrielle dismissed it with a wave of her hand. "She's about to compete in the big races, Homer. Of course she's nervous, and some people get snappish like that when they're worried. I'll wager you anything she's just fine after her first race.''

"Well—'' He considered this as they skirted a clutch of girls buying fruit from a gangly old man with a high-piled tray. "I suppose it's possible—I get moody, and Androcles snarls at everyone in sight. But everyone knows he's not doing well in extempore this season. He's like an old lion with a thorn in his paw—''

"Hey, I like that!'' Gabrielle clapped her hands together. "Good image!''

"Thanks. Atalanta's the best runner there is, and if anyone's ever beaten her in a footrace, I haven't heard about it. What does she have to be nervous about?''

"Well, not about losing because she forgot how to run,'' Gabrielle replied promptly. She slowed, then drew a deep breath. "Ohhhh, that smells *so* good! Help me remember this spot. It's where I want to eat when this race is over.'' She pointed toward a billow of smoke wafting from beneath a blue and white striped awning, perhaps ten paces back from the crowd of race watchers. "Anyway, just winning isn't her problem. What if she took a wrong step, came

36

down in a hole, broke her leg? Or she ate something bad and got sick? Or one of the people watching stuck out a staff as she went by and tripped her?''

Homer stared down at her. ''You really think she's worried about things like that?''

''I think it's possible. I mean, if I was known as the Unbeatable Atalanta, I'd probably be a wreck before every single race.''

''Well—all right, maybe. I would never have thought of any of that.'' He shook his head. ''But no one would deliberately *trip* a racer!''

''Oh? Maybe some girl who wanted her best friend to win, or a mother who wanted her daughter—people can do really stupid things for love, you know.''

''I know,'' he admitted reluctantly. ''From tales, anyway. Here we are,'' he added as he guided her toward the rope marking the end of the course. Only a few people stood here, waiting for the runners to come down the course, turn, and head back toward the finish. Inside the rope, a graybeard checked the sand over the last several paces of the course and fussed at two boys pulling a sledge piled with rocks who were smoothing the ground in preparation for the next race. Satisfied, apparently, that they weren't messing up too badly, he turned away to count the colored sticks each runner would grab before turning to sprint for the finish.

Gabrielle stood on tiptoe and craned her neck, her eyes searching the far end of the course. Homer looked that way, too. ''I can see her,'' he said. ''That yellow really stands out, doesn't it? She's the only one at the start so far, though.''

''Oh—well,'' Gabrielle sighed, then smiled up at him, one hand shading her eyes. ''So—why *did* the hen cross the cart track?''

Homer grinned. ''Because it would take too long to go around,'' he replied loftily, then ducked as Gabrielle swatted at his head.

Two more young women paced back and forth at the far end of the course now; Atalanta stood motionless, her back to the long, open stretch of sand. An argument had broken out somewhere behind the start; Gabrielle could make out several angry female voices, but none of the words from this distance. A black-haired woman in a red chiton nearly as abbreviated as Atalanta's stormed onto the course, cast a glare about her, and sat in the sand. There was movement nearer to hand: Mitradia wove her way through the sparse crowd, Nausicaa's hand in hers.

''Hi!'' Gabrielle said. ''I thought you'd left.''

''Stymphe wanted to go right away,'' Mitradia admitted. ''Even with Atalanta running. But we reminded her Nausicaa's qualified for the finals, so we *have* to stay. I saw you come this way—I hope you don't mind.''

''You can probably see the race a lot better from here,'' Gabrielle said, then turned bright pink and sent an alarmed glance in Nausicaa's direction. ''I'm sorry! I didn't mean—'' To her surprise, the girl smiled.

''You can say 'see'; I don't mind. It's just that Mitradia does it for me when my hands can't. When there aren't as many people around, I can hear what she's saying a lot better.''

''That makes good sense,'' Homer put in warmly. Mitradia gave him a sidelong look and a shy little smile; it was his turn to blush.

Both girls were flirting with him, Gabrielle thought in amusement. *Well, why not? He's nice to look at, he's friendly and genuinely nice—and he's a bard. What girl wouldn't admire a combination like that?* She glanced back up the course: two more young women were at the starting area now, but the argument was still going—hotter than ever, from the sound of things. People around them were growing restless, and an older woman turned with an exaggerated sigh and walked off. "Aren't they *ever* going to start?" Gabrielle murmured.

"It's those short chitons," Mitradia said. Her eyes were wickedly amused. "Old Xeneron—the main official, he must be a hundred—says he's shocked, and he won't let them on the course; says the judges and the men out here will be . . . ah, well, *you* know. Eulaydia—that's her in the red—says if some man is—is"—the tip of her nose was very pink—"well, that's his problem, and not hers. Atalanta just looked at him down her nose—I wish I could be tall enough to do that," she added wistfully, "and said, 'I was told there would be races today. I'm still waiting.' And then she turned her back on him and walked onto the course." She sighed. "It was wonderful. Old Xeneron couldn't think of a single thing to say."

"That would stop most people," Homer admitted. He glanced down at Nausicaa, who smiled in his direction, her upturned face openly admiring. The flush, which had barely subsided, warmed his face and throat again. "Ah—would you like to hear a little about Odysseus? I mean, since we seem to have a little time before things are settled and the race begins."

"Oh—yes, please," Nausicaa whispered. "I—all the things my father's told me about him from when they were princes, fighting pirates off the Ithacan coast. I truly love those stories, but they're really the only ones I know." Her mouth quirked ruefully. "I know it's been years since they were young princes; after all, my father is no longer a smooth-faced lad, but I still . . ." She bit her lip and shrugged.

She still sees the old Trickster as a youth, Gabrielle realized. Startling thought. Even more startling: Nausicaa had a terrible crush on the man. *Well—he's a safer idol than Apollo.* She glanced at Homer, but he'd already caught on. "But in a tale, Princess, the bard can work magic: a hero can be any age at all." He considered briefly, then launched into the story of Pegasus and Bellerophon, suitably modified. "Did you know that when he was a boy, Odysseus captured a winged horse?" He got as far as the slender but heroic youth's attack on the Chimera when a high, warbling, birdlike cry rose above the babble of the crowd, momentarily silencing him and everyone around them.

Nausicaa sighed heavily. "Oh, *no*. Mitts, can you see her?"

Mitradia stepped away from them and gazed along the shoreline, then sighed even more heavily. "I'm afraid I can. I'm sorry, bard. Gabrielle. The story is wonderful, but that's old Stymphe, looking for Nausicaa. She'll haul us both straight back to the palace if we don't join her at once, final race or no final race. In fact, she's probably angry we went off alone," she finished sourly.

Nausicaa patted her arm. "It's all right, Mitts; she has to answer to my father if something happens to me. And it's the princess thing, of course." Her mouth quirked in a wry grin, her face turned in Gabrielle's direction. "We have to remain pure, and the best way to assure *that* is a full-time person like Stymphe. She's very nice, really."

"You're much too nice about everyone," Mitradia grumbled good-naturedly. "We'd better go now."

Gabrielle wrapped an arm around each girl and hugged gently. "I have an idea. Homer, why don't you go with them? After all, you're at the Academy and a bard. That should make you safe company for a princess, don't you think?"

Mitradia's face cleared at once. "Would you? You could begin another tale on the way—and if the Stymphe can see we're coming, she won't be angry if we walk slowly. And then maybe you can finish your story."

"I'd be honored," Homer replied, with a very courtly bow. But as Mitradia turned away to whisper something against her friend's ear, he leaned close to Gabrielle. "I need an idea—anything!"

"What about the Nemean Lion?" Gabrielle began ticking off on her fingers. "Or the great boar? Or the Hydra?"

"Hydra?" Mitradia had overheard the last. She frowned slightly. "But I thought—" Gabrielle gestured toward Nausicaa with her head; to her credit, the girl caught on quickly. "Sorry. I was thinking of something else. The Hydra was a snake, wasn't it?"

"With seven heads, one immortal," Homer said. He held out his right hand to Mitradia, took Nausicaa's in his left and went into full declamatory voice as they started toward the damp line of sand at the water's edge. "The sky was blue, the meadow green, the air was warm, the ocean cool, when 'long the track a hero bold . . ." His voice faded. He had already, Gabrielle noted, picked up a comet tail of listeners; a handful of children and one or two parents followed the oblivious bard and his two eager companions. *He may not always chant with his eyes closed, but he's certainly blind to almost everything else when he gets going.* She lost sight of them almost at once; the crowd on the water side of the course was larger than it had been, and the argument at the head of the course had died away at some point in the last moments. Gabrielle caught her breath sharply. "Oh, no! What have I missed?" To come all this way, to wait so long and anxiously for this particular race, and then if it had started already—! But it hadn't, though it was clearly about to: a veritable rainbow of brightly colored chitons lined the starting area as twelve young women positioned themselves across the course. A shout from the official was echoed by an excited cheer from the crowd as the race began.

3

"Ohhhhhh." Gabrielle stuffed a knuckle between her teeth. Her throat was suddenly tight, and her eyes shone with tears as eleven women sprinted in close formation across the hard-packed sand, straight toward her. The twelfth, already several long strides ahead of her nearest competition, moved with a speed and effortless grace that explained why so many thought the woman to be goddess-gifted. Atalanta reached the turning mark, neatly snatched a stick from the official's outstretched hand as she pivoted, dug the side of her left foot into the damp sand, and pushed off. The official transferred his colored sticks to the other hand and shook his smarting fingers; Atalanta was already through the rest of the pack on her way back to the finish line.

Gabrielle shook her head in disbelief. The huntress's face had shown no sign of exertion, and she wasn't even breathing hard.

The same couldn't be said for several of those now well behind her. Just short of the turn, the pack had broken apart, and while several of the woman remained perhaps a dozen paces behind the leader, the rest trailed in a long, ragged line. The second at midpoint, the black-haired girl in the short red chiton, had a face to match her skirts and was visibly measuring her breathing: three paces, *in*; three paces, *out*. The young women half a dozen or more paces behind her looked even worse, and the last of them—a dark girl in a sweat-soaked blue tunic—gasped as she reached the official and sat in the sand as her legs gave out. The official shrugged, dropped the remaining stick at her feet, and gestured for the boys to bring the sledge back onto the course. The girl stared down at the bright blue stick; tears filled her eyes.

A half-grown boy slipped past Gabrielle to crouch next to the exhausted runner. "Amalthea? Are you all right?" The girl nodded; her face was a study in exhaustion and misery.

"I can't—think—why I did this—to myself," she panted.

He laughed shortly, without much humor. "Fortune and glory if you got lucky and passed her, remember? You won't, though. You may run like a goat, sister, but you'll never beat *that*."

Oh, that's so unkind! Gabrielle thought, and almost said so aloud. But he had a point. The girl might indeed have the tenacity and balance of a goat, but she was entirely outclassed in a race like this. She could break her heart trying to chase a dream like beating Atalanta. Better, maybe, to face that now, instead of letting it gnaw at her. Gabrielle shook her short, brown, dampish skirt away from her legs, then stepped back as the boys with the sledge began dragging it over the very end of the course, where turning feet had dug deep in the sand. Amalthea's brother helped her to her feet, then wrapped a strong young arm around her waist to guide her off the course, where she staggered and sat once more.

"I'm sorry I dragged you all the way into Athens for this, Verien," she mumbled.

"Don't be," he said. "You were there for me when I tried to bend the great bow of Hesperides, weren't you? And I didn't do any better than you did here, did I?" Gabrielle opened her mouth to say something, but the boy went on, one hand awkwardly patting his sister's shoulder. "Remember what you told me then? That it wasn't my kind of contest—just because I wanted it didn't *make* it my kind of contest. And you were right, I know that now. Next time I try for gold and glory, I'll pick something that involves swimming. Amalthea, you aren't a sprinter, that's all. You can run hilly courses and long ones—a short thing like this is for someone who hasn't the strength to go the greater distance."

Silence. The girl shoved sweat-damped hair from her face and gave him a hard hug. "Thanks, Verien. I can't think what I ever did to deserve such a brother."

He grinned; dimples bracketed a deeply bowed mouth. "You picked the right father and mother, of course. Do you want to watch the end of all this?"

She considered, shrugged, and let him help her up. "I guess not. I've already seen what she looks like from the back, running. That's enough. Let's go find something to eat, then go home."

There, didn't need to do anything at all, did you? Gabrielle asked herself. She sighed happily as the brother and sister vanished into the crowd along the seaward edge of the market. She sighed again, then turned back to eye the course. By the sounds of things up there, the race was over. No need to surmise who'd won. Her vision blurred; she ran a hand across her eyes and sniffed. *I knew I'd be moved, watching Atalanta run, I didn't realize it would move me that deeply, or that I'd feel so sorry for the others running against her. That boy's right, you can't compete with some-one who's so—so—* Even Gabrielle couldn't find words for the way Atalanta looked when she ran; not extempore, as Homer would say. Not with so much noise all around her, for certain.

Particularly behind her, she suddenly realized. There was a full-blown argument raging not far past her left ear, and the few people around her were edging away uneasily. She turned.

One of the city guards stood with his back to her, waving black-haired hands and shouting at—at a *girl*, Gabrielle re-alized indignantly. No—not really a girl, though she wasn't any taller than Mitradia, and nearly as slender as Nausi-caa—and probably no older than herself. The ends of a weblike silvery scarf that draped loosely across her dark hair trembled, and the young woman's face was so pale that dust-colored freckles stood out on her nose and cheek-bones. Her brown eyes were enormous and filled with fright. She clutched a green-wrapped bundle to her chest and tried to edge away from the man, who was easily half again her size, but even without the crested helm, but he snatched at her shoulder with heavy, hairy fingers; the girl winced as they dug in. "I saw the work you put into that bit of weavin', Arachne!" he shouted. "And you're trying to tell me you'll just *give* it to that brazen, yellow-haired, half-naked creature? Happen the queen would pay you a whole purse for cloth like that! Why, Athena herself couldn't have woven it better!"

"Hush!" If anything, the girl went even whiter. "If Athena heard you say such a thing—!"

He spat, silencing her. "Ah, to Hades with her—*and* you! *And* the wretched cloth!"

The young woman's chin came up, and her eyes were snapping as she stopped him with a thin, shrill voice that

46

carried far across the crowd. Several women who'd stopped to purchase slivers of meat on skewers from a nearby stand glanced at the quarreling pair and decided to go elsewhere. Quickly. "How dare you speak of the goddess that way in my hearing, Anteros? I know you, you're bullying me so you'll have your way and force me to sell this at the price *you* set! And then you'll 'help' me spend the coin, won't you? If you don't simply take it all! I've told you, Anteros, it's *my* loom, *my* time for the work, *my* money when I earn it! I never want any part of you again: your filthy attentions, your greedy hands—*or* your opinions!''

Gabrielle looked around her. The sparse crowd had faded away entirely—except for herself and the two who were now snapping insults at each other. No one was even remotely interested in coming to a slight young woman's aid, of course; not against a guardsman. *It isn't your business,* she reminded herself firmly. *He's one of the king's men, you don't know her, you don't owe her—* That internal argument was working just fine until Anteros snarled and tightened his grasp on the young woman's arm. She gasped, and tears of pain filled her eyes. Gabrielle closed the distance between them and cleared her throat.

"Hi!" she said brightly. "Arachne, isn't it? I *knew* it was you—that head scarf, saw it from clear across the course. And I just had to come see what you're up to these days! I simply can't remember the last time we got together. I haven't seen you in such a long time, but honestly, you haven't changed one bit!" Her voice faded; Arachne stared at her blankly—so stunned or frightened she was unable to aid her would-be rescuer in her story. The guard had already turned to glower down at the outsider. A very *long* way down, Gabrielle realized with a nervous twinge. *Oh, well, the bigger they come* . . . She eased her right fingers down the long staff and shifted the grip of her left fingers to underhand. There! She was ready, though not visibly making a threat. Yet.

"Beat it, little girl," he snarled. "This isn't your business, and I'm sick of loud-mouthed females." Gabrielle could feel anger flushing her cheeks; she held her ground and eyed him narrowly. He held up a large fist. "You want some of this after I'm done punishing *her* for giving me lip in public? I said beat it!"

"My pleasure," Gabrielle replied sweetly, and brought the staff down across his knuckles, spun it and drove the other end into his midsection. He collapsed with a whoosh of expelled wind and a groan. Gabrielle took a wary step back, another, then reached out to draw the trembling Arachne with her. "It's okay," she said softly as she pulled the girl close. "You really don't know me. I was just trying to get you away from him without making any more trouble for you." She cast her eyes heavenward and pulled a humorous face. "So, it didn't work. I guess if it had been me getting pinched and yelled at like that, though, I wouldn't have been any more help to you. . . ."

"Trouble," Arachne echoed gloomily. Her eyes remained fixed on the fallen guardsman. "He's been nothing but trouble since I first met him."

"How do you know him?" Gabrielle glanced at Arachne, then turned her attention back to the gasping soldier. "I mean, he's not your brother or anything, is he?"

Arachne primmed her lips; her color was suddenly high, the freckles vanishing under a wave of red. "He's nothing. Anteros, son of the widow Oriosa. He just got back from the eastern war—Troy, or maybe Ithaca, if you've heard of it—not that long ago. Got home the day I came in to sell Oriosa the shawl she'd commissioned, worse luck for me. *She* thinks he's Hera's gift to women, and *he* sees no reason why he should keep soldiering if he can find a wealthy wife

48

to support him." She sighed faintly. "I'm not wealthy, but I've got—well, I've got a talent that earns me my keep. Thank the gods for that, since I've no kin that I know of," she added, even more gloomily. "Stupid Anteros thinks he can exploit my weaving by yelling at me in public," she said, then shook out the green bundle and held a handful of weblike stuff before Gabrielle's astonished eyes. The weave was even finer and more complex than the scarf on the young woman's hair. Blues and greens interwoven with a silvery thread made a lacy pattern that shimmered like dragonfly wings.

"Oh—oh!" Gabrielle touched one end lightly but immediately snatched her fingers back, as if afraid to tear it.

Arachne smiled. "It's all right, you can handle it. It's much stronger than it looks. Warmer, too."

"Oh—" Gabrielle glanced at her companion in disbelief, then gently stroked the material. It slid silklike across her fingers, molding to the shape of her hand, and wherever it touched, she could no longer feel the afternoon breeze. "That's wonderful, Arachne! I never saw anything like it."

"You never will, unless it's my own patterning," Arachne said quietly. "Or a goddess's work, of course. But—it's a gift—Athena's gift, honest and truly," she added quickly and rather defensively.

"I believe you," Gabrielle said. She stroked the silken stuff one last time, rather wistfully, then pressed the loose ends back into her companion's hands. "You brought that for—"

"As a gift for Atalanta—since we're both under Athena's protection, she and I. Or—well, in my case, guidance, I suppose, since there seems to be little protection involved." She glared down at the still-gasping huddle of guard. "And because if—well, if Atalanta would wear it, it would be good for my business. Though I don't often

49

claim aloud to be so—well, so practical. Mercenary is probably a better word for it.''

"If you haven't any kin to take care of you, I wouldn't call it mercenary," Gabrielle said. "You're taking care of yourself, and good for you."

"Thanks," Arachne said, and a little of the tension went from her shoulders. "*He*," she added, scuffing a little sand in the fallen guard's direction, "spends his free time hanging around me, 'borrowing' coin, and trying to bully me into accepting him as a husband."

"Right," Gabrielle said briskly. "And why am I not surprised? Because I've met too many men like that since I've started traveling around. Oh, look, he's starting to pay attention. Pardon me while I speak to your—ah, what's the word I want?—your sponge." She drew her companion back a few more paces as Anteros swore under his breath and staggered to his feet. She waited as he flailed around and finally turned to glare hard into her eyes, then brought up her chin and lowered the staff to fighting stance. "Now, you listen to me," she said flatly, with her best impersonation of Xena's no-nonsense intonation. "Arachne's my friend, and I don't *like* my friends being pestered by the likes of you."

"I'm guard, little girl," he snarled. "You don't order guard around. And I'm twice your size; you won't get lucky a second time." He swiped at the staff with a paw of a hand; she swung it easily out of his grasp, then back into position. He frowned, visibly confused.

"Maybe it's not luck, Anteros. But it's not an order, just a suggestion," Gabrielle said sweetly, though her eyes were dark with anger. "I'm not the only one who wouldn't like the way you're treating my friend. I'm here with Xena. I don't suppose you've heard of her?"

"Xena!" Arachne whispered and gave Gabrielle an astonished look.

"Xena!" Anteros spat. "I know who *she* is, all right. In fact . . ." His eyes narrowed and he folded massive arms across his chest, though Gabrielle noticed with some amusement that he kept well away from either end of her staff. "In fact, rumor has it *she* was at Troy when we were—but not on King Menelaus' side, from what I've been told! I warrant King Menelaus and my own king would like to talk to her about that!" He clenched his fists but prudently stayed out of immediate reach of Gabrielle's staff.

She smiled, in a would-be pleasant way. "Maybe. But since Xena and I just got back from Ithaca—just a little favor for King Menelaus, something he asked both of us to check on, *you* know—I suppose he's not too worried about soldiers' camp gossip. What d'you think? Of course," she added cheerfully, "we all hear rumors, don't we? Like some of the ones I've heard here in Athens," she went on, her voice hardening once more. "About certain guardsmen terrorizing helpless women and trying to steal their livelihoods. I don't suppose *your* King Theseus would like that much, would he?"

"Ah—you're bluffing," he snapped, but his eyes were suddenly wary, and no longer met hers. Gabrielle brought her chin up, and the smile was now smug in the extreme.

"Maybe. So, if I'm bluffing, I probably really don't know Queen Antiope, either. The *Amazon* Queen Antiope," she added pointedly, and casually buffed her nails against her short Amazon-brown tunic. Doubt now creased the guard's brow. "Arachne doesn't want your attentions," Gabrielle said in a brisk, dismissive voice. "I don't want them for her—now or any time from here on. She's under Athena's protection and mine both, all right?" Anteros looked convinced—but she had a feeling he'd be back to his old ways once Gabrielle wasn't around to keep him in line. Impasse. She sighed faintly. He wasn't going to fight her now—but she was going to have to find some way to get rid of him without costing him any more face than she already had. He was the sort who'd brood on such treatment—and take it out on Arachne later. *And who knows if Antiope would even bother to put the poor thing under her protection? She might extend that kind of aid only to another Amazon. Some of them can be pretty prickly.*

"Look," Gabrielle said persuasively, "instead of bullying a coin or two out of this poor girl, if that's the kind of life you want, why don't you do it right? The war's over, and a lot of men didn't come home. Find yourself an older, wealthy widow who'd adore having a handsome young husband. Who'd shower coin and gems on him for just a few smiles?" Silence. "And by the way, you'd find it a lot easier to get that kind of soft life if you smiled and said sweet things to the lady with the money. Instead of shouting threats. Just a thought, you know."

"Ah—" He seemed at a complete loss for words; he finally glowered at Arachne, leveled a finger at her, and mumbled sourly, "She's right about one thing, weaver; you're not worthy of *me*." He spun on his heel and stomped off toward the market.

The two women watched him go in silence. Arachne finally drew a deep, shuddering breath. "Ohhhh. I don't even know your name—but thank you."

"It's Gabrielle. And you're welcome. Though, honestly, I didn't do much."

"You did enough. I—" Arachne shuddered. "Do you know, the last time I wouldn't give him money, he found a nest of baby spiders and spread them over my loom? I'm simply terrified of spiders! And d'you have any idea how many baby spiders there *are* in a nest?''

"Not nice," Gabrielle said briskly. "I don't know too many people who *do* like spiders. Myself included."

Arachne smiled, and tucked the stole back into its green cloth wrapper. "Well—thank you again." She cast a worried glance after the man. "I hope he doesn't take up your idea, though: a wealthy, older widow. If I thought I was responsible for . . ."

"You aren't, and you wouldn't be," Gabrielle said promptly. "Most wealthy widows *I* know have pretty good control of their purses, and they know how to get what they want out of a man. And they usually have influence, or at least access to higher authority. For protection, I mean. Anteros doesn't look completely stupid, either. If he sees anger will get him reported to his captain or kicked out on the street, I bet he'll learn how to smile."

"Well—he *can* be awfully sweet when he wants to," Arachne said doubtfully. "He was with me, at first; before he discovered I'm not really that wealthy. And he's sickeningly adoring with his mother."

"There! You see? Mostly, that was to get rid of him without raising more fuss," Gabrielle said.

"You certainly did that. Thanks."

"Always glad to help. After all, I've been in that kind of position myself—well, not exactly that kind, but in tight places."

"I find that hard to believe," Arachne said. "I mean, you're so—so strong and brave. I didn't know anyone could do things like that with a walking stick."

"Trust me, neither did I until recently," Gabrielle assured her. She added warily, "I don't suppose you have someplace other than your usual house where you could sleep for a few days? Just in case it—ah—takes Anteros a while to find himself a substitute?"

Arachne nodded, and sighed. "A friend of mine—a potter—has a studio; sometimes I use it because of the light. I know she'd let me sleep there, especially if I pulled her pottery from the kiln late at night so she didn't have to walk halfway across Athens to do it."

"Good. Great, in fact," Gabrielle said. "Not to scare you or anything. Just—one of those sensible things, avoiding trouble. You know."

"I can see it wouldn't hurt to learn to do just that," Arachne said. She sighed again and squared her shoulders. "I'd probably better go up that way, where the racers are, if I want to find Atalanta." All at once, she looked a little nervous.

She probably *should* look nervous, Gabrielle remembered suddenly. Walking up to a person she didn't know— a genuine celebrity—to hand her a gift that was both gift and free advertising for the craftsperson—that took nerve at any time. But Atalanta might still be snapping at everyone in sight; she might be one of those runners who didn't uncoil until after the final race. And—as she herself had told Homer a while back—the woman might have cause to be worried until she was completely done and all the races were over. She touched her companion's arm. "Listen, Arachne. There are three or four more races before the women's finals, and I'd wager Atalanta won't have anywhere to set a gift like yours while she's running. I know you'd hate it if someone stole it, right? So, why don't you just hang out here with me? We'll watch her win that last race and then I'll introduce you, okay?"

"You *know* her?" Arachne's eyes were enormous. "You didn't say—I mean, you really know her?"

"Well, sure! Well, that is, my friend does. And I talked

to her earlier, before her first race today, so—'' she shrugged casually. ''So, sure, I know her.'' Her eyes searched the racecourse; the near end had been smoothed for runners, the boys and their sledge gone—no sign of activity at the far end, and much of the crowd had dispersed. ''Tell you what—looks like they're done for the moment.'' She gave Arachne a smile. ''So, what can you tell me about this place over here—I mean, how's the food? Because I'm absolutely starving.''

Arachne gazed at her in astonishment, then broke into a shy giggle. ''You know,'' she said finally, ''you're really such a *nice* person, Gabrielle. When I left my loom this morning to come here, I was nervous, upset, angry—I knew everything was going to go absolutely wrong. Just like it started to go wrong. And all at once, I'm not scared or mad at all. How'd you *do* that?''

''She's a professional,'' a dry voice behind them remarked. Arachne caught her breath in a squeaky gasp; Gabrielle closed her eyes and sighed.

''Xena, I really do wish you wouldn't do that,'' she said wearily. She turned to see the warrior at her shoulder. Argo was trailing behind his mistress, his long, golden head resting on her shoulder. ''I mean, it's unsettling, you know?''

''Better me than someone else you'd rather not have behind you, remember?'' Xena sent her eyes to one side, then the other. ''I thought I'd tell you I'm taking Argo for grain and water and a rubdown. There won't be any more races for an hour or so. You want to eat and not miss anything, this is a good time.''

''Just what I had in mind,'' Gabrielle said. ''Where do you want to meet after you come back? Oh, Xena, this is Arachne, she's a weaver.'' She touched the near end of the woman's head scarf. Xena's eyebrows went up. ''And she has a gift for Atalanta. I thought maybe if she waited until after the final race, maybe—ah—well, you know.''

Maybe if I'm with them, this poor timid girl with an incredible talent won't wind up with her feelings crushed. Just the kind of thing Gabrielle would think about. Nice. Xena smiled. ''I'll meet you up there, where we were standing earlier.'' The smile faded. ''I saw Homer a short while ago with the two girls, arguing with the old woman about whether the girls could stay here for the finals.''

''Oh, I hope he convinced her,'' Gabrielle said anxiously.

''He seemed to be winning the argument. I was distracted about then by what sounded like a serious fight down here.'' Not *quite* a question was in her voice.

Gabrielle gently pressed her foot down on her companion's toes when Arachne would have spoken; she laughed. To her own ears it sounded almost carefree enough. ''And you thought—let me guess! You thought I was right in the middle of things, didn't you?'' She spread her arms wide and sighed heavily. ''You know, I don't *always* wind up in stupid situations like this morning, just because you aren't around.''

''I know that,'' Xena replied smoothly. ''Just—checking.''

Her eyes were amused as she tugged at Argos' rein. ''See you later. Don't forget to eat.''

''Right! Do I ever?'' Gabrielle waited until warrior and horse were lost in the crowd, then sighed gustily as she began fishing in the neck of her bodice for her coin purse. She swore under her breath; it had slid most of the way down to the lower band. ''Well—ouch!—well, she doesn't believe me, but that's all right.''

''She doesn't?'' Arachne's eyes were all pupil. ''And— that really *was* Xena, wasn't it? I—I thought she'd be taller. Or—or something,'' she finished doubtfully.

"Really, truly Xena, and she's tall enough," Gabrielle said. "And she knows I was right in the middle of whatever went on, even if she doesn't know yet what it was. Since I'm on my feet and smiling, she probably figures I came out of it okay, and she's not going to baby me, or ask me what it was all about."

"It must be nice to know someone that well," Arachne said wistfully.

Gabrielle laughed quietly. "Oh, it is. It surely is. Come on." She squeaked as the purse pinched tender skin, then drew it out. "If the meat tastes as good as it smells, it has to be wonderful. My treat, okay?"

The afternoon wore on. Two more qualifying races for the women, two more for the younger girls. A final race for the youngest girls; mothers, and a father or two, were at the finish line, cheering wildly. Xena managed a warm smile for several of the smaller girls who were staring at her armor, wide-eyed; the smile turned chill as one of the mothers threw herself and her exhausted young runner into a chariot already laden with two herd dogs and a jittery small boy clad for toss ball. A baby pouch was strapped to her back, and the interior of the chariot was a welter of game balls and sticks. Two matched golden horses reared, then sped down the tide line for whatever activity was coming up—probably a hands' worth of sun ago—for the boy (or maybe the dogs).

Right. You have your own young safe and confined. Who cares about anyone else's young winding up under your wheels? Xena thought angrily. That particular class of Athenian matron was the most infuriating: comfortable wealth, ostentatiously displayed, but never enough time to accomplish all the pointless little tasks . . . *Forget it,* she told herself flatly. *You can't change people like that. Probably nothing short of death can.* Probably someone like that would wind up arguing with Charon that she absolutely had to go back and haul one last load of beach sand for the small ones' garden area. Arrange one last urn of flowers. Cook one last dinner to rival one of Lemnos' creations. A grin tugged at the corner of her mouth as she glanced out to sea. The sun was notably lower. The final women's race wouldn't be that far off. Well up the beach to the north, she could make out a yellow-clad figure pacing anxiously back and forth, occasionally rising on her toes to peer toward the market.

Odd. Atalanta was normally arrogant and overbearing—but not the nervous type, and she'd already proven there was no one here who could beat her. *Why would she care that much about one race, anyway?*

The wind had begun to blow steadily from the south when Homer came looking for Gabrielle. "Remember Nausicaa's young fans up near the finish line? They invited us to sit with them for her final race." His eyes moved beyond her and he smiled at Arachne. "There's room for three, if we're friendly."

"Sounds great," Gabrielle said promptly. "My feet are tired. Homer, this is Arachne—she weaves. Homer's a bard at the Academy," she added. Arachne dimpled.

"I've heard of you," Homer said; his voice was admiring, and so was the gaze fixed on either her face or the scarf framing it. He stepped aside to let the women precede him up the sand. "Another one for you, Gabrielle," he added and went into declamatory mode. "I move and yet go nowhere; I wear down the mighty, and yet, a small, pale ball controls me." He paused expectantly. Gabrielle's brows drew together.

"Wait, I've got it—I . . ." Her voice trailed off.

"Tide," Arachne said immediately, then cast a sidelong glance at Gabrielle. She turned and walked backward a few paces as her gaze shifted to Homer's face; her eyes went wide as she turned back to her female companion. "Oh, I'm sorry! I mean, if it's a competition between you—"

"Nothing of the sort," Gabrielle replied warmly. "You're good!" she added. "Ah—and here we are." She slipped between two tall, gossiping men and several women—mothers of the girls running, from the sound of things—in her quest for the course barrier. The girls moved to make room; one of them divided her red and white ribbons into two bunches and pressed half into Gabrielle's hand. Gabrielle settled with a thump on hard-packed sand and separated the ribbons into a handful of streamers. "So, when's the race start?" An excited—and unintelligible—babble answered her, but one of the girls pointed toward the starting area, where seven girls were stretching or pacing. No sign yet of Nausicaa, though Gabrielle could just make out the piercing voice of her servant. And then, in a startling moment of complete silence, Mitradia's husky reply. The girl next to Gabrielle sighed in irritation.

"If that old idiot actually keeps them from running—!"

"She won't," another of the girls said firmly. "There—" she pointed excitedly. "See? Thank all the goddesses at once for Mitradia, she's more than a match for the old crow! Nausi-caa!" she shouted wildly, and waved her ribbons as Nausicaa and her companion stepped onto the track, Mitradia fussing with her end of the short rope.

Gabrielle suddenly felt a little old. Any of these girls could be a niece—or a *much* younger sister. She felt a sudden pang: Lila. *Oh, little sister, where are you at this hour? Do you smile when you remember me?* She blinked back tears. *Keeping in mind I gave you our room, you should.* Suddenly, it seemed wonderful, having such commonplace excitements as this upcoming race. She came up onto her knees, waved her ribbons, and joined the high-pitched cry: "Nau-si-caa!" Homer blinked, then smiled, and settled in between her and Arachne as the girls took their marks and the race began.

This time, however, victory wasn't assured. A tall, angular girl in a damp green tunic dashed out much faster than Mitradia, who nearly stumbled as the green-clad runner caught her elbow on the way by. A groan from the girls around Gabrielle, then a relieved shout as Mitradia managed to right herself and go on, Nausicaa right on her heels. Once again Mitradia cast her companion loose a dozen or so paces from the end, but this time the girl who'd shoved her way to the lead held it and took the coin. Nausicaa's fans were momentarily, glumly silent, then the one who'd shared her ribbons with Gabrielle sighed. "Well, that happens. And when it's Orionis, you *know* they won't call her for a foul."

"As long as her uncle's finish line judge, they won't," one of the other girls grumbled.

"Still," the first girl said, "we can't let Nausicaa know we're disappointed, can we? It's not her fault, after all." She got to her feet, stared at the end of the course, and sighed once more. "Something's up; no one's presented the coin or ribbons yet, and I can hear old Stymphe from here."

So could Gabrielle. The servant was berating her young charge. She handed her ribbons to one of the other girls, touched Homer's wrist to get his attention, and murmured, "I think maybe they could use us up there."

He rose, helped Arachne up, and led the way. There was a noticeable space around Nausicaa and her companions—other runners and their parents *and* the officials were giving Stymphe and her piercing voice a wide berth. "All this,'' the old woman flung her arms wide, ''a waste of a full day's time *and* the travel—and now you want to stay for that vulgar creature's race as well? And so she can hand you a nasty bit of ribbon? Why? You *lost*, girl!''

''My fault,'' Mitradia mumbled tearfully, and blotted her eyes on the back of one hand. ''I *knew* better than to take the mark next to Orionis. I *knew* she'd do something like that.''

''Stop, both of you,'' Nausicaa commanded suddenly. ''Mitts, it wasn't your fault, and second isn't so bad. Even if Orionis *did* swipe you on purpose, she was running as well as she ever has; we couldn't have caught her. She deserved to win.'' Mitradia gave her a sidelong, unhappy look. ''Stymphe, you're making Mitts cry,'' she went on severely. ''You always tell me it isn't right to make people feel unworthy, and that's just what you're doing.''

Stymphe drew a deep breath and would have launched another spate of angry words, but Homer stepped into the breach, took her hand, and raised it to his lips. To Gabrielle's surprise, the old woman turned pink and pressed her other hand to her mouth to suppress a thin little giggle. ''I'm so glad to see you again.'' He glanced back at Gabrielle, giving her a broad wink and a subtle gesture. *Got it,* she thought, took Arachne's arm, and moved them both quietly away.

''He's charming the old creature,'' she said once they were back in the crowd. ''He'll do it better without us around.''

''He's very nice,'' Arachne said thoughtfully. ''I—oh,'' she added in a suddenly hushed voice. ''Is—I—is that her?'' Atalanta came striding up the sand through a crowd that parted to give her room, the end official at her heels, his hands filled with prizes for the girl racers. The huntress's face was set, her eyes stormy, and her hands still

61

picking at the edge of her chiton. A frown creased Gabrielle's brow as she turned to watch Atalanta pass.

"That's her."

"Oh." Arachne was visibly losing courage. "She's—so tall. And so—so—" She swallowed, glancing at the sky and the sun, which was now quite low. "I—maybe I'd better just—"

"No, wait," Gabrielle said earnestly, and took hold of her wrist. "I told you, didn't I? Well, I meant to," she added soothingly as the weaver gazed at her blankly. "She gets nervy before her races, that's all." Homer came through the crowd just then, looking for them.

"Well, I persuaded the old woman to let the girls watch the final race—I mean—"

"Good," Gabrielle said. "Maybe we'd better find a place, too." All at once, there were people everywhere. People who'd wandered off during the girls' races were now coming back to see the renowned huntress, and others who'd come for this one race were just arriving. Gabrielle sighed. "I told Xena we'd meet her at the other end; guess we'd better go see if we can find something down there."

They did—just as the race was about to begin. Xena joined them moments later; Argo, at her shoulder, now and again tugged at her hair. Gabrielle laughed at the picture they made; Xena shrugged. "He doesn't usually get the chance to stand around like this."

Gabrielle laughed again. "You mean he's bored," she said. "Tell him I'm sorry—or I would be if this hadn't been such a great day for me."

"I'm glad you've enjoyed it," Xena replied softly, and her eyes were momentarily warm. She indicated the course with her chin. "They're ready up there." Moments later, twelve women came sprinting down the track, Atalanta again well in the lead; just as she snatched her stick from the official's hand and shoved off, however, several women at the other end of the course began to shout, and Gabrielle clearly heard Stymphe's anguished shriek over everything. "Something's wrong," Xena said shortly. "I'll be back." She swung onto Argo's back and rode out to hard sand, using her knees to urge him forward. Gabrielle was already as close behind them as she could manage on foot, Homer and Arachne strung out behind her. Dead silence now at the upper end of the course as people began to realize something was wrong, and in that silence, Gabrielle clearly heard Stymphe's cry:

"They've stolen her—stolen Nausicca!"

4

One more blessed, stunned moment of total silence greeted this terrified outburst, then pandemonium. Gabrielle clutched Homer's hand and dragged him with her, Arachne trailing, momentarily forgotten in their wake, bundle clutched to her breast. "Come on!" Gabrielle shouted. It took her several long moments to force her way through the crowd, even with Homer's help. They arrived to find a wide circle of stunned onlookers surrounding the black-clad Stymphe, who was wringing her hands and wailing in a loud, ear-piercing voice. Nearby, in a small clear area of her own, Atalanta was ripping long silver pins from her hair and tossing them in a bag held by a compactly built, sweet-faced young man with a serious expression and crisp black curls. He knelt to fumble through the bag, then handed her a narrow belt holding two pearl-handled knives, followed by a slim case of slender, short spears. Once those were in place, he shook out a finely tanned, short boarskin cloak, gave her a horn bow, and got up to fasten the enameled quiver to her shoulder and snug the cloak over all. Atalanta paid little heed to him, other than to move as he directed so he could tighten the straps on the quiver; she was too busy glaring at Xena, who stood, arms folded and eyes pale with fury, between her and Stymphe.

"Don't fret so, old woman," Atalanta finally shouted. Stymphe snuffled loudly and stared at her, blinking aside tears. "I already told you, *I* shall rescue those children, at whatever cost to myself!" Stymphe blotted her withered cheeks, shook her head, and burst into tears once more.

Xena took a step forward and held up a warning hand when Atalanta would have said something else. "You won't go alone, not for something like this," she said flatly.

"I don't take company," Atalanta snapped in reply. "And I wouldn't have *your* company at any cost. I travel alone!"

"You don't have a choice, sprinter," Xena said evenly. "There are children out there—six young girls, if I heard right. At least ten men holding them. Armed men. And if anyone knows why, they haven't said. Ten armed men—"

Atalanta laughed, but her mouth was hard, and so were her eyes. "Small odds," she said, and patted the horn bow. Xena shook her head as one of the women began to sob.

"No." She sent her eyes sideways, toward the miserable woman. Atalanta raised her chin and the corner of her lip. Xena shook her head. "I don't care about the cost to *you*. I won't see you risk the life of a single one of those children, certainly not so you can add to your own glory. Not while I'm around."

The huntress's eyes blazed, her hands clenched into tight little fists. "How *dare* you!"

"I dare."

Atalanta shook her head. "Stay here, make your noises, Xena. I'm going now, while the trail is still fresh. Don't bother following me. I can outrun *you* easily, even after both of my races."

Xena bared her teeth in a would-be smile. "Not over any distance, you can't. You're a sprinter, not a distance runner. Remember last time?" She caught sight of Gabrielle hovering nervously at the edge of the crowd, Homer at her elbow and Arachne peering warily from behind the bard's back. "Gabrielle, I'm leaving Argo with you! Find out everything you can for me about what children are gone, who took them, anything else that might be useful. Then catch up with us!" She raised her voice another notch as another of the women burst into loud wailing. "Someone— anyone! They went straight up the sand, didn't they?" One of the mothers bit the side of her hand and nodded. Xena laid a hand on her shoulder and smiled reassuringly. "We'll do everything we can to get them back safely, and quickly. Try not to worry." She turned back to Atalanta, who was now glaring at Gabrielle.

"You're making a circus of this, warrior," the runner spat. "Why don't you bring all those shrieking little girls with the ribbons, and a picnic basket while you're at it?"

"You're the expert tracker," Xena countered softly. "Why don't you get started before the tide comes in and erases what sign we have?" She glanced at Gabrielle. "Don't be too long, okay?"

Gabrielle had her arm around Stymphe; she cast a wary glance at Atalanta, but the huntress had turned away with a blistering oath. She stalked toward the shoreline—the crowd backed away to give her ample room—and squatted to gaze at the deep wheel marks. Gabrielle's eyes shifted to a spot just beyond Xena's shoulder and her mouth twitched nervously. "I can't ride Argo!"

"You can," Xena said evenly. "You haven't any choice," she added as Gabrielle would have protested again. "Not if you're going to help me—help *us*—get those girls back."

67

Nausicaa, Gabrielle reminded herself. Her own fears were small compared to what Nausicaa must be going through—torn from her nurse, grabbed by crude men and tossed into a chariot, and unable to see what was happening as she was jolted along at high speed. *At least the times I've been stuck in one, I could see where I was going.* She swallowed, hard. "I can do it," she said solemnly.

"Good. Find out what you can, then follow. And hurry."

"I'll be quick," Gabrielle promised. Xena nodded, checked her weaponry, and strode after the huntress, who was now staring intently, and rather theatrically, toward the north. Moments later, the two were gone, Atalanta sprinting like a deer, Xena running steadily, a distance back, along the hard-packed sand between rutted wheel marks. She was losing ground as the crowd closed in behind them—but not as much as Gabrielle might have feared.

There wasn't much Stymphe could tell her, Gabrielle realized after a moment; the woman was elderly, not in good health, and likely in shock from having seen her precious charge snatched by a pack of thugs. Probably her worst nightmare. The other mothers weren't much more help, except the one who'd been biting her hand to keep from sobbing aloud—and things had happened too quickly for her to have much more to add. "Three black-armored men jumped down from war chariots," she said, her gaze fixed blankly on Homer as she sought to calm herself and recall what she could. "Expensive chariots and good horses; I wondered, when I saw them, was the king here to watch Atalanta race—or maybe the queen had come. But the men—the armor was hand-me-down, ill-fitting and in poor condition; the men, dirty and ugly, and—and they knew what they were doing. They had dark scarves pulled high on their faces; I couldn't see much but eyes. Before I could move or even cry out, they had my Euterpe snatched up and tossed into the nearest car; the man who'd grabbed her was in and the driver already lashing the horses up; and they were—were gone, out to hard sand and through the crowd, out of sight before I found my voice." Homer came forward to pat her arm awkwardly. "I didn't—didn't see the rest, just the one car and the men. My Euterpe—" She gulped, and tears ran down her face.

Stymphe came alive in Gabrielle's grasp; one skinny arm shot out, a wrinkled and trembling finger leveled at the young bard, who stared at it in astonishment. "He! He's one of 'em! Part of it all! Somehow—! Don't hush me, young woman," she added in a hysterical voice as Gabrielle tried to explain who Homer was. "Who wheedled at me to let my princess stay for the last race? What was it to *him* if she was here or not, except to make another girl for those men to—for those dreadful men to steal? How much of the ransom did they promise you, boy, if you helped them?" Her voice cracked, and she burst into tears once more.

Behind him, Homer could hear angry muttering from the crowd. He spread his arms wide and raised his voice. "It's not so, I'm from the Academy! An apprentice bard, nothing more! I only wanted to see Atalanta race, and I knew the princess and her companion did as well, that's all! What girl here would have gone happily home without getting to watch that final race? Of course I pleaded her cause!"

"It's true!" Gabrielle added in a crowd-hushing, strong voice. Momentary silence. "I know Homer, he's a fine bard, not a—a—well, he's certainly not one of those men, or in league with them! He was only doing what he could so Nausicaa could be here to run her own finals, and for the last race. I—gods, Stymphe, where's Mitradia?" The old woman merely shook her head and tried to gulp back tears. "Did they take both girls?" Gabrielle demanded urgently and gave the old woman a brief, hard shake. "Both?" Stymphe drew a shuddering breath and nodded.

"Both. I—." She gave Homer a miserable look. "Mayhap he's no part of those who stole my princess, but he's at fault all the same! By now, she and I'd be halfway home to her father, and now I've got to make that journey alone and tell him—tell him—" Tears puddled in the corners of her eyes and ran down her seamed face.

"Stay here," Gabrielle ordered. "We'll get them back. After all," she added with a would-be encouraging smile, "Atalanta's the best tracker in all Greece, isn't she? Of course, she is! And Xena's—well, I don't envy those men when *she* gets done with them." She turned to Homer and held out her hand. "I guess I'd better get going. Maybe I'll see you when we get back with the girls." But he was already shaking his head.

"No, Gabrielle. I've never had an opportunity like this; I may never have one again, to pick up such a tale firsthand. I'm coming with you." Gabrielle hesitated and began to shake her head, but Homer gestured toward Stymphe. "She made me responsible for Nausicaa and Mitradia, you heard her," he said quietly. "I can't just—just go back to the Academy and wait for word of them, can I? Besides—" His eyes moved from side to side, taking in those around him. Some of them were still giving him narrow-eyed, suspicious looks.

Gabrielle sighed. *I really can't leave him here—all these frightened women and angry men—and hysterical old Stymphe to urge them on. They'd probably murder him on the spot, once my back was turned. Or have the guards— probably awful Anteros—arrest him.* A corner of her mind wondered where the guards were—but there was an uproar of some kind over in the market, the shouting and outraged cries momentarily topping even the noise around her.

No, it wouldn't be safe to leave Homer. She hadn't seen him sport so much as a nail knife in the time they'd previously spent together; he'd be utterly helpless. *But he doesn't have any idea how dangerous this journey might become; he only sees the adventure.* Now, there was irony. *I just hope he won't get strange about it if I wind up having to protect him.* But that wasn't important at the moment. Getting on Argo, and getting on her way, was. She smiled. "Well—no, I guess that would be a lot to ask. And I wouldn't dream of trying to keep you from a tale like this. I hope you can ride double."

"I can do what I have to," he said evenly, though his eyes were suddenly all pupil, and he eyed the placid Argo with visible misgivings. "We'd—better go."

"Right." Gabrielle looked down at the old woman, who seemed about ready to collapse, then searched the crowd. "Arachne?" she said sharply, her voice raised. "Arachne, are you still here?" The weaver, who'd been quietly and slowly retreating, came back into sight, her eyes wide and her color high. "Arachne, I'm sorry about your scarf."

"Don't be," the weaver said softly. Her dark eyes softened with sympathy as she looked at the weeping and frightened mothers. "I heard all of it. Get them back safely, Gabrielle. That's much more important than a mere scarf."

Gabrielle nodded and smiled. "We will. But I was hoping I could ask a favor of you. If you'd be a kind soul and stay here with Stymphe until we bring her charges back, I'd really appreciate it. See that she eats something, would you?"

"I'd be glad to help," Arachne said; she looked very shy as she shifted her bundle to one arm and came forward to take hold of the older woman's elbow. *Probably afraid of another ear-splitting set of hysterics*, Gabrielle thought. But Arachne had heart; it won through. "Stymphe, isn't

71

it?'' she asked softly. ''They'll bring back your girls. Have you had anything to eat or drink recently?'' Alternately cooing soft words and tugging gently at the woman's arm, she began to ease her away from the racecourse. ''It's all right. We won't go far, in case they find the girls right away. We'll stay close by. But you don't want to make yourself ill for when they come, do you? And don't you think you should get out of the wind? The sand's starting to blow.'' Two of the mothers followed, arms around each other for support.

Gabrielle turned away and gave Argo a long look, sighed faintly, then pulled herself awkwardly into the saddle, slid her staff into a pocket near her left foot, and tied it down firmly with a pair of loose straps. Having settled herself, she held out a hand to Homer, who eyed the tall horse with visible misgivings. He finally shrugged, slipped his foot into the stirrup Gabrielle had vacated for him, and swung up. She reclaimed the stirrup and kneed Argo, who swung around, paced evenly onto the hard-packed wet sand, then set out at a smooth canter, obliterating his mistress's boot-prints.

Gabrielle eased one white-knuckled hand from the reins to grip Homer's fingers. ''You can ease up just a little!'' she shouted to him over her shoulder. ''You still won't fall off, but right now, I can't breathe!''

''S-s-s-s-orry!'' His voice jolted as he bounced; he cautiously shifted his death grip to her skirts and the edge of the saddle. ''I'm not really used to riding,'' he added in a tight, high voice. ''Not sure I like it!''

''Trust me,'' Gabrielle replied grimly. ''I know *just* how you feel!'' Argo flicked an ear her direction, and she leaned cautiously forward, transferring one hand to the horse's mane. ''*You* pay attention to the ground in front of you, my four-footed friend,'' she ordered. ''Not to me!'' Behind her, Homer laughed nervously.

Some distance ahead, just as most signs of the city had been left behind, the beach curved westward and narrowed, then narrowed again. The ground to their left sloped up, ever more steeply, until it was a vertical stone precipice dotted with wind-ragged pines; fallen stones, scree, and boulders made footing treacherous. The sun was well behind the ridge, the air around them much cooler than it had been earlier, and only the distant light on the water, well out to sea, let them know it was still the hour short of sunset. Gabrielle sighed, drew Argo to a halt, and freed the stirrup for Homer's use before she slid from the horse's back and momentarily braced herself—and her trembling legs—against the saddle. Her voice, for a wonder, sounded normal. Calm. ''Look, it's getting too dark for me to see very far ahead of us, and frankly, if we have to go at a walking pace, I'd rather use my own feet.'' She gave Argo a smile, and his warm neck a tentative pat. ''Nothing personal, friend,'' she added, wrapping the reins around one hand and tugging the staff free with her other. ''You okay?'' she asked Homer.

Homer groaned. He was leaning against a rock, both hands digging into the small of his back. ''If that's directed to me—I'm alive. I think. Does that count?''

''It counts. You did great, honestly. Help me keep an eye on the tracks, will you? We really need to catch up to Xena and Atalanta before full dark—if we possibly can.'' She was bent nearly double, gazing at the sand; at one point she knelt to stare intently at something—he couldn't make out what, without bending very sore knees, which at the moment didn't appeal to him at all. Then she got up and peered ahead, tugging at Argo's rein to get the horse moving again.

Homer indicated the deep wheel ruts that still ran close to what had been the tide line about an hour earlier. "Can't miss those—at least for now."

"Or Xena's bootprints. I guess the narrower ones must be Atalanta's; she doesn't leave much of an impression in the sand, either. Still, once we're off the sand, or it gets darker, I—hmmm." She mumbled to herself for a moment, then shrugged. "The moon should be an early one tonight, but it won't be very big. Let's hope we won't need to use it." Momentary silence. "I can hear water—a stream. Good. I could use a drink."

"Me, too, after that ride. I'm glad you know these things." Homer hesitated, then moved to take her hand and give her a very warm smile. "Thank you, Gabrielle."

She blinked. "Me? For what?"

"Possibly saving my life back there. And for letting me have this chance. I—" He gazed down at his hands, and shrugged. "I probably won't be of much use to you or to them. Xena and Atalanta. Or the stolen girls. After all, I don't fight. Father would never let me learn. Still—"

"Oh, Homer," Gabrielle broke in as he hesitated once more. "You can't be certain how much help you'll be, and neither can I. After all, when I first started traveling with Xena, I didn't have one of these." She spun the staff deftly; his eyebrows went up. "And I seem to remember spending a lot of time getting into trouble, and her having to come save my neck." She held up the staff and started toward the running water; he followed. "Still, even back then, I could talk my way out of things, and sometimes that was a lot of help to her. Unexpected help. So don't feel like you have to be able to swing a sword to help out; it just isn't true." She glanced sidelong at Homer; suddenly, her

74

cheekbones felt warm as she knelt at the water's edge and drank next to him. Flustered, she freed a flat leather pouch from her belt, uncorked it, and eased the opening into the stream.

"Did I ever tell you about what happened when I made the mistake of telling a virgin priestess and a cave full of concerned villagers and priests that the girl was reading from a sacred scroll in the wrong rhythm? And how when I read it right, I woke three Titans?" She sighed and shook her head. "That could have been an awful mess. It was— well, it came awfully close. But Xena fought one of the Titans, Hyperion, and a bunch of really nasty thug types who'd been threatening the villagers—which was why they wanted the Titans to fight for them in the first place. Well, who knew the Titans would be looking out for Number One, rather than the people who freed them? I talked as fast as I've ever talked in my life, and it still wasn't easy."

Gabrielle glanced sidelong at Homer as she pulled the filled bag from the water and recorked it. He was openly appreciative of the tale, and she could almost hear his mind filing it away for later retelling. "Well, anyway," she said with an offhand shrug, "that's how we started out together. Xena fought, I talked. And between us, we fixed things. The two remaining Titans were turned back to stone, the thugs were run off or flattened, and the village was saved."

"Really?" He smiled warmly; she couldn't tell if he thought she was embroidering wildly on some tale from her own village or actually telling the truth. He obviously liked the story—well, that was something, anyway. She got stiffly to her feet, hung the dripping bag from the saddle, and took up the reins.

"Really," Gabrielle said solemnly as she picked her way around a pile of rubble; Argo followed, his muzzle dripping onto her arm. She sighed faintly and wiped away the cool drops. "If we were going the right direction, I could even show you the cave where they are—you can make out their shapes in the rocks. She was really pretty—Theia, the Titaness—and nice, too."

"Really!" Homer said thoughtfully. Of course, that was another bardic trick: offer to show the exact location of the tale—if only you could. But there was always a good-sounding excuse why you couldn't. Still, he seemed impressed. "When there's time, you'll have to tell me the whole tale."

"Well, sure." She cast him a warm smile, and thought, *Everything except maybe the part about Phyleus.* The young priest had nearly been her "first." Not that Homer wouldn't understand about that kind of thing—she thought he would. He certainly wouldn't be jealous, because he and she weren't *that* sort of friends. But—well, some things were a little too personal to share. *Come to think of it, I've never explained about Phyleus to Xena, either. And I have no clue about any relationships Homer had before we met. Or since—or presently.*

Some distance ahead of them, Xena ran steadily along a dusty, narrow track that bordered a dry streambed and wound slowly uphill between two steep-sloped mountains. It was nearly dark in the ravine; now and again, she had to slow to check for tracks, though it wasn't likely the men or the chariots would have been able to branch off this track once they'd ridden onto it. Most places, stones and trees would block anything but a fairly narrow human from striking out cross-country. Atalanta was still ahead of her, but she was steadily gaining on the huntress; the narrow, shallow footprints were less and less blurred by wind each time she checked. The chariot tracks, unfortunately, were clearly hours old.

One long, last climb brought her out of the trees and into an area of cracked and pulverized stone. An odd shape in the increasing gloom brought her up short: a chariot, one wheel shattered, rested at an awkward angle against the bank. The horse traces had been cut, and the horses were long gone. The rails were cool, lightly beaded with dew, and the car was empty. Another hundred or so paces further, the path moved away from the streambed, crossed smoothed, solid stone for a short distance, and then, narrower than ever, went back into soft dirt. More tracks were here, scarcely visible even when she knelt to examine them: a number of thin chariot wheels had passed here; after them, narrow boots. Xena sighed and gazed around as she got to her feet. Still no way for a chariot to leave the road; it would be smashed to bits on the stones, even if the horses could manage to pick a way through without breaking a leg or throwing the riders. She drew a deep breath, resettled her sword more firmly in its scabbard, and took off again.

The moon was just beginning to peer over the edge of the cliff to her left to shine on the sea, and great rock to give way to trees and brush, when she caught up to Atalanta. The sprinter was standing in the midst of the track, clearly waiting for her, arms folded across her chest. At her back, a clutch of five empty chariots stood midroad. A pale horse limped slowly from shade behind her and nuzzled the ground at the track's edge; a length of harness bound him to the wheel of the nearest chariot.

Sweat beaded on the huntress's brow and plastered the thin yellow chiton to her skin; her long, thin mouth was sardonic. "Xena. I *knew* I could count on you. What took you so long?"

"I'm here now," Xena replied steadily, and started to go around her. Atalanta held out an arm and shook her head.

"Go right on, if you insist. I got here too late to read the tracks or the road clearly; it was too dark to see anything except that they'd used a branch to obliterate footprints moving away from the cars, and they'd done that for some distance up the road and on both sides of it. Also, that stupid lame brute has muddled the ground all around the carts. I need light before I can tell which way they've gone—real light, not simply a torch. And I need sleep before I make another run like that last one." She shrugged. "But of course I wouldn't dream of telling *you* what to do. You want to go tearing around the woods in full dark, be my guest. The horse's skin is cool; they've been gone for some time—before sunset, easily."

"Really," Xena said flatly as the huntress paused.

"Really. Don't bother to take my word for it," Atalanta added sourly. "You ride, you've driven a chariot. Figure it out for yourself, the distances and how hard a horse can run a road like this one."

"I'll take your word—for now."

"Thank you *so* much. Take the time to figure it, you'll see I'm right. They could be anywhere. Like twenty paces behind me, or halfway to Sparta."

"Why would they go to Sparta?" Xena asked evenly.

"Why go anywhere? Why take those girls? Why take this road? Why would *I* know?" Atalanta snapped. "I doubt they're close, because sound carries in country like this, and I haven't heard anything in an hour, except you coming up the road. My own guess is that they're beyond the ridge over there." She turned to point roughly northwest.

Xena gazed at her for a long moment, then shrugged. "All right, I'll wait. I'd like to be able to see what I'm walking over, anyway." Her smile was a mirthless flash of teeth. "No offense intended. If those men were going to murder their captives, they'd have done it by now.'' Other, equally ugly possibilities hung unspoken between them.

"They'd have murdered the girls on the spot, back on that beach in Athens, if that was what they wanted to do. By now, if they'd wanted to—to—well, anything is possible," Atalanta agreed coldly.

"And if it's done, then it's beyond preventing. Agreed." Xena wasn't about to let herself be baited. "All right, we'll wait here until daybreak. You going to object to a fire?''

The huntress considered this, then shook her head. "A small one—no. A fire on this road could be anybody, I suppose. They—they might not expect someone following them yet, and they—I don't know. They aren't on this side of the ridge for certain. I would have heard or seen something.''

"Really?''

"It's what I do, remember?'' Atalanta hissed. "You want fire, we'd better start getting wood together before we have to find it by feel. And I hope you don't need anything hunted tonight; it's too dark, and I'm tired.''

"Don't put yourself out on my account,'' Xena replied with a flash of teeth. The huntress spun away and stalked across the road. Xena went in the opposite direction to see what she could find.

It took time to get enough dry wood and small bits to start a fire that wouldn't light the entire hillside—or smoke; by the time Xena got it to catch properly, it was full dark. Atalanta huddled in her boarskin cape, her dark eyes fixed on the fire. Xena dropped down across from her, felt in one of her small belt bags, and drew out a trail stick—a tough, dried mess comprised of bits of smoked meat, fruit, and herbs, rolled together and dried over an apple-wood fire. Not the greatest taste, but better than her attempts at soup

or stew, and good for filling the stomach and for energy.
"Here," she said, and held out the stick. Atalanta started
nervously, eyed the thing—or the hand holding it—warily,
then shook her head. "Go on," Xena urged. "I have several. You can pick one and watch me take the first bite, in
case you think I'm trying to poison you."

"Hah," Atalanta responded sourly, and snatched the
stick. She turned a little aside to sink her teeth into it—shy
about eating with anyone else, Xena thought, or unwilling
to let her despised comrade see how desperately hungry she
was. *She doesn't eat enough to keep a butterfly alive. Look
at her—all bone and skin, no muscle anywhere except her
legs. I don't care what goddess has blessed her, or how
fast she can run, that isn't healthy.* "Thank you," the huntress mumbled finally. "Tough—but it tastes good. I hope
it isn't half lard," she added warily, and stopped chewing.

"Just enough to hold it together. Here—take another,
you worked for it."

"I—"

"Go on," Xena urged. "It won't make you fat."

"Fat." Atalanta shuddered and let the half-eaten stick
fall. Xena sighed under her breath, retrieved the stick,
wiped it off, and held out another.

"You need something in your stomach, particularly after
a day like today. You need the energy, all right? You want
to find those girls tomorrow and get them back to their
mothers, don't you? You ought to know you can't do it
without food. Real food. But this will hold you over." *Until
Gabrielle gets here,* she added to herself. Atalanta seemed
to have forgotten about *that* little detail; it could stay forgotten until the girl actually got here. Avoid another spat,
at least for the moment. Atalanta took the second stick, bit
off an end and chewed, her eyes fixed blankly on the
ground just in front of the fire.

Xena shoved another dry branch into the flames and found herself hoping Gabrielle was still carrying her favorite soup starter—the leather bag filled with sun-dried vegetables and a few bits of travel stick, a handful of barley, and whatever herbs she had at hand to kill the taste of the leather bag. It had kept the two of them fed on more than one night when they'd been between villages at full dark. Better yet, maybe the girl would have had the forethought to stop at one of the streams she'd crossed coming here so she could add water to the mix; if so, it could be poured into the pot strapped to Argo's ample rump and then heated. It wasn't exciting, or even particularly tasty, but it was certainly better than her own cooking. With a few slices of dry bread tossed into the pot, it made an extremely filling soup.

But, she admitted to herself, the necessity of riding Argo had probably driven everything else from Gabrielle's head. If Gabrielle had to track down water up here, it would take at least an hour for the dry stuff to soften and become soup. The warrior scowled at her half-eaten trail stick. *Amazing. I'm sitting across a campfire from someone I detest—someone who can barely stand to be on the same mountainside with me. We're waiting for dawn so we can track down dirty thugs who'd dare kidnap young girls—and all I can think about is food. Dear gods and goddesses, Gabrielle's finally gotten to me.*

Her mouth quirked, and she turned away to hide a smile. Atalanta would surely assume it was somehow directed toward her, an intended insult, and start another argument. At the moment, the quiet was particularly nice.

It lasted for at least another hour. The moon had broken free of the distant sea, and the tops of the taller trees were frosted with pale light; the fire had burned down once, and Xena had gone for more wood. Atalanta finished her trail stick, pulled the boarskin close around her, and sank into a moody study of her sandals. Silence, except for the soft snapping of the fire. Thin clouds rolled in from the south; the moon appeared to be flying across the sky as it sailed in and out of cover.

The lame horse roused them both, whickering softly. Atalanta rolled her eyes, but Xena was already on her feet, striding toward the road. She reached it just as the moon broke clear once more. The bluish light bleached Gabrielle's hair and Argo a ghastly white. A third figure limped at Gabrielle's side.

Gabrielle caught sight of Xena and waved. "Hi! Hope we aren't too late. I brought dinner and—and I brought Homer. I think they were gonna lynch him back there on the sand, it was getting crazy. Well, I thought, you really shouldn't waste a good bard, right?"

Xena smiled; behind her, she could hear Atalanta cursing steadily and inventively under her breath. "Main reason I keep you around, Gabrielle. Besides your traveling stew, of course." The smile broadened. "I'm glad to see you again so soon, Homer. You already met Atalanta, didn't you?"

5

"I'm glad you took me at my word and made a picnic of this," Atalanta growled. Xena chopped a hand her direction for silence and followed it up with a warning glare. Gabrielle, unusually sensitive to mood this night, laughed nervously.

"Listen, I also brought you Argo—and hey, nothing personal, horse, but she's all yours. And vice versa. I may not be able to *stand* tomorrow, let alone walk. Human legs weren't meant to spread that far apart, you know?" She turned to her companion and asked anxiously, "Homer, are you going to survive this?"

"I'm dead," he moaned.

Gabrielle gave a weary smile and patted his shoulder. "Hey, a little food, a little conversation around the fire, a good night's sleep, you'll be fine." The eyes that met Xena's were worried, though; she turned away, freed the pot and the leather bag from the saddle, and limped toward the fire. "I'm earning my keep. I want you to know the stew's been soaking since the foot of that cliff, so it should only need to warm up."

Xena took the reins and led Argo around the fire, slowing to murmur in Atalanta's direction, "Remember what I told you earlier: only a fool annoys a bard. The resulting stories are usually wildly comic, easily repeatable, and not at all amusing to the fool." Atalanta gave her a searing look, then turned away to glare at the fire. "Fine. Be that way. You have two bards here, it's your choice," Xena added. "If you've got any sense, you'll come off the sulk and think of this as the chance for two heroic tales about the fabled huntress for the price of one." The fabled huntress cast the warrior another black glance, but by the time Gabrielle and Homer staggered up to the fire, she had composed her face and even managed a faint, shy-looking smile for both before she bent to gather a handful of sticks to feed to the fire. Her eyes were mutinous, but neither Gabrielle nor Homer was in any condition to notice.

Gabrielle cautiously eased herself down, winced as her backside made contact with hard and rocky ground, then settled the blackened pot against the fire and concentrated on pouring cold stew makings from the bag into the pot. "There. That won't take awfully long, it's been soaking since—well, it sure feels like forever." She smiled in Atalanta's direction, but the woman's attention seemed to be fixed on the flames. Homer sat down beside her. "Homer? You sure you're all right? I mean, you're moving even more slowly than I am, and I *know* how bad I feel."

"Mmmm." He had only just managed to get himself settled. "I'm sorry, Gabrielle; I—" His color appeared rather high, though that might have been a trick of the fire. "You know my father—a little about me. He wanted me to be a bard so much, I never—well, I've never been on a horse before today."

Gabrielle gazed at him in astonishment, and even Atalanta looked surprised before bending back to feed the fire. "You—really?" Gabrielle demanded.

He shrugged and wouldn't meet her eyes. "I told you. He's a carpenter, and a good one, but he wanted so much more for me. He wanted me to be a bard from the first time I told a tale—"

"When you were five," Gabrielle said softly. "I remember, see?"

"Five," Homer agreed quietly. "I'm—please understand, it's all I ever wanted, too. But it meant changes in my life. Suddenly there were new rules, things I had to do each day, things I couldn't do. He meant it for the best, I know he did," he said unhappily.

"Homer, I've met Polonius," Gabrielle said, even more softly. One small hand cupped his chin and forced his eyes to meet hers. "He loves you very much, and of course he wanted the best for you. He just didn't know how to go about making your dream come true. All of that—those new rules—they set you apart from the other boys in your village, didn't they?"

"Right from the first," Homer said. His hand came up to rest on hers, and he smiled briefly. "I couldn't go into the fields with the other boys, couldn't serve as a crowscare just before harvest, couldn't participate in any of the harvest fest races—might somehow injure my voice, you see—couldn't ride anything from a donkey to a horse, for fear I might fall and hurt myself."

"That would be hard on a boy," Gabrielle said quietly. "On anyone. But at least you had your stories."

He smiled. "I did. And it was nice, honestly. Father'd come in at night, and after we ate, he'd sit back with some bit of carving or something, just keeping his hands busy, while I told him a story—sometimes one of the myths that I knew, often something I'd made up myself during the day. It was lonely sometimes, but not always—especially during the hot days of summer. The other kids preferred sitting in the shade and listening to tales, so I was pretty popular then.''

Atalanta was gazing at him from across the fire, but as Gabrielle shifted, the huntress got up and walked away. Gabrielle's eyes followed her briefly. Homer, who was biting his lip as he cautiously kneaded his fingers together, didn't seem to notice. Silence. ''Well, I'll tell you what,'' Gabrielle said finally. ''That was brave of you, getting up on Argo and coming with me. I would have been petrified.''

''I was,'' he admitted ruefully. ''If I'd had time to think, I probably wouldn't have done it.'' He glanced up at her and smiled briefly, then went back to massaging his hands. ''So it wasn't really bravery at all, just—not thinking.''

''You can call it what you like—I know what I think.'' Gabrielle held a hand over the contents of the pot. ''Warm but not boiling—it's ready when you are,'' she announced.

The stew didn't last long. Gabrielle swabbed the bottom of the pot with a handful of grass and set it aside, then stretched out on her back with a stifled groan. ''I'm gonna hate the morning,'' she mumbled, and closed her eyes.

''You'll be fine after a few minutes on your feet,'' Xena told her. It was the first thing she'd said in hours. Atalanta licked stew from her fingers and gave the warrior a cold, sidelong look. ''So, Gabrielle, tell me what you learned back there.''

''Well—it wasn't much, I'm afraid.'' The girl spread her hands in a broad shrug. ''The usual thing. You know, it all happened so fast, no two people saw the same thing. What I got was a bunch of really grubby down-on-their-luck types—worse than Kalamos and *his* bunch, the kind who probably wouldn't be good for much beyond stealing help-less little girls," she said indignantly.

"Never mind, Gabrielle," Xena put in. "Getting angry won't help anyone right now. What else?"

"Well, the carts and horses and everything—that was new and shiny, expensive stuff. Stolen from some noble or another, I'd say." Atalanta started, and Gabrielle glanced in her direction; the huntress shook her head and began sucking her fingers, as though she'd burned them.

"Good thought," Xena said approvingly. "If necessary, we can find out who in Athens might be missing some expensive chariots and everything that goes with them— and if he had a reason for hiring pond scum to drive them and kidnap girls from that race." She scowled at her hands, then eyed Gabrielle. "It doesn't make sense; men of that class don't drive chariots. It takes skill and training."

"Well—sure." Gabrielle considered this, then nodded enthusiastically. "I should have caught that; after all, I've ridden in a couple of the things . . ." A corner of Xena's mouth quirked.

"You sure have."

"So whatever they might be—the guys who grabbed the girls, I mean—the guys who drove are professionals."

"I'd think so. What else?"

"Else . . . hmmm." Gabrielle's brow furrowed briefly. "Not much. They covered their faces, everything but the eyes, according to one mother." Her face was suddenly solemn as she remembered the mother in question. Euterpe's mother. Where was Euterpe at this hour? Was she sleeping, dead, scared, in tears? *I must have seen her run, but she could have been any of them, eager young girls trying to copy their hero. Atalanta.* Their hero sat like a stone, staring at the fire, still absently rubbing her fingers. Oblivious.

87

"All right." Xena's words broke an increasingly dismal train of thought. "So possibly they didn't want to show their faces. Which might mean they're known in the market."

Gabrielle shook herself. "Good point. Still—why?"

"We'll find that out tomorrow, won't we?"

Gabrielle eyed her solemnly. "Let's hope we will. One day is more than enough. Those poor girls, the women waiting for them, the fathers . . . it's dreadful."

Xena's eyes were grave. "I know. It's something you can't make better by dwelling on, though. Think of something else to talk about, why don't you?"

Something else . . . what else was there, just now? Gabrielle wondered unhappily. Homer patted her shoulder, then shifted his weight cautiously, and smiled at Atalanta.

"I couldn't help noticing your cloak," he said in a clear shift of topic. "It's a beautiful hide."

It would have taken a harder woman than Atalanta to withstand such an assault of youthful charm, Xena thought. After a moment, Atalanta smiled back at him, then shrugged, trying to be casual. "It's boar—something I got in Caledonia," she said. Homer's eyes went wide and his jaw dropped.

"That boar? *That*—that hunt?" he breathed. She nodded. "I've heard about it, the way one does—bits of rumor and so on. But never—I mean," he added carefully, "I know you have your own personal bard. I'm certain he's already set the tale in verse for you, and I'd never dream of trying to steal his fire, but—" He gazed down at the ground, then glanced back at her.

To his surprise, and Xena's astonishment, Atalanta laughed aloud, a delighted young girl's laugh that erased years from her face, and clapped her hands together.

"You're sweet," she said in a shy girl's voice. "What do they call you, bard?"

"Ah—ah—ah—Homer," he stuttered; the tip of his nose was suddenly very red.

"Homer. Well, I'll tell you, Homer. Endymion is a very passable bard, but he doesn't care much for *my* tales. He prefers tales of pure heroism like Orpheus' journey to rescue his beloved Eurydice from Hades, or just—well, love. He doesn't like telling violence—and the boar of Caledonia certainly was a nasty brute." She pulled a log from near the fire, settled it behind her back, and clasped her hands around one knee; her gaze was fixed on something beyond the road and the abandoned chariots. "Four times the size of a normal boar and of an evil temper," she murmured. "It killed cattle and men at will, trampled the fields—"

"They say a goddess sent it to punish the king for not remembering to decorate her shrine," Homer put in as she paused. "Though I thought it unkind of the goddess to make an entire kingdom suffer and starve for the mental lapses of one man."

Atalanta shrugged. "It's as good a tale as any, I suppose. I thought the beast simply came down from the mountains after the heavy snows two winters ago. However it came, it was there, tearing Caledonia to shreds. The king was desperate; nothing he'd tried had worked, so someone suggested a great hunt. Word went around, the way it does." Her gaze slid sideways and fixed on Xena. "I'm surprised *you* weren't there."

Xena shook her head, and the corner of her mouth twitched. "I heard about it, but I wasn't much interested. I was up north, helping some villagers. I'm not a hunter or a hero, anyway." She turned away and fed sticks into the fire.

"There were a lot of us," Atalanta went on after a moment. Her eyes were warm, her voice suddenly soft and almost dreamy. "Some of the bravest and handsomest young Greeks, well muscled, weapons-crafty, yet still at that golden age when sunlight touches the skin with love and the beard does not yet darken young cheeks. The brothers Castor and Pollux . . . young Pirithuos, and his friend Theseus . . ."

"You *know* the king?" Gabrielle demanded, her eyes wide.

"Well—" Atalanta smiled faintly and shrugged. "I hunted with him. We never spoke, though. Odd, in a way, since *he* married an Amazon. He certainly couldn't have been affronted by my presence, or afraid of me. Like some."

"Yes. You were the only woman, weren't you?" Homer put in softly. "That must have been—I can't imagine it."

"It wasn't very pleasant," she said. "Not at first, especially. I already had something of a reputation as a huntress, of course, or I wouldn't have dared set foot in the palace. But most of the men there were older, set in their ways. You know the sort," she added sourly and lisped in a high, angry voice: " 'Let your parents raise and train you, then ride in a covered litter to the home of *my* mother and stay within those walls to the end of your days, taking care of *me*.' It's Menelaus and his kind, poisoning men's minds, if you ask *me*," she added in an even angrier voice. "They treated me like—the *nicest* thing most of them said was, 'Go home and play with your dolls, little girl.' "

"How unfair! That would hurt," Homer said.

Gabrielle sat up next to him and shook her head. "Of course it would hurt—but I wouldn't think about that at the time. It would really make me angry. Mad enough to want to prove myself."

Atalanta's gaze rested thoughtfully on her. "You really aren't stupid, are you? That's just what it did. Well—it made me angry enough to demand an audience with the king, so I could invoke my right to stay in the hunt. The call hadn't specified *male* heroes only, after all. But the king was a weakling.'' Her eyes were dark with remembered humiliation. ''Bullied by his wife, Althea, who tried to swaddle her only son from anything that might possibly hurt him in any fashion. *She* said—well, never mind what she said.'' She closed her eyes and sighed faintly. ''I argued for—it seemed hours. It might have actually been. Castor and Pollux were starting to take my side against some of the other men, they were shouting I should at least have a chance since I'd come so far and wanted it so badly. Some of the others were shouting that I'd wasted an entire day with my whining, that by now the boar could be dead and the feast begun. And Queen Althea was whispering in the king's ear, pressing him to send me home to my mother.''

She brooded on the fire. '' 'Send her home to her mother, with a message to put her in some decent skirts.' That's what *she* said, and when Castor—Pollux— You know,'' she said with a faint smile, ''I never *could* tell them apart! One of them was trying to get the king's attention, and Althea was about to have *him* tossed out, and that had his immortal brother up in arms. Then all at once, the prince came into the chamber.'' She drew a deep breath, let it out as a long, quiet sigh. ''Prince Meleager interceded, and his mother was caught in a proper trap. She couldn't deny her son—her perfect, priceless, only child—anything he really wanted, and what he wanted was—well, was me.'' She shrugged. ''So I got what I wanted, a chance to prove myself. And Meleager—well, he wanted me in the hunt, but for all the wrong reasons. It was maddening: I had my sights fixed on the boar, on tracking him and finishing him and winning out over everyone else there, and at every turn, there was Meleager. Everywhere I went, all that evening:

next to me at the feast, next to me during the entertainment that followed. At my side when we gathered the next morning to begin the hunt. I wasn't interested in—in *that*.'' Unexpectedly, she blushed a deep, fiery red. "Well, I wasn't," she added shortly. "And, of course, *he* wasn't really in love, or so I thought at the time. He was young for his years, I thought, and moonstruck.'' She wasn't paying heed to her audience at all; the words and the thoughts were inwardly directed. Gabrielle glanced at Xena, who rolled her eyes and shrugged.

With a start, Atalanta came back to the moment; her color was even higher as she glanced in Homer's direction. "I didn't care about that—Meleager, his mother, the others involved—about anything, so long as they let me into the field with the men, so long as I could be part of the hunt. It was so important, nothing else mattered. Well, we were out of the palace as soon as the sun rose, and found destruction and prints everywhere, almost to the castle walls in one place. Sign of the boar everywhere—but no boar.'' She held up her hands, making an enormous oval. Homer blinked. "No mistaking *his* prints for a normal pig's, either. Or the damage he'd left—the smell of death all around us—dead, bloated cattle and sheep everywhere, too many to burn, and the herders terrified to go into the fields to deal with them anyway.'' She came back to the moment with a little start and another brief smile for Homer. "You can see why Endymion wouldn't want to cast this into verse.''

"It wouldn't need to dwell on detail like that," Homer began, then shook his head. "Unimportant. I'm sorry, I didn't mean to interrupt you. Go on, please.''

"Well, we hunted most of that day, splitting into smaller and smaller groups, until finally it was me, Meleager, and another boy—I never knew his name, poor thing. The ground was boggy where we stood, the hour late and humid, no wind, and so of course, insects everywhere. I remember thinking the smell of dead beasts and mud and flowering weeds all combined was so awful. My legs and feet ached, and my arms were covered in bites. And I remember thinking how stupid that so many niggling, trivial things should interfere with something as important and heroic as this hunt.''

''I understand,'' Gabrielle said earnestly, and when Atalanta glanced at her, she nodded.

''Well—perhaps,'' the huntress conceded. Her eyes remained fixed on Gabrielle for a long, thoughtful moment. She shook herself then, and turned her gaze back to the fire. ''Well—where was I? Oh, yes. I was following fresh trace, when all at once the boy shouted, then screamed. He came flying out of the brush, and right on his heels was a massive, mottled blur. The ground shook. The boy's scream was cut off—'' She closed her eyes, then swallowed. ''The beast stopped maybe ten paces from us, and when I meet Cerberus, I swear he will seem not half as fearful as was that boar: as high at the shoulder as I am, bulky as an ox but fast on its feet, and terrifyingly agile. Hairs like that''— she held her hands nearly a forearm apart—''bristled from his snout; his eyes were''—she closed her eyes and shuddered—''were red, like dried blood. Evil. I looked into them and saw my death, saw the manner of it. It nearly froze me where I stood. But I think it couldn't decide which of us it wanted first, and that gave me my only chance. It settled that horrid gaze on Meleager and took one step forward. I threaded an arrow, drew back the bowstring, somehow calmed my breathing enough to steady the bow, sighted, and shot. The arrow lodged just behind the boar's shoulder, a deep wound but not a killing one. With a roar that momentarily deafened us, he wheeled and charged back into the brush. We followed at once, of course.''

"You—followed?'' Homer demanded breathlessly. "You went after a wounded boar of any size? Into the brush, where you couldn't see anything?''

Atalanta nodded, then licked her lips. "We didn't dare lose him. He was still a deadly threat, and it would be on my shoulders if I sent him straight back into the others in such a state. It would have been on my shoulders if he killed someone because I had only wounded him, and not made an instant kill. I was running as fast as I dared on that boggy, uneven ground, so of course Meleager lagged behind me. Though not by much,'' she added, and her mouth briefly softened. "When we got to open ground again, the boar was down, a dozen of our forces surrounding him, four spears and a handful of arrows in him. He was badly bloodied but still a danger. Castor, I think it was, caught hold of the beast's head and pulled it back so Meleager could cut his throat. We lost two hunters altogether—*only* two, as the better heroic tales will tell you—but the boar was dead.''

Her mouth tightened. "At the feast that night, they tried to honor Meleager with the hide because it was he who'd actually killed the brute. He refused it, and insisted it be given to me for drawing first blood. His mother—'' She shook her head and managed a smile. "Well, you wanted the tale; there it is. Pity I'm not a better teller.'' She stood abruptly and strode from the fire.

Homer stared after her. "Meleager—the name's familiar,'' he said vexedly. Gabrielle tapped his arm.

"He's dead. He died that very night,'' she said. "I've heard four or five different explanations of how he died, but it's all because he gave the hide to *her*, and his family and the other hunters were outraged.'' She turned to gaze after the huntress. "Poor thing. How awful to love a man and then have—have that to remember him by.''

Xena stirred. ''Maybe she didn't really love him, Gabrielle. Not everyone has your heart, you know. More likely she feels guilty because she didn't care for him at all. If she feels anything,'' she mumbled to herself. Gabrielle looked at her in confusion. ''Never mind, it's not important. I'm going to check on Argo, then I'm coming back to get some sleep. I'd suggest you two do the same; we'll be on the move before the sun's up tomorrow.'' She left the fire in the other direction. Gabrielle sighed.

''But the look in her eyes, just now. Atalanta's, I mean. I think she loved him—and probably didn't realize it until too late. Or maybe she did know but couldn't have told him. She just doesn't strike me as the kind of person who could openly say 'I love you.' '' She glanced at Homer. ''You know—like your father. Some people hold things in because they don't know how to say that without feeling foolish. Maybe she's one of those.''

''I know,'' Homer replied softly. ''That would be terribly sad, wouldn't it?'' He took her hand and held it lightly for a long moment, then shifted into bardic voice:

''Hold me gently in your hands,
Echo words I'll never say.
When my sentences are uttered,
You will carry me away.''

Gabrielle stared at him. ''I—Oh, wait, it's a riddle. And a good one,'' she added after a moment. She eased her hand from his and gazed down at both of hers as she thought hard. ''When my sentences are uttered—oh!'' She gave him an impudent grin. ''Scroll, of course.''

He rolled his eyes and smiled back. ''Of course. You *are* good; I tried that one at the Academy, and only Docenios got it.'' He shrugged. ''And I think only because he had a handful of scrolls at the time.''

Out in the darkness, Xena rubbed Argo's neck and stared back toward the fire. ''Very nice story,'' she murmured. Some of it might even be true. The hunt itself—well, the Caledonian boar hunt *had* taken place; details about it were sketchy and often contradictory. Possibly Atalanta had won the hide just as she said—though it was also possible she'd bought a large skin from a tanner.

No one had ever said Atalanta wasn't clever, and she was most certainly conscious of her image. Probably her latest boy-bard had concocted most of that heart-wrenching story from whole cloth. Once Atalanta realized she couldn't shake her unwanted companions, it might have occurred to her to appeal to Gabrielle's soft heart—and Homer's.

She's still a manipulator, and she doesn't care who gets hurt, so long as she comes out of things with her reputation as a hero unsullied. She might have fooled the others, but not me. Not after the last time.

On the other hand, it would take a professional actress to fake the emotion—the stark fear—she'd seen on Atalanta's face just now.

Argo lipped her fingers. ''Sorry, fellow,'' she murmured. ''I was ignoring you, wasn't I? I'd like to know what she's up to. Too many things about this whole mess just don't add up.''

Homer was lying flat on his back next to the fire, his eyes closed, when Xena returned. Gabrielle was curled on her side next to him—they were sharing his short wool cloak. She looked up as Xena sat down again, then slipped from beneath the cloak to sit, cross-legged, at her friend's side. ''We'll find them, won't we?''

Don't frighten her. At the moment, Xena wasn't certain what they'd find when they caught up to the kidnappers. Best not to share her fears. "We'll find them, Gabrielle. Soon."

"I hope so. I mean—I know you said not to worry about it, but I can't think of anything else at the moment. And I just can't think why anyone would—would do that, can you? I mean—Nausicaa's father's probably rich; he's a king, after all, and Phaecia is one of those island kingdoms where everything's always all right, for some reason. You know, locusts don't eat the crops, the fish fall into the nets, the fruit drops from the trees and doesn't get bruised when it falls. So he could pay a lot of money to get her back, and he probably would. But those men just rode up and grabbed girls at random, the way I heard it. And most of the mothers didn't look rich or anything." She bit her lip. "I know there are other reasons for stealing girls, but— such *young* girls!"

The warrior shook her head. "Don't tell yourself horror stories before you sleep, Gabrielle. You need rest, so you're ready for tomorrow. And that won't help the girls at all. Don't try to live their story; live your own."

"Don't—where'd you get that?" Gabrielle demanded. Xena smiled apologetically.

"It's something I've learned over the past few years. We'll catch up to them, get them away safe—and then we can worry about why, about who was involved, and why."

"I—all right. Thanks." Gabrielle smiled; Xena leaned over to tousle her hair.

"Any time. Get some sleep."

Just out of sight, shrouded in her boar cloak and tree shadow, Atalanta stood very still. *I knew she'd be suspicious of me, whatever I did. And that girl's too quick-witted in her own way.* She tugged hard at her hair. *But everything's still in place. I can still salvage it.*

She looked away from the fire and turned to pace between the trees. Everything had gone just as she'd intended. Why, of all people, had Xena chosen to show up at the women's footraces? *That girl, of course. The look on her face when she first met me . . . don't they realize how—how uncomfortable it makes me to see that much worship in someone's face every single time?* Or how hard it was to keep up the appearance of someone worthy of that look. She sighed very faintly, pulled the cloak closely around her arms, and stared gloomily at the abandoned chariots. *All right,* she ordered herself finally, *go over it one more time. So far everything is just fine; it will stay that way. Xena's suspicious, but that's only her way. She'd look at me like that no matter what I did, or said, any time we met, under any circumstance. It's fine; I don't like her either. Not after last time.*

Probably the best way to deal with Xena would be to return to the fire and sleep—or try to. She was exhausted, and her legs ached from that last hard uphill run. *The price you pay for having to reach this place first, to make certain there was nothing amiss when Xena got here. Time to go back to the fire and sleep.* She turned to look that way. Xena sat where she had earlier, feeding small sticks to the fire; the eager, chattery girl was no longer sitting next to her, her place taken by the fresh-faced young bard. He used his arms a lot, more than Endymion. *Not as—well, as pretty,* she thought. Probably not quite as young, either, by a year or more. They got too serious as they reached man's years. *Wait a little out here,* she decided. She didn't want another session like that last with Homer. The boy had probed too close to her heart with his questions, awakening emotions she'd rather have left fallow. Better to wait until he slept once more.

Homer glanced at the armor-clad woman next to him, then back to the fire. "I hope you don't think I'm presumptuous. But Gabrielle told me so much about you—"

"I'm sure she did," Xena said. Her eyes moved to the sleeping girl curled on her side under Homer's cloak, and she smiled. "She's told me about you, too." A companionable silence passed then; wind soughed through the treetops and the fire crackled.

"She beat me in the competition, you know," he said finally. "For placement at the Academy. Her story—it was wonderful."

"She told me about it—and about your slave. I forget the name. It was a good story. You earned your place, Homer."

"I—thank you. I—just wanted to say, while she's asleep, I didn't think ahead very well, and if I'm in your way, well—I'm sorry. I'll do my best not to be underfoot. I just—" He swallowed, then stared at the ground. Xena waited him out. "I told her I never had the opportunity before, in all my life, to see a heroic tale in the making. I know it sounds selfish—those poor frightened little girls out there somewhere, and here I sit, thinking about the wonderful story I can make of it all."

"Oh, I don't think that's exactly true," Xena said. "And you aren't in the way. Not in my way. Once I would have said just that." She smiled, and her eyes turned to the sleeping Gabrielle. "And then she decided I needed her. Well, she was right. It took me a little longer to realize that, of course. These days, I see a larger mural, like the ones made up of all those tiny bits of enameled clay. Things aren't solved just by brute strength, or valor, or even by words.

Sometimes it's a mixture of all that—'' She broke off and shrugged. "Words aren't what I do."

"It's all right," Homer said quietly after a long moment. "I understand what you're telling me. At least, I think I do. Thank you."

"Of course." Xena sighed faintly and stifled a yawn against the back of one hand. "I'm going to take my own advice and get some sleep. If you're smart, you will, too."

"I can try," Homer said. "But first," he added diffidently, and shifted into the bardic voice.

> "In with a breath and out with silence,
> ending with age or ills or violence.
> It's yours to spend wisely, or to squander.
> Some lay roots while others wander.
> Gods may get in the way,
> But they made you to run,
> Give your all 'til it's over, and
> The battles are won."

His eyes met hers, then shifted away.

Xena shook her head. "I don't do riddles, you know. Gabrielle'd like that one, since the answer is obviously life . . ."

To her surprise, he gasped, then broke into quiet laughter. "You know, I'm about to say something I should not ever say," he managed finally. "Certainly not to a warrior. You're much more clever than you think, Xena; don't sell yourself short."

She smiled faintly. "I don't. But I got lucky on that one."

"Gabrielle's told me about you—the kind of team you make. How it was in the beginning and how things have changed since."

Silence. Xena finally shrugged and said, "Oh."

Homer nodded. "Yes. It seems so odd to me, sitting here and talking to you like this." He cast her a quick, sidelong glance. "I mean, you're a warrior; I've never so much as struck anyone in anger in all my life. I grew up in a sleepy little village; we never saw war, danger—anything like that. While you—"

"It's not quite like that. I had a quiet childhood. I grew up in a village, in a world, where everything had been the same for generations. That all changed in a moment, the day raiders attacked us. We had no weapons, no chance at all. I saw my brother murdered by brutal men. And no one would do anything. I can understand now why they didn't want to fight. Some of them were too afraid, but most thought they were doing the right thing, that it would go that much worse for them and their families if they fought back. But I *knew* if we didn't do something, we'd all die anyway, and it infuriated me that men I'd known my whole life were telling us, 'Be patient, the king will rescue us, the gods will save us—' The king was at least two days' ride from us, and the gods didn't seem very interested in helping one small village." Her eyes were dark with remembered pain; silence held for a long moment, then she shook herself.

"Well, all right. It was a black hour, and someone had to do something. That"—she shrugged and cast him a faint smile—"that someone turned out to be me, and that decision started—well, like any decision, it changed my future." Silence, a long but comfortable one. "You can have that story if you like."

"Thank you." Homer yawned widely. Xena's jaws ached, and she turned away from him. "I think the best thing for me would be to try for more sleep. As you reminded me—reminded us—tomorrow comes early and goes long. Thank you.''

"Of course," Xena murmured. "Settle in as best you can. The wind will probably be strong by dawn."

Homer glanced at Gabrielle, then back at the warrior. "I hope you don't mind if we—I mean, it isn't anything—" His voice faded as Xena shook her head and smiled.

"I know it's not that kind of relationship, but it's not my business. Keep each other warm; you'll sleep better for it and be less stiff in the morning." Her smile widened. "A *little* less stiff."

"Morning." Homer contemplated it unhappily, but he obediently turned and cautiously, gently, took back a portion of the cloak from Gabrielle, who now slept on her stomach, the cloth pulled under her right shoulder.

Xena's eyes searched the surrounding road, slopes, woods, and distant silvery sea. Atalanta must be somewhere around, but she was beyond anything but a diligent search. *She's not worth that.* Probably waiting for everyone around the fire to fall asleep before she came back. The warrior banked the fire with a thick chunk of oak, then got to her feet and retrieved her seldom-used cloak from the pack at Argo's feet. Ordinarily she wouldn't need it at this time of year, but the combination of sea and mountain slope might make for chill wind or fog by morning.

The sky was a clear, cloudless blue, the air damp and cool, and the sun still below the horizon when Xena tugged at Homer's cloak. "Time to go, you two," she ordered. A pair of heartfelt groans was her only answer. "Up," she added, and gave the cloak another tug. It came away in her hand. Gabrielle sat up, eyes still closed, and wrapped her arms around herself; Homer mumbled something and curled into a tight little ball. "Atalanta's out on the road looking for a sign, which way they went from here. Hurry up."

"I'm dead," Homer muttered as she walked away. "Dead men don't go anywhere, not before the sun's up, anyway."

"Dead men don't talk, either," Gabrielle informed him through a yawn. "Ohhhh," she added as she staggered to her feet, "I *knew* I was gonna hate this!" Five short, cautious steps away from the fire; five back. She bit her lip, turned, and tried again. Gabrielle glared at Argo, who was quietly cropping grass a short distance away. "See if I ever get on *you* again!" It was easier walking back to the fire.

Barely. She held out a hand to Homer, who groaned as he took it; she tugged hard, and almost fell into him.

"Sorry," he mumbled. "Try again."

She braced herself and pulled, this time bringing him to his feet. "Walk a little bit, if you can," she said through clenched teeth. "It'll help."

"If that's a joke, it's a very poor one," he said, and moaned as he put weight on his right foot. "I don't think I'll ever walk again."

Gabrielle eyed him sympathetically, then winced as she bent forward to massage her legs. "I think you'll have to, actually. Or sit here forever."

"You can't think how wonderful that sounds at the moment." Jaw set, Homer took three slow, awkward steps that brought him to the nearest tree, eased himself around, and leaned against it. "I asked for this, didn't I?"

Gabrielle managed a pained smile for him. "No—you asked to come with me. No one would ask for *this*. Here, lean on me. We'll walk around the fire a couple of times. If it makes things any better, I don't think we'll be going very fast today."

"It helps—I think." He set his jaw and concentrated on walking for several moments. "Why slower?"

Gabrielle waved her free arm to take in the steep mountain-side, overhanging cliffs, windblown trees. "I wager even Atalanta can't run in that."

He eyed the terrain with misgivings. "I must have been mad," he said.

"It won't be so awful, honestly," she assured him. "And there'll be plenty of chances to rest, especially if the trail isn't very clear."

"But—why up there?"

"Well, those men abandoned the chariots here, so they obviously took to the countryside. They'll have to be

104

tracked, and that takes time.'' She frowned. ''I wonder if we have time to eat anything before we set out. I'm starved.''

Atalanta stood very still in the center of the road, her back to the chariots, eyes searching the nearest high ground. The surface of the road had been swept clean in both directions; she'd checked. Nothing to see except the prints of the lame horse, and now her own. She turned as something metal clicked against something else: Xena was moving between the cars, glancing into the interior of each. She finally shrugged and came on. ''So—you've searched. What did you find?''

''Not much,'' the huntress admitted. ''There's a tree branch just up there.'' She pointed to a notch in the steep ledge that bordered the east side of the road. ''Obviously what they used to cover their traces. They must intend for anyone following them to think they went that way—so they probably didn't.''

Xena eyed her sidelong. Atalanta glanced at her, then went back to her visual search of the mountain. *She can't possibly see anything up there, with the sun below the horizon out there, and everything still in shadow.* ''Maybe they're stupid and they really did go that way. Are you going to be able to tell?''

''If they manage to stay on dry, hard rock, probably not. But I know this country, it's not continuous stone. They'll have to move onto dirt, or grass, or a game trail, and when they do—'' Her voice trailed off, and she sighed. ''It's going to take time.''

''Well, then, we'd better get started, hadn't we?''

Atalanta cast her a sharp look; her mouth thinned with displeasure. ''Wrong. *I* look first, starting at that notch and working back this way, parallel to the road, until I find

105

some trace of them. *Then* we go. If you're all up there tromping around, you might cover sign and never know you did it. I'm the tracker, remember?''

''Oh, I remember,'' Xena said softly; her eyes were cold slits.

Atalanta turned to glare at her. ''What's that supposed to mean?''

''Nothing at all. You want to start looking alone, you'd better start now; they've had all the time they need to get ahead of us.''

''They had to stop at some point for rest,'' Atalanta said flatly. ''I'll call out when I see something. Keep your chattery little friends out of my way, all right? This is going to call for concentration.'' Xena closed the distance between them in a bound and fastened one hand in the throat of the yellow chiton. The huntress's mouth sagged, and her eyes went wide and nervous.

''I warned you once. Normally, that's all anyone gets. Six frightened little girls out there somewhere are buying you a second opportunity. It won't cost you much to be nice to Gabrielle *or* Homer, but it's going to cost you plenty if you treat her like dirt.'' She let go of the other woman's garment and gave her a little shove. ''Go concentrate. And remember what I said.'' Atalanta tugged the chiton straight, turned on her heel, and strode away. Xena watched as she crossed the road, then entered the narrow cut in the ledge she'd pointed out earlier. She vanished among thick brush and towering stone almost at once. Xena waited an additional count of ten, then turned back to inspect the carts and the road around them more closely.

She worked slowly, steadily, from the notch back down the road, checked each of the abandoned chariots in turn, but there was nothing to see except brush marks in the dust, overlaid here and there with Atalanta's narrow prints or the horse's marks. No identifying markings or paintings on the cars themselves, or on what was left of the harness. Nothing special about the wheels, nothing left on any of the floors. She climbed into the sole wicker car last of all and knelt to peer closely at the inside walls. A long, pale hair had been caught in a broken reed—but she already knew the girls had been carried here. *And it could be old, the owner's hair, if he wears it long—his wife's* . . . She swore and returned to the road, brushing off her knees.

"Hey, is it all right if we come over there?" Gabrielle hovered on the edge of the road. Behind her, Homer was walking slowly from a nearby tree to the fire pit; he reached it, turned and started back, his eyes narrowed, his mouth set.

"Sure. There's nothing here."

Gabrielle turned to watch Homer's progress and nodded enthusiastically as he neared her. "Keep that up, you're doing great!"

"Sure am," he grumbled. "In another year, I may even be able to walk normally again."

"Well, you're doing a lot better anyway," Gabrielle said. She patted his shoulder as he turned away from her to limp toward the fire pit once more. She crossed the road, peered doubtfully into the wicker car, then looked up at her friend. "Nothing at all, huh? Terrific." She looked around. "Where's Atalanta?"

"Trying to find which way they went," Xena said evenly. "She said there was sign of them that way"—she pointed toward the notch—"but that it was probably a ruse to mislead us."

Gabrielle studied Xena's face for a long moment, glanced over her shoulder to see where Homer was, then lowered her voice. "There's something wrong, isn't there? I mean—besides the obvious something."

"Why?"

"It's your face. You're giving me that look that says you're pretty angry and you don't want me to know." She sighed and hung her head. "I guess it was pretty stupid of me to bring him along, wasn't it?"

Xena shook her head and wrapped an arm around her companion's shoulders. "That's not it at all, Gabrielle. He's obviously in no shape for a trek like this. But if you'd left him behind and something happened to him because of that . . . You did the best you could in an impossible situation."

"Thanks—I think," Gabrielle said doubtfully. "But—if it isn't Homer, or something I've done, then what?" She paused, searching for the right words.

Xena shrugged. "It just doesn't add up. Like you said last night, why take a bunch of little girls and run for it? It couldn't be for ransom, unless they aren't looking for much money. They weren't priests of some obscure little cult looking for sacrificial victims—"

"*I* thought of that last night," Gabrielle said in a small voice.

"I knew you would. I hope it didn't keep you from sleeping. Not for fortune, not for a god," Xena went on thoughtfully. "And it couldn't be for their company—I'd wager most of them have been in hysterics since they were grabbed. So—why?"

"And why bring them this far, if it's for ransom?" Gabrielle asked.

"Why take them out of the city at all?" Xena countered. "I don't like it, and I can't put my finger on why I don't like it." Movement high to her left caught her eye; Atalanta had clambered up a steep ledge and was waving vigorously. "I guess that's our call," she said.

Gabrielle squinted, then with an oath shielded her eyes

as the sun rising behind her sent brilliant shards of light from water-slicked stone high on the mountain. "What's that she's holding?" She paused. "Guess we'll find out when we—how are we supposed to get up *there*?"

Xena touched her shoulder to get her attention and pointed toward the gap. "Get your things, go that way. She'll have marked the way. I'll be waiting for you."

It took time. The huntress was visibly trembling with the need to be gone when Homer and Gabrielle finally scrambled onto the steeply tilted ledge. "Here," she said briefly, and held out a short length of rope, knotted with a loop at each end.

Gabrielle took it. "That's Nausicaa's, isn't it?" Homer nodded.

Atalanta eyed the heavens, then the still and silent warrior at her side, and nodded. After a moment, she said, "It hasn't been here long."

Gabrielle tied the bit of rope around the strap of her lumpy bag and sighed. "Well, that was an exciting climb." Behind her, Homer groaned very faintly. "Which way from here?"

Atalanta shoved the boarskin cloak back across her shoulders and pointed down the ledge and along a narrow ravine that cut roughly northeast. "There. Old streambed; it's dry now but rough footing. Watch where you step; you break a leg and—"

"I get the point," Gabrielle broke in hurriedly. "Let's go."

The morning passed slowly; footholds in the ravine were treacherous indeed, and signs of the passing men and children faint and few and far between, even for Atalanta's keen eyes. As time wore on, and the day grew hotter, Homer lagged behind. Gabrielle dropped back to keep him company. "Leave markers if you jump out of this thing," she called ahead. "I'd probably miss where a whole herd of centaurs went by, the way I feel right now." Xena merely waved a hand at her and kept going; she had stayed on Atalanta's heels the entire morning. "Remember, I'm the one carrying the lunch!" she added. The last word echoed from the rocks below them, and she clapped a hand over her mouth as Atalanta turned to glower down at her. "Here," she said to the panting bard as the two women vanished around a bend not far ahead, "this is as good a spot as any for a quick rest."

"Are—you sure—that's a—a good idea?" he asked. Gabrielle dropped onto a flat, shaded stone and patted the rock next to her for answer. He collapsed beside her.

"Something I learned from Xena early on," she assured him. "You go farther in the long run, faster, and with a clearer head if you rest once in a while."

He leaned forward, his forehead against his hands. "I'm sorry," he mumbled.

"You shouldn't be," she said. "You're doing better than I did at first. Besides," she added, "think of the great story this will make!"

"For people who like horror stories," he replied. Gabrielle chuckled, and he began to laugh. "Well—maybe *long* years from now, when I've forgotten how *awful* the backs of my legs feel right now." He sat up straighter and looked around them. "It's so *quiet* here. I don't think I've ever been anywhere so quiet." Gabrielle sat still for a long moment, then nodded.

"It feels odd to me, too; after a village, you know." Another companionable silence. "I wonder where they are."

"The girls? They can't have gone too far, can they? I mean, imagine having to drag or carry a girl like Mitradia through here." He frowned. "I wish I knew *why* they'd done it."

"That makes three of us," Gabrielle said. "Maybe all of us; Atalanta wasn't saying much about it, was she?"

"Just that she'd get them back . . ." His voice trailed off; he settled his chin on the palm of one hand and stared blankly into the distance. "Funny. Odd, rather. What she said to the old woman—it sounded, well, bardic. Like she'd rehearsed what to say, maybe, or someone had written a speech for her—" He broke off, glancing sidelong at his companion. "But that's foolish. Forget I said it."

"No," Gabrielle said slowly. "You're right, it *was* odd. But she's—she seems like such an insecure person. Maybe she's daydreamed about what she'd say or do in certain circumstances. Didn't you ever know anyone like that?"

"Yes," he admitted. "But—insecure?"

"You heard her story last night," Gabrielle said. She shifted uncomfortably. "I wish rocks weren't so hard, you know? Her story—I mean, it just—everything she said, almost every single word, I could just *see* the scared girl under the hero, the one who doesn't believe she's really that talented, or that good, or that worthy of praise. No matter what anyone tells her."

"I—well, I guess," he said doubtfully. "It seemed to me a lot, taking on not just the boar but the king, the queen, those stubborn old men—and for nothing but a chance at fortune and glory. Why would anyone?"

"Hard to say; I don't think like that," Gabrielle said. She sighed and got to her feet. "I guess we'd better get moving before we lose them entirely."

"Let's not do that," Homer said promptly. His eyes were wide as he edged off the rock and slowly got himself upright.

"Oh, we're not lost or anything," Gabrielle assured him

111

cheerfully. "I can find our way back to Argo any time; I've got a great bump of direction. But since we've come this far, I want a chance at thumping at least one of those guys. They're caused a lot of heartache." Homer eyed her with as much dismay as he'd earlier shown the mountain. "It's okay," she added, "Xena's a match for any ten brutes, even on a bad day; I'll be lucky to get in one good thump. And they won't come anywhere close to you." Silence. She glanced at him, and her coloring was rather high. "Look, I didn't mean that like it sounded."

"It's all right." He sighed. "I hadn't thought about fighting when I asked to come with you. I don't object to—"

"Don't," she urged, and he fell silent, eying her in confusion. "I mean, don't feel like it's something wrong, that you don't fight, or don't want to, whatever. It doesn't mean you're not as good as anyone else."

"Oh, I know that."

"You may know it, but you don't feel it," Gabrielle replied. "Look, I told you about when I first got together with Xena, and at the time it was great fun and adventure, all that. Well, it was also pretty maddening—it still is, sometimes, because so often she still winds up protecting me, or rescuing me from some stupid situation that, if I were really as good or as clever as I'd like to be, I wouldn't have needed protection or a rescue from." She considered this, frowned, glanced back at him. "Does that make sense? Good. Anyway, I *want* to fight. My village was attacked by Draco's men—you've heard of Draco, I imagine?"

"Everyone's heard of Draco," Homer said.

"Xena saved us. Saved me. I was this far"—she held her thumb and index finger a hair's width apart—"from losing most of my skin to a bullwhip; that close to being run off with every other young village girl and turned into a slave. That—that does something to you." She went on

112

after a moment, "Well, it did to me. I didn't want to be afraid like that ever again; to know that some goon with a sword and a whip could break me, body and soul. And then, to see Xena take on all those—those—it was amazing. She was wounded and she *still* broke heads. I'd never seen anything so impressive in all my life. It was—well, yes, it *was* Fate that brought us together." Silence.

"You didn't have the same kind of introduction to the outside world, Homer: you were luckier in some ways. Once I would've said you'd lost something by not having to learn how to fight. Well, I've seen both sides, and though I know she was wrong about me, personally, I understand better what Xena tried to tell me at first. There's a—an innocence that shouldn't be broken. People who don't have to, or don't want to, shouldn't be forced to fight by circumstances, or by what others will think of them if they don't." She glanced at him again; the tip of her nose was pink. "I'm not saying this very well," she said with a nervous little laugh. "Some bard, huh? What I mean is, I think it's good you don't fight. And if you really meant what you said, I think it's great you don't mind being a guy and having a girl with a big stick defend you—if it comes to that."

Silence. The ravine had widened just around the bend; Homer caught up with her and took her hand. "I'd be lying if I said I didn't mind at all. I feel—inadequate, and I haven't felt that way since Father convinced me to alter my tales according to the audience reaction. But I realize that's—impractical. Foolish, even. No one can master everything. And"—he squeezed her fingers—"and since it's you protecting me, I don't mind *quite* as much."

Gabrielle turned to face him, her eyes bright; her hand squeezed his in return. "Homer, you're the sweetest man I ever met."

● ● ●

A distance away, Atalanta had emerged onto hard stone that was probably a waterfall early in the year, when the stream-bed below them was full. Thick, spiny brush was every-where. She glanced over her shoulder quickly; the warrior had lost a little ground on the last steep ascent, but not much. The huntress scuffled at the ground before her, where a little dirt had drifted across the rock, then moved to in-spect the brush. By the time Xena hauled herself onto the broad ledge, the other woman was bent double to inspect the heavy growth at close range. "They came up here. I *told* you we hadn't lost them," she said sourly and pointed to the scuffed-up dirt.

"How'd they get off this without getting torn to bits?" Xena demanded.

Atalanta snorted in exasperation. "Maybe they grew wings and flew! Leave me in peace so I can figure that out, will you?"

"Whatever you say," Xena murmured sardonically, but when the huntress straightened to glare at her, she'd already turned to gaze back the way they'd come. No sign yet of Gabrielle and Homer. The boy had been a mistake from the start. Soft. *You're getting soft yourself; indulging Gabrielle the way you do.* Still, the girl asked for so little—and so seldom. And usually with her heart in the right place. *A bard torn to bits by an Athens mob—there'd be an interesting addition to Xena's evil mythos,* she told her-self. And of course, if Gabrielle hadn't insisted they come to Athens for the races, the huntress would have been on her own out here, searching for six little girls . . . Xena frowned, then half-turned to eye her companion sidelong; Atalanta was still checking the brush—to see if branches had been shoved aside, or maybe checking the dirt for prints, who knew? *It's been almost as though she's in-*

114

vented this as she's gone along, she thought. Something was wrong . . . But the thought wouldn't form properly; she had only a sense of the wrongness, not of *why.*

Maybe, with luck, that would come. Atalanta stood up and rubbed the small of her back. "This way," she said flatly, and was gone through a narrow, and previously invisible, opening in the prickly brush before Xena could respond. The warrior swore under her breath, bent three branches in swift succession until all were pointing the direction the huntress had gone, and dove after her.

Midday came and went; the land around them grew, if anything, more tortured and more difficult to pass. Homer was walking more easily, but now Gabrielle was limping after turning her ankle on a loose rock. Atalanta lost the trail as the sun reached zenith—on a ledge twice the size of the Olympic stadium—and then again not long after that when the kidnappers apparently thought to pull the trick of obscuring their trace with a branch again. Both times she found it quickly. A third time took longer: late afternoon sun lay golden on the woods and reflected in blinding shards from a fast-moving stream, rock-bordered on both sides for some distance.

"I *told* you!" Atalanta snarled as Xena gazed at her. "There is absolutely nothing to track! There's nothing to take prints or show passage! Do you want me to produce proof out of whole cloth?" The huntress balanced on rocks midstream just short of a low waterfall. She'd spent the past hour searching the banks on both sides, all the way to the next waterfall—an impassable mess comprised of stone overhangs, fast-moving, chill water, and two shallow caves that went nowhere. Xena, who'd gone downstream, had had no better luck, and the impatience that had driven her since dawn was threatening to shift into temper. *Be easy,* she warned herself. *It's likely she's done just as she said; anyone would be angry, being outwitted like that. I would. I am.*

"All right, I believe you. Fine. So where do we go next?"

"How should I know?" Atalanta demanded furiously, her cheeks blotched and mottled with uneven color. She shook her head, drew a deep breath, and let it out through her nostrils. "I'm not angry with you, *any* of you. I just— I don't have an answer at this moment! And I'm *sorry* if that doesn't please you!"

"It's not the answer I wanted," Xena said evenly. "You can't help that, I understand that. Come down from there, eat something."

"Another of those awful, fat-laden sticks of yours?" Atalanta inquired sharply as she slid down to join the others. Xena's mouth quirked sourly.

"Nuts and berries if you can find them instead. Food and drink. Even a hero needs those, you know." The fire of anger kindled again in the woman's eyes; Xena sighed. *I can't help baiting her; she can't help reacting. Great.* She turned to give Gabrielle a look; the girl was visibly exhausted, and the boy was even worse off. Yet Gabrielle was still unusually sensitive to mood.

She smiled, spread her arms wide in a peace making gesture, and said, "I've got a bunch of trail sticks in here"—she patted the lumpy bag—"but I also have some dried grapes, things like that. Some baked wheat and oats and dried apricots and honey cakes, *you* know—energy without the animal tissue, if you're avoiding it. Not quite as hard on the teeth either," she added as she held out a small square. Atalanta accepted it, sniffed cautiously, then took a bite. "Good, isn't it?" Gabrielle asked, and took a large bite out of her own.

"Not bad," the huntress allowed. But she turned aside, her back to the others, before she took another bite. Xena glanced at her back, then looked at Gabrielle, but Gabrielle had already turned away to offer something to Homer. The apprentice bard was pale and visibly in a lot of pain, but keeping it to himself. *Odd. How can anyone be—embarrassed to be seen eating? Everyone has to eat—you die if you don't.* All at once she remembered Thisbe. Thisbe'd been older than her and—well, large all her life. Until she'd been trothed to Pyramus. Somehow, she'd managed to control her appetite. She'd grown slender. Then thin. Then—gaunt. Her mother and father had been pleased; Pyramus, if she recalled correctly, delighted. Thisbe had died two days short of the wedding ceremony, so thin her bones showed through her skin.

She wouldn't eat with others, either. I remember that: she was ashamed... She glanced sharply at Atalanta, who had stuffed half the oatcake into her belt. *Half an oatcake—that wouldn't keep a dryad alive.* But Atalanta seemed, suddenly, very much alive. She glanced skyward, and her mouth curved with visible satisfaction; she clambered back up the stones next to the waterfall with an ease and grace that made poor Homer both groan and stare in admiration. She gazed eagerly all around, then pointed—dramatically, of course, Xena thought, and cast her own eyes heavenward. "There! Dear goddess, why didn't I see it before? That way—there! Hurry! They aren't that far ahead of us!"

7

Gabrielle stared at Xena as the huntress pulled herself up the steep stone wall and vanished. "Did you see or hear anything new?"

Xena shook her head. "No. All the same—" She whirled around as a horrified scream tore at the air, easily topping even the roar of the waterfall. "Wait here! I'll be back!"

"Right!" Gabrielle called after her; the warrior was already finding handholds on rough stone, and moments later she disappeared after Atalanta. Gabrielle stared anxiously at the rock barrier and bit her knuckle; when Homer came up behind her and touched her arm, she started violently. He jumped.

"What do you think that's—all about?"

"I wish I knew," Gabrielle murmured; her fingers closed on his arm, and his free hand covered hers. "I guess we'll know pretty quickly." She swallowed hard. "I hope it's—I mean, it can't be—I mean—"

"I know what you mean," he said quietly. His eyes, like hers, were fixed on the waterfall and the tumble of massive stones flanking it. And on the woods above it.

It seemed forever, but could only have been moments, when Xena reappeared, overhead and some paces northeast of where she'd climbed up. She cupped hands around her mouth and shouted, "Don't come up this way!"

Gabrielle's eyes closed and she bit her lip.

"Why?" Homer shouted, when it became clear his companion was momentarily beyond speech.

"Just—don't!"

"Please, I have to know!" Gabrielle yelled. "It's not—not the girls?"

"No! There's no sign of them, but there're dead men everywhere, it's a—it's not a pretty sight," Xena finished grimly. "I can see part of a trail from up here, goes around that way! You'll have to jump the stream, then you'll see it!" She turned and vanished once more. Gabrielle gazed at Homer, her face pale, her eyes wide and frightened. He stared back at her, and finally swallowed.

"I guess—we should go," he said doubtfully.

"It's all right," Gabrielle replied. She walked toward the water, then upstream a few paces, looking for the best place to jump across. She jumped, waited for him, then led the way; the noise of the waterfall filled the air, making conversation difficult until they rounded a pile of spray-drenched boulders. "I mean—I didn't mean all right; something bad must have happened up there. But she's not—she wouldn't lie about something like that; it wouldn't help anyone. But"—she licked her lips—"but if *she* says it's not a pretty sight, then—"

"Then it's not one I want to add to my visions," Homer finished grimly as she hesitated. "I hope you're right—about the girls, I mean." Gabrielle nodded firmly, but her eyes were bleak. *She just might not have found their bodies yet.* She wouldn't think about that—would try not to, she told herself more honestly. She blinked and tried to force a smile for Homer, who looked awful. His eyes kept straying to the steep hillside on their left. "Look," he said after a moment, "I think she was right about the trail. There's some kind of clear spot, that way, between those two oak trees. See it?"

"See it," Gabrielle replied, and followed him across water-smoothed stone and through a deep drift of fallen leaves, into cool and shaded woods. "It's not much of a trail," she said moments later as Homer paused to look around them. "All these years of fallen leaves on the ground, any space between the trees will look like a path. I've gotten seriously lost places like this."

"No, it's an old hunter's trail," Homer said. "See the mark there? Shoulder level," he added, and touched three faint, half-healed knife slashes in the bark of a slender aspen.

She looked at him, puzzled. "How'd you know that?"

He shrugged and smiled. "We had hunters in my village, an uncle of mine among them. He taught me a few things, though of course," he said as the smile slipped, "I never got to hunt with him."

Gabrielle wrinkled her nose. "You haven't missed a thing," she said firmly. "Hunting's messy. Well," she added with a sigh, "I don't want to go on at the moment, but I guess we don't have a choice." It was his turn to look puzzled. "I'm hoping Xena finds someplace to meet us beyond—ah, away from—well, *you* know. That may not be possible, though. Just—just a warning."

"Oh."

"I know she'll do her best; I mean, she knows I don't do bodies well. Or blood."

"Blood." Homer's eyes closed briefly, but when Gabrielle eyed him sidelong, her eyes worried, he managed a faint smile. "Don't care for it much," he said in a would-be casual voice. "We'd better go, get this part behind us. Before—before I lose my nerve." His smile was forced; she patted his arm as they set out again. Silence as they moved from the aspen to the next marked tree; after five or so, the sound of the water was a very faint rumble. Somewhere far overhead, a bird warbled, and beyond it a raven uttered a harsh, pebbly croak. The leaves weren't very deep here, and the trail was much more visible, though it wound in and out of trees and brush in such a fashion that they couldn't see very far ahead.

"I wonder what happened up there," Gabrielle said finally. "The girls—"

"She wouldn't lie about something like that, isn't that what you said?" Homer asked. He sounded nervous again.

He was probably thinking the same thing she'd thought about the girls. No point bringing it out in the open, Gabrielle thought, and shook her head. "And I meant it, too. But where are they? I—I'm worried. What if someone attacked the kidnappers, and the girls scattered and ran? We could be days finding them all, and we might be—be too late to find them in time. We're a lot higher than where we slept last night, you know. It'll be pretty cold up here, and—"

"And the girls were dressed for a race on a warm beach," he finished as she hesitated.

"And there's the small matter of food and drink: I know how to look for water, and if I really *had* to, I could probably remember some of the wild plants my mother showed me back when she was training me to be someone's wife, so I'd be all right, lost. But—but a scared young girl!"

"A *blind*, scared young girl, you mean?" Homer asked gently. Gabrielle nodded.

"Any of them, really. But if she got separated from Mitradia—it's bad enough for the rest of them, but Nausicaa can't even see which way—I mean, she could walk right over a cliff without knowing it was there!''

Silence. Homer laid a hand on her shoulder and drew her to a halt. ''Don't underestimate the princess, Gabrielle. She's never had the use of her eyes. I'm sure she's learned not to simply put a foot down without testing the ground before her, and it's obvious she uses her other senses to compensate for the lack of vision.''

Gabrielle sighed faintly. ''You're right. I—guess it's because I've never had to deal with anything like that myself. Not being able to see, I mean. So I don't think of people like Nausicaa as able to take care of themselves. Stupid of me.''

The trail petered out on mossy stone; Homer slowed, then looked around until he found the next marked tree, a goodly distance away. ''That isn't stupid, any more than it's lack of feeling. Most people are busy living their own lives; they don't think about problems of that sort unless it's their own problem, or—like Mitradia, because she and Nausicaa are so close.''

Gabrielle blinked rapidly, then surreptitiously blotted her eyes on the back of her hand. ''Gods and goddesses, I hope they're still alive!'' She cast a glance at the sky and shook her head. ''It's getting late. We'd better keep moving.''

But five paces on, she halted once again, and when Homer would have said something, she laid a hand on his mouth. ''Listen,'' she whispered. ''Did you hear something?'' Silence. He finally shook his head. ''Not very loud,'' Gabrielle whispered. ''A moan—there!'' The sound was faint, either distant or weak. She glanced at him; he nodded, and when the sound was repeated, pointed between the trees, just off the trail, where tall bushes cast a deep shadow. Gabrielle shifted her grasp on her staff, then looked at Homer once again. "Stay behind me," she said softly. "Not too close, in case I need to use this, okay? But don't get out of sight, either."

"All right," he said doubtfully. Gabrielle cast him a smile, and he nodded. The smile slipped as she strode forward, checking the brush warily, pausing every other step to listen. Behind her, Homer swallowed hard, then cautiously followed her. *Beloved Muses,* he thought unhappily, *what am I doing here?*

The moaning was louder now. Gabrielle hesitated, looked back at him and held a finger to her lips, then eased soundlessly over a bed of pine needles and stopped short. Silence. Then a weak, tremulous voice said, "Thank the gods, girl!"

"It's all right, Homer," Gabrielle said. "Come on." He set his jaw, then eased into the open behind her. A scruffy, red-bearded bear of a man sat with his back to a broad-trunked fir, hands bound behind him; blood had dried in his thick, reddish-gray hair, and a trail of it ran down his forehead and cheek, but he didn't seem injured otherwise. At the moment, he was eyeing Gabrielle with astonishment, but it was rapidly changing to irritation as she stood and gazed down at him.

"Well?" he demanded finally. His voice was deep, rather hoarse, as though he didn't use it much. "Aren't you going to free me?"

Gabrielle smiled, but her eyes remained hard. "Not a chance in this world. You were one of the men down in Athens yesterday, weren't you? Snatching little girls?"

He opened pale brown eyes very wide, in an apparent attempt to look like he had no idea what she meant, but his lips twitched nervously. "Little girls? What would I want with little girls?"

"Right," she replied sardonically. "You're so good at

acting, why don't you go down to the amphitheater and put on one of the masks? Little girls," she repeated flatly. "You either helped steal them, or you were one of those who did—well, whatever got done up there," she finished lamely and pointed toward the distant ledge with her staff.

He turned away from her and spat. "Don't know what you're talking about. I'm a hunter, I live in the village just down there."

"Right," Gabrielle repeated crisply, her voice now dripping sarcasm. "What's its name?" He looked up at her blankly. "The village you live in," she explained sweetly. Silence. "You're an awfully bad liar. Girls," she said, and spun the staff neatly, stopping the end just short of his nose. "Unless you'd like your kneecaps moved to the backs of your legs?"

He laughed. "You couldn't do something like that, little girl." He didn't sound or look very certain of that.

Another, deeper voice answered him. "Maybe not—though I wouldn't wager on it. Of course, *I* could," Xena said flatly as she stepped into the little clearing. Gabrielle sighed and cast her eyes heavenward, then relaxed. Homer was backing slowly away—from her or from the prisoner, she couldn't be certain which; his face was utterly white. Not far from him, Atalanta came out of the trees, and if anything, she was paler than he was. Her hands and her lower lip trembled.

"What—I mean, who is that?" she demanded warily.

"We just now found him, just like that," Gabrielle said. She watched the huntress from under her lashes. *Something really is wrong; she isn't acting the way she should be.*

Atalanta cleared her throat and with a visible effort pulled herself together. "Oh, well, he doesn't look like he'd know anything," she said quickly. Walking slowly toward the man, Xena chopped a hand, motioning for silence.

When she stopped, her boots were nearly touching his feet. He glanced up at her, then stared across the clearing. The huntress backed up a step, set her bow and quiver on the ground by her feet, gave Xena's back a wary glance, sharply eyed Gabrielle, then turned a little away from her so she was directly facing the bound man. Homer, some paces away and apparently forgotten for the moment, stared in astonishment as Atalanta's fingers moved in a swift sequence of gestures.

Dear goddess, what is she up to? Those were the same kinds of hand signals his uncles used to communicate when they were close to game! *But that would mean—!* He couldn't complete the thought. He glanced at Gabrielle, but her eyes were fixed on Xena and the man at the warrior's feet. Atalanta now stood very still, arms folded, but her whole body was tense. *Like a deer ready for flight,* he thought.

Xena eyed the bound man, her face impassive. The silence stretched. He licked his lips; his eyes flickered toward the huntress. Atalanta's hands moved again; he blinked once, slowly, then fixed a blank stare on the ground by his feet.

The raven cried from somewhere almost overhead; Gabrielle jumped. Xena shifted her weight. "Gabrielle?"

"Xena?"

"This is how you found him?"

Gabrielle nodded, then realized Xena wasn't watching her, and said, "We heard him groaning, found him just like this. *He* said he was local, a villager out hunting."

"Well, it could be true," Atalanta began; Xena glared her into silence and turned back to the bound man.

"It's a lie," she said softly. "There's no village within a day and a half of here."

"It's so obscure, he doesn't even know its name," Gabrielle said. He glared at her, then lowered his eyes again and set his jaw.

"Fine," Xena said, even more softly. "You tell me who you are, what happened up there, why you're here like this, and maybe I'll let you live. If I even think you're lying, you'll regret it."

"I told her," he said sullenly. "I'm a hunter. There's three villages within four hours' walk of here. Mine's called Vista—"

The warrior went to one knee beside him and gripped his neck; her hand twisted. He yelped, and Homer closed his eyes. "I warned you," Xena murmured against the man's ear. "Now, you've got maybe a minute left to live. I just cut off the blood to your brain. You can tell me the truth, or I can just step back and watch you die." She smiled unpleasantly. "Your choice."

Dead silence in the small clearing; then he drew a shuddering breath and gasped, "I'm sorry—I can't—!" But his eyes had moved beyond her. Gabrielle turned as Atalanta shrieked in fury.

"You fool! You thrice-damned fool!" She spun on one heel and fled through the trees. Xena leaped to her feet, chakram in hand, and threw; it ricocheted off two trees, then sliced the air between two others to rebound off a third. It caught the huntress square on the back of the head. Hard. Xena retrieved the flying weapon before it could wedge itself into the tree behind her, then knelt once more beside the gasping, sweating man and said, "Well?"

"I'll—tell you, I swear," he gasped. "Don't—let me die." She gazed into his eyes, shrugged, and reversed the pinch. He caught his breath on a sob and sagged into the trunk.

"Make it good," she said flatly, then held up a hand for silence. "Wait. Gabrielle?"

"Right here." Gabrielle was staring in shock at the fallen huntress.

"You still have that piece of rope *she* found?"

"Got it."

"Go drag her back here and tie her feet with it. Good knots. Then watch her closely." Gabrielle shook herself, dropped her bag to the ground, and knelt to untie the length of rope. "Do it now, before she wakes up. Get her weapons, make sure you have all of them before she wakes up." She turned back to the prisoner and leveled a finger at his nose. "You—talk. I'm listening. Who are you?"

"I'm Ixos. It—it wasn't supposed to have happened this way!" he protested, a whine edging into his voice.

"I'm sure it wasn't. Where are the girls?"

"Gone—*she* said they'd be safe, though! Swore they would! At least, until—"

"Who's she—Atalanta?" He shook his head. "Who, then? And safe until what?"

"Horrid creature." He closed his eyes and shuddered. "Woman's face and hair—beautiful face, long, wild hair like dark gold. Lion's body and—and wings! I swear, I'm not making that up!" he added hastily as the warrior eyed him in visible disbelief.

Homer cleared his throat; Xena glanced at him. "He's not," said Homer quietly.

"If you say so," she said doubtfully, then glared at Ixos, who swallowed and closed his eyes. "What else? Safe until what? And where did they go?"

"Up the mountain, just over the top and partway down. The road goes east and north toward Thessaly. "She—she's holding it now, she said. The Thessaly road. She said to say that." He looked up as Gabrielle backed into the clearing, dragging the still unconscious and bound Atalanta.

"Said—said to tell *her* that the Sphinx was looking forward to a proper duel, with a proper opponent."

Gabrielle checked the rope holding the huntress's ankles together, then bundled the javelin case, bow case, quiver, and sword belt together, binding them with the belt. They made a sizable burden; she scowled at it, then rummaged under the boarskin once again. Four long-bladed daggers joined the pile. She sighed, shoved the knives into the case with the javelins—except for one, which went into her own belt—then got to her feet and reclaimed her staff. "You aren't making a lot of sense, Ixos," she said. "Start at the beginning, why don't you?"

Ixos looked from her to Xena, back again, then sighed and gazed at his feet. "All right. She's—I helped raise her. After her father set her out on a rock. I mean—we were hunters, Neneron and I. We'd shared a hut on the other side of the slope, eastward slope, I mean, almost a day's walk from here—shared it for years, and it suited us fine. Well, I went out to check my lines and found—found her." He looked at Atalanta, and his gaze softened momentarily. "She wasn't above a few hours old," he added indignantly. "Well, I'm no wet nurse, but what could I do? Leave a child—a helpless baby—to die? I took her back and—" he sighed. "It wasn't easy, two hardened men raising an infant, but we managed, somehow. I mean, look at her."

"Thanks," Xena said flatly, "I'd rather not. Go on. And don't take all day!"

"She left us—four years ago, it would be. Wanted to make someone of herself. Couldn't understand that, myself, but—well, couldn't argue with her, either." He gazed at the fallen huntress, and his eyes softened. "Never could argue with her. Trouble was, she wanted to be a hero, do all these great deeds, have people talk about her. But it didn't make her happy, even when she got what she wanted. She had all this—competition, she called it: this Hercules fella with Zeus for a father, and Prince Theseus, down in Athens. She thought she'd stand out, only woman hero around, but there's this—'' He paused, trying to remember something. ''This female, name of—''

''Name of Xena,'' Gabrielle said dryly. She smiled. ''But you've already met.''

He looked up at the warrior, and his already pale face went ashen. ''Oh.''

''Go on,'' Xena said flatly. ''And speed it up; there are some scared little girls out there somewhere, remember?''

He sighed. ''I didn't want to; I mean, she *had* the boarskin, she's a wondrous archer—taught her myself, but she's long since passed my skills by!—fast runner, she doesn't *need* to create things like this to be known! But she's always been so aware of her—her image, she calls it; said a women's footrace every two years wasn't going to make her anyone special. And—well, she insisted. And I just couldn't tell her no. Neneron couldn't either.'' He swallowed, and his eyes were suspiciously bright. ''What's left of *him* is up there. Thirty-five years we were together; never thought he'd cross the Styx before me, and in so many pieces.''

''Let's see if I have this right,'' Xena said after a moment. ''Atalanta had you and some other men steal girls from that beach so *she* could rescue them and be named a hero?'' She gave the fallen young woman a chill, appraising look. ''And then what happened?''

''It wasn't supposed to happen this way!'' Ixos protested weakly. ''She told us where to go to steal the chariots. The king's guard doesn't bother to watch the king's carts and horses very closely—it was dead easy. Then we did ourselves up as rough as we could—''

''We?'' Xena demanded.

"Me, Neneron, nine boys from around where she grew up. You know the sort: bored by village life but not willing to learn a skill well enough to leave the village for something better. Louts with no ambition. Did ourselves up rough," he repeated, "covered our faces, and drove down the sand. My word, you think that was easy? Controlling carts and horses like that! 'Specially with all those shrieking little girls? Managed, though—and once the horses had a clear way ahead of them, it wasn't so much work. We left the carts where *she* told us, cleaned all sign from the road, took the girls back down a way, over rock; there's a path comes straight up here, hardly any distance at all if you know where to find the start of it.''

"And Atalanta took us on a long, false trail this morning," Gabrielle said indignantly. "I guess to mislead us, right? Except—she couldn't know we'd be at the races, could she? Or right on her heels yesterday afternoon?"

"Was always a chance some father, or maybe the city guard, would be there to follow her. She planned it well," Ixos replied loyally, then glanced up at Xena and bit his lip. "She had a plan in place to mislead you—mislead anyone trailing her, you know—to give us time to reach this place and stow the girls up here, warn 'em to stay put, and give 'em a hard enough threat they'd do it. Then we were to steal away, down to the Thessaly road, and no one the wiser. Atalanta shows up, rescues them, takes 'em back to Athens, and she's a hero. And no one's hurt. Maybe a little cold and hungry, but what's that? They're all the more grateful—"

Xena sighed loudly, silencing him. "I never heard anything so stupid! She's touched, and you're no better, Ixos. All right, it's done, and we're wasting time. What happened up there?"

"Wasn't supposed to go so wrong," he mumbled unhappily. She tapped his arm, hard; he winced and went on. "We got the girls in place, the shallow cave just short of where the waterfall drops down. I started warning 'em, and the boys were already backing off, when all at once, there were these men everywhere, real armor, ugly weaponry and—and *her*. I tried to tell the creature—I mean, there was a chance it would work, wasn't there? Tell her Atalanta's coming for them, she's a bad enemy, don't mess with her—All at once, the creature was interested—*really* interested, I could tell. She gave orders, I couldn't make 'em out, but then one of the men grabbed me and"—he swallowed—"and I saw what they did to the others. The girls tried to run, but other men and that lion thing cut them off, got them all together, bunched up, like. And—and when it was all over, *she* came to me and said, 'Ordinarily, I'd simply eat nice young prey like this. But it's boring on the Thessaly road, and I haven't had a decent challenge since that brute Oedipus was fortunate enough to guess the answer to one of my best riddles. I need a better adversary—one with a hero's name. Tell her, if she wants these children back alive, she'll have to come to my lair at the bald peak just above the crown of the Thessaly road, and we'll riddle for them.' That's all I remember," he said unhappily. "I think the man holding me hit me; I woke up here with blood in my eyes and my head pounding."

Xena cast up her eyes and sighed. "It's ridiculous enough to be true," she muttered. "But this creature—what *is* it?"

"Sphinx," Gabrielle and Homer replied in chorus. Xena motioned for silence, then pointed at Gabrielle, who made a reasonably succinct story of it. "Immortal—can't be killed or wounded—body of a lion, wings of an eagle, woman's face and hair. Has a nasty habit of blocking roads

132

and demanding that travelers who'd get around her answer a riddle. When they can't, she eats them.''

"Oedipus must have answered her," Homer put in.

"Must have," Gabrielle replied. "Let me think: What comes on four legs in the morning, two at midday, and three at night?''

"Man," Homer said promptly. "Because man crawls as a babe, walks upright as a grown person, then leans upon a cane in his age.''

"Glad to see *you* wouldn't have been the Sphinx's lunch," Gabrielle said with a smile; it faded at once as Xena cleared her throat meaningfully. "This is awful! The Sphinx! I mean—she might have the face of a woman, but her appetite's all—well, all lion!" At her feet, Atalanta groaned and stirred; Gabrielle drew back, eyeing her with alarm. Xena shook her head, stepped over Ixos' legs, and went to one knee, putting herself at Atalanta's eye level.

"I never did like you," she murmured softly, her eyes pale daggers. "Especially not since *last* time. Right now, I'm ready to turn you into the same kind of bits of men we left up there." She jerked her head toward the ledge. "How *dare* you play with the lives of innocent little girls?''

"I? I dare? He's lying, if he says that!" Atalanta shouted indignantly as she struggled partway upright. Xena gave her a shake, and the huntress subsided. Xena glanced at Ixos; he'd gone wide-eyed and pale. She leveled a finger at his nose.

"You're about that far from *dead*," she hissed. "Both of you. Give me one decent reason not to kill you.''

"You wouldn't dare!" Atalanta yelled, but she winced away from the warrior's hard look. Ixos sighed and shook his head.

"Go ahead and kill me," he mumbled. "Maybe I can catch up with Neneron before he pays Charon to take him over, and we can go together.'' Atalanta stifled a sob, but when Xena glanced toward her, she was dry-eyed, her jaw set.

The warrior smiled; it wasn't a nice smile. "Oh, no," she said softly. "You aren't going to get off that easily. You took those girls from their mothers and fathers—you're going to help us get them back. Gabrielle . . .''

"Yeah?"

"Stay here, keep an eye on him—on both of them. I'm going to see if I can sort out which way they went."

"You can't track half as well as I can," Atalanta said defiantly. "I can fix things! I thought you were supposed to care so much for the weak and the oppressed, but you—!''

"Shut up," Xena said evenly. "It's true—everything he said. Isn't it?" Silence. The huntress wouldn't meet her eyes, and after a moment, she nodded. "Fine. You're coming along, too. But I'll do the tracking. At this point, I wouldn't trust you to tell me water runs downhill." She looked at Gabrielle, who was pale and still, then at Homer, who stared into the distance, his mouth moving though no words came. "Keep an eye on her," she told Gabrielle. "I'm going to search for tracks up there. Don't get soft and do anything you'll regret, like think about letting her go.'' She glared down at Atalanta. "She isn't worth it.''

"I won't," Gabrielle said flatly. A long, uncomfortable silence lay over the small clearing as the warrior vanished from sight. Ixos had drawn his legs up and sat staring at his knees; Homer seemed to be of two minds, perhaps trying to decide whether he should stay here or back away entirely and return to the Academy. If he could recall the way they'd come. Atalanta lay motionless, her eyes fixed on the ground just beyond her splayed fingers, her legs bound in rope that wrapped twice around her ankles and culminated in a huge, complex knot.

Gabrielle bit back a sigh. *She looks so—vulnerable. So thin and young and helpless. And yet, what she did—* "Why?" she demanded suddenly. Homer started; Ixos looked up abruptly. Only Atalanta remained motionless, finally gazing up at her. Her mouth quirked.

"Why? What do you mean, why? Why does anyone do anything?"

"I'm not interested in blind philosophy," Gabrielle said angrily. Homer and Atalanta gazed at her in astonishment. "If I wanted that, I could have gone down to the Agora in Athens and listened to a bunch of dull old men play questions and answers. I want to know why anyone would terrorize innocent young girls—including a *blind* girl!—to satisfy her own quest for fortune and glory!" Silence. Gabrielle glared down at Atalanta, who stared at the ground before her hands. "I—I was—I wanted to be proud of you! To watch you run and see something glorious and golden and wonderful. I *did* see just that when you ran! Why would you spoil that by—by doing what you did? I—Atalanta, honestly, I want to know!"

A long, chill silence. Homer looked from Atalanta to Gabrielle, to Ixos, and back again. *That poor man! Of all of us, he's made the dearest purchase, and he has less coin to pay.* His eyes touched, thoughtfully, on Atalanta. *And she's the one who cost him, and all for spoiled, stupid pride.* A thought brushed over him. Achilles was supposed to have been one of the greatest Greek heroes in the war for Helen. But Stallonus had met the man—the sullen, spoiled creature who'd been so indulged by his mother that he couldn't see beyond his own nose—or his own desires. Suddenly, the young bard was almost trembling with realization: *Oh, Muse, now I know I can create a new telling of this great tale!* But if one girl died here—*I may not ever be able to compose verse again, without remembering it. Or to compose at all.*

Atalanta's voice drew him back to the present. "You wouldn't understand! Why should you?"

Gabrielle shook her head. "I'm trying to! Don't you see that? I—just tell me, *why?* What's worth that much? You put those girls in danger—"

"There wasn't going to *be* any danger, it was planned!" Atalanta shouted. She caught her breath on a sob and turned away. "It wasn't supposed to happen this way," she mumbled defiantly.

"There isn't a military leader in all history who hasn't said that at some point," Homer put in quietly. Gabrielle glanced at him, surprised. "I've studied these things, the Academy stresses them, and they're right; it's one of the great components of tragedy: failed tactics, blundered strategy, stupid mistakes. Any leader who's lost a major battle will say just that: 'It wasn't supposed to happen this way.' " His ordinarily mild eyes were fixed accusingly on the fallen huntress. Atalanta looked up at him, then immediately away. Her shoulders sagged.

"Maybe you didn't plan for this to happen," Gabrielle said. "It doesn't matter. Didn't you think what it would do to a young girl, to be snatched from her parents by masked men and taken away, up the sea, across a hard, cold land? Don't you know what most of those girls must have thought—have feared? Not death, girls at that age don't think of death so much. Even if no man laid a hand on any of them, even if they survive all this, what do you think their dreams will show them, for years to come?"

Atalanta squared her shoulders and brought up her chin in defiance. "Why should *I* care what any other girl thinks or feels? My father carried me from his house while my mother was still bleeding from my birth; he set me on hard,

136

cold stone in hopes I'd die! I've borne scars like none of those girls will *ever* know, borne them all my life! All those wide-eyed, giggling little girls, you saw them,'' she added bitterly. ''Maybe a dose of reality is just what they need. I had it from my first hour in this world—''

''Got it,'' Gabrielle replied crisply. ''All right, you started out hard, you suffered, so everyone else should have it just as hard, right? Like no one else in the whole world had something go wrong? Like I didn't? Or *he* didn't?'' she added, with a glance in Homer's direction. Atalanta gazed from one to the other, shrugged angrily, and glowered at the pine needles under her hands. ''All right,'' Gabrielle went on quietly. ''That's—that's ugly, that your father would do something like that. Nastier than what happens to a lot of people. But you grew up with love; look what Ixos did, because he loved you too much to say no to you! And you ignore that much love, so you can keep all that hate for your father alive?'' Atalanta's lip curled, and she looked away. ''Why hang onto a part of your life you can't control? It's past, it's done. And because you won't let go of it, your father's won after all, and you've lost. Haven't you?'' she demanded as Atalanta stared at her blankly. ''I don't call that much of a life,'' she added mildly.

Atalanta bit back a sob, shook her head, and burst into tears. Homer cast Gabrielle a nervous look; the girl shook her head, hard, and he retreated. She waited; the huntress finally blotted her eyes and drew a deep breath. ''All right,'' she mumbled finally. ''I'm *sorry!*''

''Don't be sorry,'' Gabrielle said. ''Be useful. Help us save those girls. Oh!''

''Oh?'' Homer asked warily.

''Oh!'' Gabrielle said once more. ''Dear gods and goddesses, I forgot, the Sphinx! How are we going to get those girls away from her?''

8

Xena was back with them moments later. As she drew a knife, both Atalanta and Ixos eyed her nervously; but she merely used it to free his hands. He remained where he was, eyes still fixed on her, his fingers gingerly pressing raw wrists as the warrior walked over to the huntress and stared down at her. Atalanta sat up and spread her arms wide.

"Go ahead," she said bitterly. "I don't care. I'd rather die than have anyone know that I—"

"Oh, no," Xena replied evenly, her ice-blue eyes very bright. "The Sphinx wants you. You're our bargaining coin."

"You wouldn't!"

"Wouldn't what? Hand you over to her? In a minute, if it would get those girls back safe. Gabrielle, untie her."

"I won't go," the huntress mumbled rebelliously. "You can't make me go."

"You might be surprised," Xena said. "You'll walk right in front of me, you'll do exactly what I tell you, or you'll be even sorrier than you are right now. Than you

139

think you are. But I don't intend to just feed you to the Sphinx. You might think that way; I don't do things like that.'' Silence. The huntress eyed her in patent disbelief. ''I'll even make a bargain with you. You cooperate with me—with us. You do exactly what I tell you, when I tell you, you do whatever it takes to help us get those girls back home safely. At whatever cost to yourself. In return, I won't tell anyone that you were responsible for the whole stupid mess.'' Stunned silence. Gabrielle and Homer both stared at her.

Atalanta finally looked up; tears beaded her lashes, and her cheeks were wet. ''Why?'' she whispered. ''Why would you even bother?'' She flushed. ''You're lying! You'd say anything, just to get me to—!''

''It's not a lie,'' Xena overrode her flatly. ''I'm trying to get your help, willingly if I can. Saving those girls and getting them back to Athens is the only important thing. If I can avoid letting them know what kind of a person you *really* are at the same time, if I can let them hold onto something—believe me, I would never do that just for you. But I'd do it for them.'' Another silence. Xena stared down at Atalanta, whose eyes were fixed on the ground between her hands. Gabrielle was scowling at her jumble of knot, trying to remember how to undo it. ''We don't have all day,'' the warrior said sharply.

''Working on it,'' Gabrielle mumbled. She backed one end of a loop through another. Atalanta sighed very faintly; her shoulders sagged.

''All right. I'll do it. Whatever it takes. I swear. I didn't mean for this to—''

''Save it,'' Xena told her. ''What you meant doesn't count for anything at this point. It's done.'' Gabrielle unwound the last loop, then used the rope to bind Atalanta's formidable weaponry to her bag strap. She moved the bag around so it lay against her back, then got to her feet. Ixos eyed her staff warily and pushed himself upright. "Let's go," the warrior said. Atalanta stood slowly and carefully, then backed away from Xena, who indicated the direction with the knife. "I found traces of the girls up that way, but if *he* isn't lying, we know where to find them anyway. You," she said as Ixos sidled past her, "you know how to find this place in the Thessaly road she was talking about?"

"I can find it."

"Good. You better not have lied to me about that," she added evenly.

"I'm not—I swear it by Neneron's shade," he vowed as she gave him a cold-eyed look.

"You'll join him sooner than you expect, if you are," Xena said. "Go up there with your precious ward, so I can keep an eye on both of you. I'll be right behind you, so don't try anything." Ixos nodded, then moved stiffly toward the trail; he patted Atalanta's arm as he passed her. The huntress gave Xena a measuring, wary look, then turned to follow him. "Gabrielle, you and Homer stay behind me," Xena said sharply. "Keep an eye out for any sign of trouble. It's possible all Ixos' men aren't dead, or that some of the Sphinx's men stayed behind for *her*." She fell in directly behind Atalanta, who cast a nervous glance over her shoulder, then moved up to join Ixos.

One slender, long-fingered hand slipped into the old hunter's; he patted the hand gently, then wrapped his own fingers around it. "There, princess," he murmured, "we'll mend it somehow. There'll be a way." She merely nodded; Xena cast up her eyes and muttered a nasty curse under her breath.

Behind her, Gabrielle slowed to let Homer catch up to her as the trail widened just enough for them to walk side by side. He wrapped an arm around her shoulder. "Are you all right?" she asked in a low voice.

"I'm—I don't know how I feel," he said frankly. "Do things like this *always* happen to you?"

"Things happen," Gabrielle answered with a shrug. "But this is stranger than most." She gestured with her head toward the three ahead of them and slowed a little. "It's going to be up to us—you and me—to figure out how to deal with her. The Sphinx, I mean. Riddles," she said gloomily, "I don't think I'll ever want to hear another riddle as long as I live."

"Well," Homer said after a moment's thought, "it doesn't sound to me like we'll have much to say about any of this. Unfortunately. If she wants to contest the matter between herself and Atalanta, I mean."

Gabrielle laughed briefly. "Oh, she thinks that's what she wants. We'll just have to convince her otherwise." Homer eyed her sidelong. "Think about it," she added as he eased her around a pile of stones that had fallen from the ledge high above. "She's obviously a very proud creature, all the tales say so. And what she told Ixos—"

"If he was telling the truth, that is," Homer put in.

"He was. I could tell. No one lies to Xena when she puts that pinch on them. When you're that close to death, you just—well, you don't."

"Mmmm." Homer swallowed. *I really must have been mad, leaving Athens,* he thought. *And if Father ever finds out—* Probably he would; likely the Academy would dismiss him for having just taken off—if they hadn't already done that. Either way, they'd inform Polonius. Who would immediately go through the roof. *I'll never hear the end of it.*

Gabrielle hadn't noticed his sudden quiet; she was concentrating on the increasingly steep and rough trail and on what she was talking about. "Anyway, she's vain. The Sphinx, I mean. So we can work with that, make a real contest. At the very least, we need to coach Atalanta with some *really* good riddles." She tripped, nearly bringing the distracted Homer down with her. "Hey, are you all right?"

He shook himself and let go of her. "Just fine. Wasn't paying attention to my feet was all."

"Good. We both need to think hard."

"Uh—sorry?"

"Riddles. Good ones. What do you have?"

"Well . . ." His voice trailed off. "All right. Twickenham came up with this one last week; I've altered it a little:

> I am quick as I pass by,
> Faster than great Zeus on high.
> I can chill Helios' light.
> I touch the Titans, who brush the sky.
>
> I am plain, I am not shy,
> I shriek and wail, I scream and cry.
> There is not one who escapes my eye.
> Still, one day I, too, must die."

He paused. Gabrielle frowned, shook her head, then said, "Wait. Shriek and . . . wail . . . Wind!" She glanced at him, and he nodded. "Good one. Change 'wail' to something else, and it would be even harder. I like the touch with the Titans."

"From your story last night," he said with a faint smile.

"Nice extempore work; I wish I were better at that. Really. You know, I hate climbs like this," she added sourly, and shifted the staff so she could grab at crumbling rock and pull herself up. The trail was the faintest depression in soft stone, and it had suddenly risen very steeply. "Hey,

143

we're falling behind," she exclaimed, pointing up and ahead. The others were out of sight, over the lip of the ledge.

Homer worked his way around Gabrielle, up a little higher, and craned his neck. "Not really. I can just see the top of Xena's head; they're on level ground again, I think. Come on." He held out a hand and braced his feet to pull her up. "There's a better set of holds here, and after this little bit, we're almost done." He pointed to the long slab of sandstone blocking their way; someone had cut foot- and handholds in it. Gabrielle sighed, then clambered up. The others were about twenty paces ahead. Xena glanced over her shoulder as Homer and Gabrielle reached level ground.

"Hurry up, you two," she called back.

"Coming!" Gabrielle shouted breathlessly. She was quiet for some moments. Homer brushed scraped fingertips against his tunic, then shook dust and tiny stones from his sleeves. "All right," Gabrielle said in a more normal voice. "Try this one:

'Tis fit to be tied—or worn, cut, or hit.
It can move as I move—or not give a bit.
It can't die,'cause it's already dead, don't forget.
And it comes between me and my friends. What
  is it?"

"I like the rhythm of that," Homer said. "It's— hmmm." He was silent for some time as they crossed a meadow dotted with slender rowan and a few brushy willows. To Gabrielle's relief, there was no sign of any violence here, and Homer seemed to have forgotten about all those dead men—about that—at least for the moment. *Poor man, what an awful time he's had of it. He's gonna think I'm bad luck or something.* She glanced around them cautiously as she remembered Xena's warning, but there wasn't anywhere within a hundred paces of them for even one man to hide, let alone an army or a creature the size they said the Sphinx was. "Hmmmm," Homer said again. "I can—it's *almost* there, if I could just— All right," he sighed finally, "what is it?"

Gabrielle blinked, momentarily lost. "What is—? Oh. Leather, of course."

"Of course," he muttered. "Fit to be tied—already dead—oh!" He eyed the three just ahead of them. Atalanta was walking very stiffly, her shoulders tense as though she expected a blow from behind at any moment. "You think she'll be able to learn the lines? I mean, she isn't bardic trained, she's a hunter!"

"Don't know," Gabrielle replied thoughtfully. "We'll have to work with her, that's all. Or maybe there'll be another way. Look," she added, and pointed with the staff. "Is that a road up there, just through the trees?"

Homer stared in the direction she indicated, then shrugged. "All I can really see is that oak woods. And a— what's *that?*"

Ixos stopped dead in his tracks and Atalanta uttered a muffled shriek. Xena eased to one side and then around them as an enormous man-shaped being came out of tree shade, heading straight for them, a much smaller person at his side practically running to keep up.

"Oh, no!" Gabrielle exclaimed as Xena swore and drew her sword. Familiar dark, grubby pants and shirt, familiar shape. Familiar awkward stride. "Oh, no, tell me it isn't—!"

"It is," Xena replied flatly. "Stay back, all of you," she ordered. "I'll take care of this." She strode across open ground. Atalanta turned to run back the way they'd come, but Gabrielle had closed the short distance between them,

145

staff at the ready. The huntress caught her breath in a startled squawk. Gabrielle smiled and jiggled the ends of the staff.

"I wouldn't, really," she said. "I'm sorry, but Xena'd only find you later, and she'd be—pretty upset with you. Besides," she added, as Atalanta glanced over her shoulder at the enormous creature now almost upon them, "I know him personally. He isn't going to hurt you."

"That's a Cyclops, little girl!" Atalanta hissed. Her face was a muddy color; her eyes, enormous.

"That's a *blind* Cyclops," Gabrielle corrected her gently. "And he's not very smart to begin with."

"Who would blind a Cyclops?" Homer asked, then shook his head. "Don't tell me, I can guess."

"Right in one," Gabrielle replied cheerfully. She gazed thoughtfully beyond Atalanta. "I wonder who the fellow with him is. The big guy was a loner last time I saw him." Her nose wrinkled as the afternoon breeze shifted. "I don't think he's washed those pants since I saw him last, either." Atalanta stared at her blankly, then sighed, shook her head, and dropped down to sit cross-legged.

"Everything was fine," she mumbled. Ixos knelt next to her and patted her hand; his nervous gaze was fixed on the giant now no more than twenty paces away. "I had everything under control. The woman is a curse, I swear it. *Last* time she crossed my path, everything went—"

"Last time?" Gabrielle asked curiously. The huntress cast her a black glance.

"Ask *her*; I don't have to tell you anything, not one single thing! Ask her about it—if we don't all get turned into lunch, that is," she snarled, then fell silent. Gabrielle shrugged and looked over at Homer, who was staring blankly at the creature who now towered over Xena, grubby hands clenched into fists at least the size of her head.

"All right?" Gabrielle asked. He started, then managed a faint, nervous smile.

"Assuming I survive this journey, he'll make a tale all by himself," Homer said. "But how could anyone get close enough to a Cyclops to blind him?"

"Ahhhhh—well, that's a long story," Gabrielle said quickly. Her cheeks were noticeably pink. "And not exactly polite enough, let's say, for the mass market. I wonder who the little guy is," she added thoughtfully.

Some twenty paces away, Xena eyed the Cyclops's companion with delight. "Mannius! I haven't seen you in—"

"Not since they ran you out of your own camp," Mannius broke in. He was a full head shorter than Xena, a neat and compact person; next to the Cyclops he looked small indeed. Thick, dark curls bounced as he tipped his head to one side and smiled, a crooked grin that was even whiter against the dark, neatly trimmed beard and moustache. "I hope you know I didn't have anything to do with that. I've missed you," he added quietly.

"I know you didn't. And I've missed you, too, Mannius," Xena countered softly. "But—what are you doing here? With *him*?" The Cyclops snorted, and she fanned the gust of dreadfully bad breath away from her face.

"Man's got to eat, you know," Mannius said with an apologetic smile. "And I know you didn't keep me in camp for my mighty thews and sword prowess."

"I've always liked the way you talk, Mannius," Xena said, and her eyes were warm. "All those big words."

"Always glad to entertain my favorite warrior princess," he replied. "Well, once you were gone, I didn't last long; they tossed me out a few days later. Of course," he said thoughtfully, "there wasn't much left of your army anyway, by the time I got booted out."

"Why am I not surprised?" Xena murmured.

"Yeah. All that brawn, not a brain in sight. But I was at loose ends, so when I left camp, I decided, why not go visit my old mother up in Thessaly? My rotten luck, I walk up the old highway, right into the Sphinx."

"Sphinx—you mean, you're with her? *He's* with her?" she asked warily. She glanced at the Cyclops, who was snuffling the air and glaring in the general direction of her voice.

Mannius executed a neat little bow. "At your service," he replied cheerfully. "Everyone needs an outer perimeter of defense, right? Well, that's what I convinced her."

"Yeah," Xena said. "You could convince almost anybody of almost anything, couldn't you?"

"Well, the alternative wasn't one that made me very happy. Anyway, since she lost the contest on the road to Thebes, she's gotten cautious. Guess she doesn't much like vanishing in a puff of smoke—hurts, or something. And it sets a bad precedent."

Xena laughed deep in her throat. "Yeah. Precedent. You and those words."

"Well, she'd already acquired the big guy here. Since I talked her into keeping me around, she's added a genuine guard company—they mostly hang out close by. Me and the big fella, we do the perimeter stuff. It's quieter, and the company's a lot better."

"Sounds like she handpicked some company," Xena said with a wry smile.

"One or two you might know, if she hasn't had 'em as a late night snack. Some of 'em don't learn fast enough that you don't criticize the boss when she's that big and that—ah, voracious." Mannius glanced up at his towering companion. "How you doing up there, Flyer?" The Cyclops grunted. "Say hello to your old friend Xena," he said persuasively. The Cyclops scowled, his single eyebrow lowering over the cavern that had been an eye.

"Hullo," he said finally, resentfully.

"Hello," Xena replied, her eyes fixed on his face, the sword at the ready and her free hand on a dagger. Mannius spread his hands wide.

"Hey, you don't have to worry, Xena. Flyer here has become a changed Cyclops since I joined forces with him."

"Oh, yeah?" Xena asked. "He's picked up a name, anyway."

Mannius grinned, dimples bracketing his generous mouth. "Well, I couldn't just call him Cyclops; it sounds rude. And even blind, when he carries me and I guide him, he can move so fast it's almost like he's flying."

"Mannius, you're insane. This guy hasn't changed a bit since I saw him last."

"Hey, Xena, it's me, remember? I'm a master of words. He and I've talked all this stuff out; he's not even a little like he used to be." He gave a mock bow, but Xena's eyes remained fixed on the Cyclops, who was still glowering. "And we've been together—how long, Flyer?"

"I lose count." The deep voice rumbled, vibrating Xena's bones. "Plenty of time, though. Xena, if I could still eat human flesh, I would—"

"Now, Flyer," Mannius cut in soothingly. "Remember what I taught you."

Flyer sighed heavily; Xena batted at the gust of horrid breath. "I remember," he said dully. "Eating meat is not good for your stomach, for your heart, for your voice; it is wrong to kill humans or any living things for meat. All things are touched by gods." He scowled in the direction of his small companion, who spread his arms in a wide shrug and grinned. "Stupid notion," he growled. "Meat is good! See these?" He bared a formidable array of teeth, tapped long canines with a grubby finger. "These are teeth like wolves, and dogs, and panthers, and bears have! Like humans have. They are made to rend meat! The gods gave me such teeth for a purpose. I quit eating people because you drove me mad with your big words and arguments. I don't give up meat altogether. Got it?"

"Fine, good, all right," Mannius said hastily. He gave Xena an apologetic grin. "We're working on it," he murmured. "Besides, he has something of a point. Sheep are stupid enough; they aren't much more intelligent than tubers anyway."

"I remember you and your arguments about not eating meat," Xena said. "You really haven't given it up, have you?"

"In this region," Mannius said gloomily, "if you don't eat meat, you could starve. I mean—dry bread stolen from villages two days' walk away? Yeah—I eat sheep. And some fowl. And an occasional fish. He," he added with a jerk of his head toward the Cyclops, who was testing the air again and scowling mightily, "I consider him a success story. It hasn't been easy, but I've actually convinced him to quit eating people. He's grown rather fond of mutton—and one of these days, he may even let me cook it for him first."

"Mutton," the Cyclops mumbled.

"One whole sheep, I swear," Mannius told him. "It's marinating as we speak. But it's yours only if you leave Xena and her companions alone."

"Companions!" the Cyclops said sharply. "I knew I recognized that scent! It's—it's that chatty bit of food! I remember her!" He directed what should have been a daunting glare in Xena's direction. "She swore she was out to kill you!" he said accusingly. "That if I'd let her go, she'd bring me back both your eyes, both legs, and a—"

"Let's not get greedy," Mannius interposed hastily. "And remember, you don't eat young girls anymore, do you? Remember what I told you, how we worked it out?"

"Don't eat girls," the Cyclops mumbled gloomily. "Don't eat people. Eat sheep." He sighed heavily. Xena fanned the air in front of her face, and even Mannius wrinkled his nose fastidiously.

"Be nice, and you'll get stag tomorrow," Mannius said. The Cyclops considered this, then smiled.

"Stag." He scowled in the general direction of his slight companion and demanded, "How much stag?"

"Everything but my percentage," Mannius replied smoothly. "Two chops for me, and you don't get to comment on how I cook them."

"You do funny things to food," the Cyclops complained. Mannius folded his arms and waited. The Cyclops sighed again; Xena turned away, coughing harshly. "All right. Two chops, no comment."

"Good settlement," Mannius applauded him.

"Some deal," Xena said dryly. "So he gets a sheep or a stag, you get a couple of chops. What else you do for him?"

Mannius grinned crookedly. "It's not such a bad deal, Xena. He's my meal ticket, and I'm his Seeing Eye thug. So I have to ignore his breath, and sometimes his table manners aren't so good—he's no worse than some of those I hung out with back in your camp, right? Little guy like me doesn't always get to choose who pays his tally, does he?"

"Always could count on you to land on your feet, Mannius," Xena said softly, and her eyes were warm.

Mannius nodded. "I don't do so bad. But Xena, what are *you* doing all the way out here? Last I heard, you were

151

somewhere south and west of here, kicking stupid Kalamos out of some village.''

''News travels fast,'' Xena murmured. She sent her eyes sideways to take in the small company behind her. ''We're looking for a few young girls. But you're quick, you probably guessed that already, didn't you?''

It was Mannius' turn to sigh. ''I—yeah, I guessed as much. They warned me someone was looking for those girls. I don't know who the other three over there are, but the skinny thing on the ground must be the virgin huntress, huh? Listen to me: the Sphinx has put out word to everyone guarding her borders—which includes me, of course—*and* Flyer, of course,'' he added as the Cyclops rumbled high above him, ''that when the huntress shows up, she gets grabbed and brought to the Thessaly road. I shouldn't be standing here gabbing about old times with you.''

Xena smiled faintly. ''You know you aren't going to overpower me, even with his help. And I've got help over there. Why don't you just forget you saw us?''

''Forget,'' the Cyclops rumbled ominously.

''Let me handle this, Flyer,'' Mannius said quickly. ''You know, Xena, I have to admit I don't like this whole situation. I mean, she finds a spot on the road where the late afternoon sun hits, takes over, then asks riddles of travelers and eats anyone who doesn't give the right answer— which is just about everyone who gets asked. Now, I can live with that; she's a carnivore. The face doesn't control the appetite. Besides, I know better than to argue with someone who's immortal and eats as much as she does! But this: taking those little girls hostage, just so she can bargain herself some fame and glory, what's that? It isn't right.'' He lowered his voice and took a step toward her. ''One of them's as blind as *he* is—who could use a poor little helpless thing like that as a bargaining stick?''

"You're going soft, Mannius," Xena remarked. He laughed, but his eyes were dark.

"Yeah—maybe I was soft to start with, but I can't go with this deal of hers. Maybe I can't confront her, but there are other ways, right? Hey, Flyer," he added quietly, "you and me—we're gonna let Xena and her friends go, right?"

The Cyclops cleared his throat ominously. "Let the chatty food go free again? Why should I?"

"Because," Mannius explained patiently, "you gave up eating humans, remember? And because I won't let you have your share of the stag tomorrow night if you *do* eat her."

"Oh." He considered this, then finally shook his head. "I get my share raw, none of your fussing with the meat?"

"This once," Mannius said even more patiently. "But next stag you eat, I cook it to rare stage; you'll see how much better it tastes once it's had a little heat, all right?"

"Rare. Sounds foolish." The Cyclops bared his teeth at Xena. "I still say you cheated when you blinded me!"

"Probably did," Xena replied evenly. "You cheated whenever you ate a villager, though; it evens out."

"Hah!" He blew a gust of air her direction; Xena quietly held her breath.

"Ahhh," Mannius put in. Xena's breath came out with a whistle. He smiled at her. "Correct me if I'm wrong, but I rather think we've been useful to you, Xena. So, maybe for old times' sake, you wouldn't mind—when you get to the Sphinx, you wouldn't mention that you saw either of us? Just a minor detail, really."

Xena smiled, then closed the two paces between them and kissed him gently. "Mannius, you take care of yourself. All right?"

"I've been doing just that," he said quietly. "And you—be careful, will you? She's not to be trusted."

"The Sphinx? I don't intend to trust her, any more than I trust that huntress over there." Xena turned and walked away. Behind her, she could hear Mannius talking to the Cyclops.

"My friend, that's quite a woman."

"Women," the Cyclops replied dreamily. "I still remember how good they taste." He spat noisily. "That Xena's all muscle; probably too tough to chew anyway."

Xena strode across open meadow and waved a hand to her companions. "Come on, road's that way." Atalanta growled something under her breath that made Homer blink and stare, then got to her feet. She eyed the massive Cyclops warily as they started past him and his guide, cast Gabrielle a very sour glance, then hurried to catch up with Ixos, who was practically running. He slowed once the odd pair was well behind them, and stopped when Xena stepped into his path. She bared her teeth at him in a mirthless smile, and motioned him ahead of her.

Gabrielle shielded her eyes and eyed the sun with resignation. "It's getting awfully late," she told Homer unhappily. "We're gonna be lucky to find the road *and* the Sphinx before night falls." She shivered. "I'm not particularly wild about the idea of meeting her on a dark road, if you know what I mean."

"Not what I had in mind when I asked to come with you," he said gloomily. Gabrielle laid a hand on his arm, and he managed a smile. "I'm not—I'm *trying* not to complain," he said.

"You're doing great. Honest."

"I'm not. I'm stiff and sore, and so far I haven't been any use at all."

"Oh, sure you have," she protested, but he shook his head.

"You don't have to lie to me, Gabrielle. You were ready to hit that man Ixos; you would have struck Atalanta if she'd tried to run just now, wouldn't you? I've never hit anyone in my life—I can't imagine hitting anyone."

Gabrielle eyed him sidelong and considered this gravely. "Well, don't try," she said finally. "Sometimes—understand me, when I first saw Xena fight, in my village, there wasn't anything I wanted so much as to learn to fight just like she does. I'd still like to be able to do half the things—a quarter of them—that she does! Still—sometimes I wish I'd never learned as much as I have. Fighting for your very life, or fighting to save someone else, you're so busy you don't have time to get scared or sickened. But sometimes it's unpleasant things, like today. If I'd had to hurt Ixos, to get the truth out of him, I'd have done it, but I wouldn't have liked myself for it." They plunged into the shade of a grove of ancient oaks. Xena had moved ahead of Ixos on open ground, but now she paused to ask the man something. The hunter pointed; Gabrielle stared, but the shade was too deep for her to make out much around them. Xena shook her head, then finally stepped aside to let Ixos and his ward lead the way once more. "Besides," Gabrielle went on, her voice determinedly cheerful, "I don't think there's going to be any more fighting, really. It's more—thinking and planning, and then talking. I'm still better at talking, and that's what you do, so it's up to us. Where's he leading us, anyway?" The ground on both sides of them began to rise sharply; ten paces, and they were in a deep rift overhung with bracken and moss. A trickle of water meandered down the narrow floor, making footing hazardous. "This better not be a trap!" she called out; her voice echoed.

"It's not," Ixos called back. "It's the best way to reach the Thessaly road without—" His voice rose to a startled squawk, and Atalanta yelped as four men slid down the east bank, and half a dozen more charged down the ravine floor, straight at them.

Xena's high battle cry bounced off the walls of the rift; she shoved Ixos one way, Atalanta the other, and raced upstream to meet the attack. She leaped high, legs snapping out at the last moment, and the two men who'd thought to catch her between them fell in a sodden heap. Another went sailing over her head to land with a splash and a groan in a shallow pool.

Gabrielle shifted her grasp on the staff and shouted, "Homer, stay with me!"

"Give me back my bow!" Atalanta yelled.

"Not in here," Gabrielle shouted back. "Too close. You'll hit one of us. Here," she added, and held out the long-bladed dagger she'd stuffed in her belt. "Watch where you put it!"

"Shut up and fight!" Atalanta replied sourly, setting her shoulder at an angle against Gabrielle's; the two formed a barrier to a narrow depression in the sheer stone wall.

Gabrielle shoved Homer behind her, then lunged, ramming one heavily armored thug in the midsection; the staff rebounded sharply, and the man laughed as he swiped at the staff with a gauntleted hand. But she'd already pulled back, and this time she swung the staff in a vicious arc, catching him beneath his ear. He stumbled back into the brute who was trying to pull himself out of the pool, and both went down with a splash. Beyond them, Xena yelled and wrecked three men with her spin kick, then vaulted over a fourth and drove her elbow into the back of his head. All at once the two men just short of Gabrielle were the only ones still conscious; both were trying to stagger off amid the slick rock. The smaller one, now dripping wet, tapped his companion's arm and gestured urgently; the other glanced upstream, where Xena stood, sword at the ready; across from him was Gabrielle, staff doing a lazy circle in the air, and next to her Atalanta crouched over a bleeding man. The huntress stood slowly, a red-bladed dagger in her hand. The two men turned as one and fled down the ravine.

"Let them go," Xena shouted as Gabrielle moved away from the wall. "And *give* me that," she added angrily as she snatched the dagger from Atalanta.

"I gave it to her," Gabrielle said warily. Xena's mouth quirked; she bent to rinse the blade and handed it back to Gabrielle, then hauled Ixos out of hiding.

"It wasn't—I wasn't—!" he stuttered. "I swear, I didn't have anything to do with that!" She rolled her eyes, shoved him aside, and headed up the ravine, stepping over unconscious and wounded men and gesturing sharply for the others to follow. Once in the open, she turned back to wait for them to catch up, then shoved Ixos ahead of her once more.

"I hope for your sake that's true," she said softly. "Get moving."

It was very quiet in the ravine; Xena followed the subdued hunter and his ward. Some paces back, Gabrielle put Homer in front of her and kept a wary eye on the way behind them. The sun was low and tree shadows long when they finally clambered out of the rift to stand on a broad, steep mountain road.

"Fine," Xena said. It was the first thing anyone had said in some time. "Which way, hunter?"

"That—" His voice died. Xena turned to look; Atalanta clapped a hand over her mouth. Gabrielle edged around the tall huntress so she could see.

"Oh!" she breathed. "She's—she really is big, isn't she?" Twenty or so paces up the road, at its crest and across most of its breadth, the Sphinx sprawled, golden and glorious in the late afternoon sun. Flanking her, several seasoned fighting men paced or stood, weapons at the ready. The tallest of them didn't reach her furred shoulder. Gabrielle swallowed hard as the Sphinx yawned, exposing glittering canines and a mouth that would easily hold four men—or possibly the Caledonian boar itself. Xena looked at Gabrielle, who shrugged, trying to be casual. "Well," she said, "I guess there isn't any reason to be standoffish, is there?"

"I can think of one or two for leaving here right now," Atalanta whispered, her voice trembling.

"I can think of six better reasons for staying," Xena replied in a low voice. "Between her forepaws—look."

Gabrielle squinted, then caught her breath. Between the enormous lion's feet, she could just make out a small, frightened huddle of children. Standing apart, just short of a shining, exposed claw, were Nausicaa and Mitradia.

Atalanta stopped and folded her arms. ''I don't care what you say *or* do,'' she said flatly. ''You can't make me face that!''

''I told you, you haven't got a choice,'' Xena hissed.

''I'm—I'm with Atalanta,'' Ixos put in, his voice much too high. ''I'm not going anywhere but back down that road, as fast as I can.''

''It's—ah, not wise to run from something like that,'' Gabrielle said quietly. She was watching the Sphinx and her young captives, head tipped thoughtfully to one side. ''I mean, look at those wings. She'd have you before you got five paces.''

''I won't,'' Atalanta said flatly, and sat in the middle of the road. Xena swore a blistering oath and turned to drag her back to her feet; Atalanta struggled, but with little success, as the warrior dragged one arm behind her back and hauled her, kicking and cursing, to her feet.

''Gabrielle,'' she said sharply, ''hand me that piece of rope.'' No reply. ''Gabrielle?'' She turned; Gabrielle's bag and staff were on the ground almost at her feet, but Gabrielle was a good twenty paces away, heading purposefully toward the Sphinx, Homer right behind her. "Gabrielle!"

"Be right back," Gabrielle replied over her shoulder. "Just setting the ground rules. All right?"

"All right," Xena growled under her breath. "I swear, I'll—" Atalanta tried to twist away from her, and Xena swore again and shook her, hard. "Settle down," she said sternly. The huntress sat still, panting and staring blankly. Ixos gazed down at her, then glared at the warrior.

"You didn't have to shake her so hard," he said evenly.

"Shut up and sit down next to her. There's enough to worry about here and now—you're not going to distract me." She glared him into submission, waited until he'd settled on the road and taken the girl into his arms, then turned back to check on Gabrielle.

This time I just might wring her neck, and— She sighed, and some of the anger went out of her. Someone was going to have to do the talking here. And Gabrielle hadn't misjudged the size of those wings. The Sphinx could probably have picked her off even from this far away in the blink of an eye. *Still, those are eagles' wings. Eaglelike.* There wasn't an eagle alive with wings like that. *None now, at least,* she reminded herself grimly. But eagles were day birds. Maybe, if they could stall this contest long enough, it would be possible to grab the girls. *Lions hunt at night,* she reminded herself gloomily. If Gabrielle had just hung around long enough for them to come up with a plan! *I wonder what she's saying up there.*

At her feet, Atalanta moaned and stirred in Ixos' arms. "Keep her quiet, and keep her down there with you," Xena said evenly. "Or I'll flatten her again. Got it?" Silence. She looked down at him; he eyed her angrily but finally nodded. "Good."

•   •   •

"Wait!"

Gabrielle turned to glance over her shoulder; she frowned slightly.

"Homer, you shouldn't be here. I mean, if she decides—well, you shouldn't be, that's all."

"I have to," he said. "I'm afraid, yes. But I know how I'd feel if I did nothing, and hid back there, and then if she decided to—."

"No one's going to get eaten," Gabrielle put in hastily. "But someone's got to talk to her and set things up."

"Talking's what I do, you said so."

"I'm not so bad at it myself," she replied mildly.

"I know." He managed a faint, shaky smile. "So between us, maybe we can fix things up right." The smile faded. "I'm not going to go back and leave you alone here."

"Well, then I'm glad to have you," Gabrielle said. Sunlight was suddenly warm on her back, and the Sphinx very near indeed. The great beast with a woman's face stretched and yawned widely; Gabrielle's jaws ached, and she set her teeth together to keep from yawning herself. Four girls sat in a huddle between the enormous paws, and one of them was crying steadily and hopelessly. Mitradia, who had been whispering something in Nausicaa's ear, straightened and smiled.

"Oh! I'm so glad to see you, Ga—!"

"I'm glad to see again you, too." Gabrielle cut her off sharply, then turned a dazzling smile on the Sphinx. "I heard you want to see me. My name's Atalanta, and there was something about a contest. He wasn't too clear about it, though, and—"

"Shut up!" the Sphinx snarled. Homer paled, and Gabrielle kept the smile in place with a great effort. "You aren't Atalanta; even I know she's a huntress and a runner." Dark green eyes moved beyond Gabrielle to the three

161

people down the road. "That's Atalanta, the skinny thing."

"Hey, I'm not so overweight as all that, you know!" Gabrielle protested indignantly. The Sphinx laughed and bared her teeth. Gabrielle took an involuntary step back and said, "All right, I'm not Atalanta. But, you know what? You don't really want Atalanta."

"Who says I don't?" the Sphinx demanded ominously.

"I do. I'm Gabrielle—you've heard of me, I'm certain. I'm the personal bard and soothsayer for Xena—that's her down there, the, ah, not skinny one with the black hair."

"Why would I have heard of *you*?"

"Well—you've heard of Xena, haven't you?" The Sphinx growled under her breath, then finally nodded. Gabrielle patted her chest in a self-congratulatory gesture. "So, I'm the reason you've heard about her. She has an adventure, rights a wrong, saves a village, rescues a child or two, slays an ogre—and I cast it into iambic pentameter—or whatever form fits it best; some adventures don't fit well with iambic pentameter . . ." Her voice faded as the Sphinx eased forward and glared directly into her face.

"Why are you here? I sent for Atalanta: I've heard of *her*. She's famous. When I outriddle her, everyone will know I'm the greatest of all time!"

"Well," Gabrielle temporized, "they'll know you beat Atalanta." The Sphinx was still staring at her. "I wish you wouldn't do that," she added vexedly. "Makes it hard for me to remember what I'm trying to say to you."

"You talk too much," the Sphinx muttered. "Why are you here? I won't ask you again!"

"Here? Ah . . . here! Because you may not have heard of *me*—or my very famous companion here." She indicated Homer with a deep bow and a flourish of her arm. "But we've certainly heard of you. Why, there probably isn't a bard in all the land who wouldn't be honored to engage in a contest with you!''

''Some have,'' the Sphinx replied meaningfully; she gazed into the distance and a smirk turned the corners of her mouth. ''Some of them were fairly tasty, too.''

''Nice to hear that,'' Gabrielle muttered. ''Well, anyway, since you want me to come to the point: Atalanta's a runner; she doesn't know a riddle from a—from a—well, she's no good at them. Now, I'm one of the best, and this—well, there isn't anyone greater at riddles than Homer. You've heard of *him*, of course,'' she added. ''He's the king's bard, the bard of all Athens.'' The Sphinx gave her a confused look. Homer opened his mouth to protest, and Gabrielle stepped on his foot. ''King Theseus,'' she explained. The confused look didn't change. ''Of course, before that, he was bard to King Menelaus—and Queen Helen.''

''I've heard of *them*. They're in Sparta,'' the Sphinx said. ''I left Sparta years ago; not enough travelers.''

''Well—sure,'' Gabrielle replied. *Doesn't even know Helen left Menelaus for Paris, or that she didn't come back!* She filed the thought for later examination and went on. ''Well, the thing is, now instead of a girl who doesn't know the first thing about riddling, you've got two experts—not as good as you are, of course, I'm sure, but still, we're about as good as it gets. Right, Homer?''

''Right,'' he echoed faintly, and eased his foot from beneath hers.

Gabrielle turned back to the Sphinx, who was showing signs of restlessness. ''So, my question is, why should you settle for winning a contest against someone like Atalanta, when you could best the two greatest bards in all Greece?''

''Hmmmmm.''

''Keeping in mind, too, that if you eat Atalanta when she loses, there isn't that much there to eat.''

163

"Good point," the Sphinx conceded. She eyed Gabrielle sidelong. "No one deliberately sets out to be eaten. You're planning to trick me!"

"No way," Gabrielle said firmly. "I think too much of your talent and your prowess to do that. An honest bard would never attempt trickery to win a contest. What we're offering is, we come up with three riddles between us; you come up with three. Best two of three wins it. And—well, you get your choice between us. One gets to take the girls, and he—or she—goes back to Athens to cast the tale of the Great Contest into verse, for all the world to hear in amazement. And the other is—well—" she shrugged. "Lunch. Or dinner."

Silence. Even the sobbing girl had stopped crying so she could listen. The Sphinx frowned and gazed down the road. "I need to think about this—stay where you are," she ordered. "Only a fool would try to run."

"Wouldn't dream of it," Gabrielle replied cheerfully.

"She's lying, your Greatness," a gritty voice broke in. A dark-haired, ugly man in old leather armor came from somewhere near the creature's left flank and stopped just short of Gabrielle. She blinked; his face was as scarred as any she'd ever seen, and he was missing most of his left arm. *Must be good with the one he's got left,* she thought. "If she's with Xena, she's lying. They're trying to pull something."

"Be still, or be appetizer," the Sphinx hissed. He glanced up at her and went quiet, but he stayed right where he was, within sword's reach of Gabrielle. She ignored him, met Mitradia's eyes, and winked at the girl, who tried to smile at her, then whispered something in Nausicaa's ear. The blind princess whispered something back and Mitradia nodded, then returned Gabrielle's wink. "Probably you *are* up to something," the Sphinx went on after a long moment.

"Most people are; usually it's trying to get away from me alive. No one does."

"Ah," Gabrielle said. "But if *no one* does this time, then there's no one to tell the tale and spread the story of your greatest conquest, is there?" She glanced at the one-armed man and smiled contemptuously. "I suppose you could let *him* do it, or something—but there isn't a bard anywhere else in the whole world who could do you justice in Dorian like I can, and Homer's the absolute master of Ionian."

"Three riddles each—why three?" the Sphinx demanded.

"What's the point of one?" Gabrielle countered. "One riddle, you either guess it or you don't, and bang! It's all over, isn't it? This way, you've got something—a story worth telling and a contest worth participating in."

"Three," the Sphinx said thoughtfully. "All right. We'll do this your way." She smiled; Gabrielle tried to swallow past a very dry throat. "I like your looks."

"Ah—thanks!" She paused. "I think. Are you ready to get going on this now?"

"It's nearly sundown. And you've probably already chosen your riddles. You think to best me by trickery, don't you?"

"Hadn't even occurred to me," Gabrielle said.

"Hah! We'll begin when the sun reaches the tops of those trees tomorrow. Don't think of escaping tonight, any of you," she added pointedly, "or I break my fast on very young meat. I hope that's not a riddle beyond your grasp."

"Nope—got the idea. I don't suppose you'd let them come sleep with us, or—anything like that?" Gabrielle's voice trailed away as the Sphinx bared very sharp teeth. "I was afraid you'd feel that way about it. Well, then, I guess we'll see you in the morning." She looked at Mitradia, who managed a shaky smile before backing cautiously between the creature's paws, drawing Nausicaa with her, as the Sphinx muttered something Gabrielle couldn't quite catch. The one-armed brute scowled at her for one more long moment, then turned on his heel and went back the way he'd come. Homer tugged at Gabrielle's sleeve, and bowed to the Sphinx—her mouth quirked in amusement. Gabrielle backed away, turned, and walked down the road, Homer at her side.

"Beloved Calliope, just let me keep my knees from buckling until we get back to the others," he mumbled. Gabrielle squeezed his hand.

"You did really well—really and truly well. I'm proud of you," she said quietly. "Don't walk any faster; we don't want her thinking we're scared."

"Aren't we?"

"Well, we don't want *her* thinking it. I've got to talk to Xena; I think I have an idea."

Light was fading rapidly in the trees around them; Xena was on one knee, rummaging through Gabrielle's pack as Gabrielle and Homer came up, skirting Ixos, who still sat in the middle of the road, Atalanta in his arms. Her eyes were still tightly closed, but her lips were moving—steadily cursing, from the looks of things, Gabrielle thought. The old hunter looked up at her, rolled his eyes, then looked away. Xena shoved the pack aside, got to her feet, folded her arms across her chest, and turned toward her traveling companion. *That* look, Gabrielle thought nervously. The silence stretched. "Ah," she managed finally, and to her surprise, her voice sounded almost normal. "Ah, I think we got everything set up all right; no surprise we couldn't get the girls back over here, but I did try."

Xena looked at her for a very long moment. Finally, she sighed faintly and said, "I'm still trying to figure out how it was going to help anyone if you just walked up to her and got eaten.''

"I wasn't gonna get eaten!'' Gabrielle protested. "No one's gonna—''

"Gabrielle, talking's what you do. *Eating* is what she does. Keep that in mind, will you?'' Xena spun away and glowered down at the bag. "You have any kind of something to fix for dinner in there? Because somehow I have the feeling game might be a little scarce around here.''

"Good one,'' Gabrielle laughed. Xena glanced back at her, and the laugh died an instant death. "I—yeah. It'll take a while. I didn't figure on two nights in a row, but I can feed us.''

"Good,'' Xena said flatly. "Keep an eye on those two; I'll be back in a few minutes.''

"Ahhh—I hope *she* doesn't think you're taking off,'' Gabrielle said. "Because—''

"I'm going to scout both sides of the road for firewood,'' the warrior broke in. "She'll be able to see me at all times. You keep our two helpers there under control, all right?''

"Got it,'' Gabrielle said. She knelt to rummage through the bag, grumbling as she straightened the contents. A string of dried vegetables and a few hot peppers needed to be untangled from her spare bodice; the shallow cooking pot probably wasn't very clean, but a surreptitious swipe of her hand cleared the worst of the grit, and it really didn't smell too bad. Water might be a problem. *Guess I didn't think of everything up there.* Well, it would have taken someone twice as good at talking as *she* was, to have gotten everything in. Everything caught up to her between one breath and another, and she had to stuff her hands between her knees to keep them from shaking.

"Gabrielle?'' Homer leaned over her shoulders. She managed a smile for him. "Everything all right?''

"As close as it's going to get under the circumstances," she said brightly. "Think you can stand my cooking two nights in a row?"

"My father used to cook for me. I can eat anything. Almost anything," he amended carefully. "Except maybe those salty, hairy little fish some bakers put on their flat bread along with the rounds of dried sausage and the goat cheese before they bake it."

"Anchovies?" Gabrielle's nose wrinkled. "No one really eats those on flat bread, do they? Actually," she added thoughtfully, "I guess if there was enough cheese to hide the taste, I could . . . Well, anyway, it isn't anything like that. More soup. Provided we can find water. Guess I should've asked *her.*"

"She probably has a mind above such mundane matters," Homer said. "But if Ixos knows this area, then he'll know where water is. If—" He swallowed. "If I go for water, and I have a bucket in hand, surely *she* won't think I'm trying to run for it."

"You're the world-famous bard Homer," Gabrielle reminded him. "World-famous bards don't run away." She suddenly caught at her head with both hands; her eyes closed. "Oh! Oh!"

Homer eyed her anxiously "Gabrielle? Are you all right?"

"I—I can see it!" she gasped, then shook her head and blinked at him. "I almost could. Ohhhh. My head aches. Um—what's a catalog of ships?"

"A—?" He blinked at her, his jaw hanging. "A what of ships?"

"I don't know," she said, "but it's important. It—somehow, it's part of your legend."

"My—legend?" he echoed.

"I don't know," Gabrielle whispered, and let her eyes

close again. She could see it so clearly, line upon line, verse upon verse; children in odd, bright clothing seated in pale-walled rooms on hard wooden benches, other children staring at black walls covered in white squiggles that must be writing, reciting lines. *Lines he wrote. How wonderful.* She managed a smile for the wide-eyed, wary Homer, and shrugged.

"What are you talking about?" he asked finally. "Was that a—a vision? You never said you have visions."

"Sometimes I do. I think. You know how visions are," she added with another shrug. "They don't always tell you anything you can use—or tell it to you straight."

"I don't know anything about visions, except what the tales tell me," Homer whispered. "Catalog of ships—I'll remember that."

"Well, I hope it's something useful." She got to her feet, the string of dried vegetables dangling from one hand and the pot from the other as Atalanta shoved free from Ixos' arms and tried to struggle to her feet. Gabrielle stared briefly at her hands, then shoved the pot and stew starter toward Homer, caught up her staff, and closed the distance between her and Atalanta in a bound. "I wouldn't, if I were you," she said.

"Wouldn't what?" Atalanta snapped. "Wouldn't try to keep from being turned into that creature's—next meal? I suppose you look forward to it as a new experience! Forgive me if I'm not as open-minded as you are!"

"I wasn't thinking about that so much," Gabrielle said. "I was thinking more about those six girls up there; one of them was crying when I got there, and still crying when I left."

"Crying doesn't prove anything, and it doesn't get you anywhere," Atalanta replied sullenly.

"That isn't true," Gabrielle said. "It releases pain; it—

well, it does a lot of things. Just because it didn't soften your father doesn't mean it's a useless activity.''

''How dare you!'' the huntress demanded furiously.

Gabrielle shook her head and dropped down cross-legged onto the road. Ixos reclaimed his grasp on his ward, who gave him a black look but subsided in his embrace. ''Atalanta—I'm sorry. I don't like shoving myself into other people's private affairs, it embarrasses everyone, including me. And obviously, you.'' There was a long silence. ''Look, you've fooled everyone around you for years. Castor and Pollux, Meleager—all those guys on the boar hunt had you figured for this really tough little thing, didn't they?''

Atalanta stared at her for some moments, then turned away. ''They thought—they *said* they thought—that I was the hardest, bravest female they'd ever met,'' she said finally.

''Fine. You fooled a bunch of young male would-be heroes. You know, they can be both the hardest and the easiest guys in the whole world to fool—they're all so concerned with their own male thing, the ego, hiding their own nerves, making sure the other guys see them in the bravest possible way. At the same time, they're all so scared someone else is gonna show 'em up. A girl like you—a genuine girl hero—shows up and demands to be part of the party, and has the weapons and the skill to back up the demand, half the time they're gonna be scared silly a mere girl's gonna show them up, and the other half they'll be wondering how they're gonna—ah—gonna—well, you know.''

Atalanta's mouth quirked. ''*Virgin* huntress,'' she said quietly, then giggled. ''Oddly enough, that part's still true.''

Ixos blushed painfully. ''Atalanta! I should hope it was!

170

You're unwed, after all, and—and dedicated to—''

"To Athena," Atalanta put in gravely. "Papa, I—I think Gabrielle and I need to talk a little. I'm sorry," she added. "Uncle Nenny, everything—I'm not trying to hurt you—''

"Princess, it's all right," he said at once. "It wasn't your fault."

"It *was* my fault. If I hadn't come up with this mad scheme, Nenny'd still be alive and both of you planning your next—next hunt." Her eyes filled with tears; she swore angrily and blotted them on the backs of her hands. "But remember what you both said, just before I left you. That I needed a—another woman to talk to? Not things like—like *that*—but—just to talk?" Her color was high; so was Ixos'. "Please, Papa. I'll come find you in a little."

"It's all right, Princess," he replied. "I'll be right here." He sighed faintly and mumbled under his breath, "I haven't anywhere else to go, after all. Not now."

Atalanta got stiffly to her feet and blotted her eyes once more. "He won't survive this," she whispered. "And it's my stupid, stupid fault. Poor Nenny was half-blind the past year or so, and—''

"You can't take responsibility for anyone but yourself," Gabrielle broke in firmly. Atalanta blinked tear-starred lashes, then shook her head. Gabrielle insisted: "I mean it. I left behind a village, a father, a mother, a younger sister, a betrothed—to follow Xena. What if because of that, because I wasn't there, something awful would happen to them? I could have thought of it that way. Just as maybe you should've thought about what would happen if you persuaded those two old men and a bunch of stupid, bored village boys to help you out. But those boys had the choice of saying no, and so did your—so did Neneron and Ixos."

"They never said no to me, all my life," Atalanta broke in tearfully. "I knew that, and acted on that knowledge."

171

"That was still *their* choice," Gabrielle said. "Just like it was *your* choice to become a huntress and a hero. There isn't one of those little girls up there right now who isn't resting easier because you're here to rescue them."

"Oh, goddess, don't put a burden like that on me!" Atalanta cried out.

Gabrielle shook her head. "I'm not. You put it on yourself when you chose the path you took. Maybe the goddess did mark you early on, but that doesn't need to be a horrible burden. Xena's been marked for that kind of attention by Ares—not my idea of a soulmate. But even so, she hasn't been kept under his influence, has she?"

Atalanta shook her head furiously and pounded long-fingered fists against the trunk of a nearby tree. She winced and shook them out with care. "Let's not talk about her right now—all right?"

"Whatever you want. Look, Atalanta, I'm just trying to help. To understand you. Most important, to help you and me—all of us—get those girls home safely."

"I don't know what you think I can do," Atalanta whispered. "You've seen me—at my very best," she added bitterly. "You know I'm no more a hero than—than that Cyclops is."

"Well," Gabrielle objected mildly, "he might be a hero to someone. Maybe even to the little guy traveling with him, who knows? Thing is, all it takes sometimes is the look: you had that right from the start. Put the appearance on and people will believe, because they want to believe. You can do it. You've already proved you can."

"I can't—not here."

"Of course you can." Gabrielle laughed suddenly and spread her arms wide; Atalanta eyed her tearily. "Look, if Homer—who's never been allowed to so much as *blink* at danger—and I can face off with a nasty, mythological, immortal being who has a nasty taste for raw humans, and come away with the upper hand, are you gonna tell me someone as well trained with weapons as you are can't at least pick up her javelin case and *look* heroic? To please a captive—'scuse me, bad choice of words—audience?''

"Oooooh!" Atalanta wrinkled her nose and suddenly began to giggle. For the first time since Gabrielle had seen her, the huntress looked, and acted, like a girl only a year or so short of full womanhood. "That was *awful!* Now I know why I don't keep company with a woman bard!''

"Hey!" Gabrielle grinned. "If I had a choice of bards like that boy you had in Athens! Well—''

A strong voice interrupted her. "You'd probably lose your—ah—your ability to occasionally view the future, wouldn't you?" Xena dropped a loose load of firewood to the road; a rope-bound bundle of kindling followed. The sound of wood rattling onto the dry, hard surface echoed from tree to tree, then finally died away. "We gonna eat sometime tonight?" she added dryly.

"You see any water out there?" Gabrielle countered as dryly. Xena eyed her for a long moment, sent her eyes toward the huntress, then finally shrugged.

"Small spill over a decent length of stone. How much you need?" She took the shallow pot Gabrielle thrust at her. "How long's it gonna take to cook this?''

"Full dark!" Gabrielle shouted after her. "Or longer, depending on how long it takes you to bring me a pot of water.''

"Your humble servant," the warrior replied sarcastically. "You think only the Sphinx is hungry," she added as she vanished down the darkened roadway.

"I know *she* is," Gabrielle mumbled to herself. *Can't believe I did that—not only confronted a bored and hungry carnivore but told her I'd make a better lunch than Homer*

173

would. . . . Homer! Suddenly, she realized that her vision sense was talking to her—not only talking, but demanding she listen. It was about the war for Helen, of all things. *I was there; I talked to Helen, fought Menelaus' warriors, saw the Horse firsthand—but I was too close to it all, including poor Helen. I wouldn't mind telling Xena's part of that story, if she'd let me. Homer'd do such a wonderful job of the rest of it. Find the time, if you aren't on tomorrow's menu, to tell him the whole story.*

Gabrielle shook herself and got to her feet; Atalanta was eyeing her curiously. "Well, never mind. I just—act like you aren't afraid, for those poor girls up there. Who knows, it might even stick to you."

"I don't believe it," Atalanta said flatly, but a small, embarrassed smile tugged at her mouth. "But—all right. I'll try."

It took time to get the fire to burn hot, then die down enough so she could shove the pot into a sheltered corner. Wind blew steadily down the road, coating everything in dust. Gabrielle scooped out a small spoonful, tested a tuber. "Just about," she promised.

Xena sighed faintly. "Gonna be full dark before it's ready, right?"

"Sorry. It's the wind, you know."

"Not your fault." Without warning, she leaped to her feet, her eyes flashed, and she stepped onto the road. Half a dozen men were coming toward them, the Sphinx at their back. They halted in a ragged line. The Sphinx sat on her haunches. Atalanta froze; the branch she was shoving into the fire trembled briefly, then steadied as she drew a deep breath and positioned it. Ixos edged closer to her. Homer, who had fallen asleep moments earlier, sighed faintly and rolled onto his side, away from the light.

"Great," Gabrielle murmured. "Something to block the wind, finally!" Atalanta cast her a startled glance across the flames, then clapped a hand over her mouth to stifle something that might have been hysterical laughter. Gabrielle settled the pot more firmly, dropped the spoon on a warm, flat stone next to the coals, and turned to see what was going on.

On the road, Xena stood very still, her eyes moving from one shadowy figure to another. "You might at least make some light," she said finally. "I like to see who I'm talking to."

"Light," the Sphinx rumbled. One of the men crouched at her feet and began to fumble with flint and tinder; moments later a torch spluttered and caught. And then a second, and a third. He passed one to the man at each end of the line, and kept the last for himself. Xena took a step forward and smiled.

"Well, well. Old home week, isn't it? Philimos. Kodro. And—how nice." She didn't look the least bit pleased. "It's my old friend Zakon. What's left of him." She looked up to meet the Sphinx's eyes. "There's a purpose to all this? And where are the girls?"

"They're safe—and warm, and fed. But they aren't your concern. *He* is." The creature gestured with her chin. Gabrielle squinted against a sudden swirl of smoke as the one-armed man in grubby fighting leathers took a step forward. "He tells me you're the one responsible for his . . . condition."

"He thought he knew more than me about how to take a ridge," Xena countered softly. "I don't put up with that kind of insubordination from common soldiers, not when it costs me time and men. I wager you don't either."

"I told you she'd have a lie ready," Zakon said smugly.

175

"Shut up, Zakon," Xena snarled. The Sphinx rumbled ominously and two of the torch holders paled.

"He's not your underling anymore, warrior. He's mine—and I take care of what's mine. He says he wants vengeance. . . ." She was abruptly silent; Xena was laughing.

"Vengeance!" she managed finally. "Zakon, you never did have much for brains! I could easily have killed you back in camp that day. You couldn't get near me, even with two good arms!"

"I'm bored at the moment," the Sphinx said. "Very bored." The woman's face *looked* bored; as Xena eyed her sidelong, one vast eyebrow went up. "You know how these things are," she added in mock apology. "When there's nothing to see or do—you want to eat."

"You do," Xena echoed flatly. Her gaze moved to Zakon, who was smirking broadly.

"*I* do," the Sphinx replied. "Of course, I don't doubt you could simply take him the way things are. But if we evened them somewhat . . ."

Gabrielle was on her feet and next to Xena in one smooth movement. Xena cast her a sidelong glance and muttered, "Get back over there; I'm really gonna be hungry after I get done with this fool."

"It's cooking all by itself," Gabrielle said out of the corner of her mouth, then addressed the Sphinx. "Ground rules again!" she said brightly. "I mean—I can see your point, but how do you plan to even things out? Because if you—ah—cut her arm off, then it isn't even any more, not if she's bleeding and all that."

"Hadn't thought of that," the Sphinx said thoughtfully, and snarled wordlessly at Zakon, who was trying to protest. "All right. Suggestion?"

"Easy. Tie one hand behind her back," Gabrielle said promptly.

"Right hand," Zakon demanded.

"I could take you any time, either hand," Xena purred. The Sphinx looked from one to the other, then flopped bonelessly onto the road, human chin resting on enormous paws, and sent her eyes in Gabrielle's direction.

"Do it," she ordered.

"Do it—right! You bet. Be right back," Gabrielle added. She scurried across the road and knelt to fumble in her pack. There was a slight delay as she struggled with the knots on Nausicaa's length of rope. "I swear I just put a simple over-and-under in this thing," she grumbled. It finally came loose, and she scrambled back onto the road. Zakon stepped in front of her.

"Wait a minute!" he demanded loudly. "I want to see this bit of rope, make sure it isn't fake or something!"

"Oh, sure," Gabrielle retorted. "I always carry a bit of magic rope around with me. Doesn't everyone?" She held it out, let him tug at it. "Want to watch me tie it, too?" she asked sweetly. He probably would have said yes, but one of the men behind him broke into raucous laughter.

"Hey, Zakon!" another jeered. "Thought you said you could take her with *your* hand behind your back! What's the matter? Scared?"

"Just making sure it's all done right," he shouted back. With a sour glance at Gabrielle, who was unsuccessfully biting back a grin, he slapped the rope aside and stepped back to draw an ugly, knobby mace from his belt. He eyed it with satisfaction. Gabrielle turned away and looked up at Xena. "I hope I didn't mess things up for you."

"You did fine." Xena squeezed her shoulder. "I liked your suggestion a lot better than his." And as Gabrielle looked at the rope, then eyed her companion uncertainly,

Xena put her right arm behind her back, turned so it was facing Gabrielle, and wiggled her fingers. "Fix it to my sword belt; it won't go anywhere."

"It better not!" Zakon yelled. He'd secured the mace and was now testing the air with his sword—a thick-bladed affair with a grip of leather-wrapped metal bands that encircled his hand.

"I told you," Xena said as the blade sliced the air with a hiss that made Gabrielle wince and nearly drop the rope, "I never did need two hands to take you."

"Ahhh—" Gabrielle was busy at her back, working a complex wad of knots even larger than the one she'd wrapped around Atalanta's ankles. "Listen," she whispered, "I bet you can flatten him in one whack. But—ah—keep in mind, our furry friend there wants to be entertained."

"I won't forget," Xena said quietly. "She wants a show, she'll get one. Watch your back, and keep an eye on our skittish friends over there, will you?"

"Got it," Gabrielle said. With one last tug on the rope, she backed up two paces, then turned and headed for the edge of the road. She had barely turned back to watch the fight when Xena's battle cry cut the night air. Four thugs backed hastily away and the Sphinx sat up, the tips of her wings quivering above her head, her eyes wide and very bright.

Zakon laughed and held his sword at the ready. "You can't scare me with noise, Xena! Come on—" He stopped short, his mouth hanging open; the warrior had launched herself into a tight double flip that carried her over his head. She made hardly a sound as she landed behind him and whirled around, smacking him hard with the flat of her blade. He howled with pain and outrage, spun around, and slashed where she'd been. Too late. She was already airborne, this time coming down so close to him that her near foot flattened his. He yelled again. "Fight fair! You know I got bad feet!" He started halfway around, then back the other way. Xena was behind him, behind him again, then right in his face, sword between her teeth; her left hand backhanded his blade aside, then came back hard in a ringing slap to his face. He reeled and blinked, tightened his grip on the sword hilt, and with a yell charged her. Xena sidestepped and tripped him as he rushed by. He staggered to regain his footing, blinking dazedly. Xena waved her empty hand in front of his eyes, then backflipped away from him to retrieve the sword she'd let fall to the road. She wasn't even breathing hard. A corner of her mouth quirked; she seemed to be enjoying herself.

"You're making a game of this!" he shouted breathlessly.

"You prefer I just stand here and kill you on the spot?" she asked evenly. "You forgot just how good I am, didn't you Zakon? And how lousy you are?" He swore furiously—and incoherently—and charged straight at her. Xena sidestepped at the last possible moment, gripped his shoulder as he passed, and flipped him onto his back. The air erupted from his lungs in a loud gust. He opened his eyes to see a sword held very steadily, just short of his nose.

"What do you think?" she asked conversationally. "Take your nose off and make you even uglier—if that's possible? Or maybe just hack off your other arm? You can always fight with your teeth, you know."

Zakon gasped for air and swore helplessly. "You're making a game of it! Damn you to Hades, Xena! You think it's easy finding work as a one-armed fighter?"

"So go be a one-armed goatherd, or a one-armed baker,"

she said indifferently. "No one's forcing you to do this kind of stuff."

"It's what I do," he replied stubbornly. "It's all I've ever done."

"You won't be doing it anymore if I kill you here and now, will you?" she asked.

"Or if I do," the Sphinx put in smoothly. Zakon's eyes rolled sideways in a vain effort to make out the bulky creature. She didn't sound very happy, he realized uncomfortably. Not that she ever sounded happy—but this was definitely the *other* voice.

To his surprise, Xena flipped her sword away from his face, and stepped over him to confront the beast. "He amused you, didn't he?" she asked. "I think that's worth letting him go." A long silence. Men eyed each other sidelong, and the Sphinx stared beyond Xena, her thoughtful gaze fixed on the fallen Zakon, who lay motionless where Xena had left him, lips pressed together and eyes closed.

To his astonishment, the creature began to laugh, a sound like stones falling downhill, but indisputably laughter. His eyes flew open. "Amused," the Sphinx repeated. "Yes. That was—most amusing, warrior. Kept my mind off food very nicely." She turned the impassive look back to motionless Zakon. "I'm not hungry now," she said. "In the morning, I doubtless will be. Go away, now." Zakon scrambled to his feet, backed warily away from her one slow step at a time, fumbling his sword back into its sheath with a shaking hand, feeling for the mace, which had fallen from his belt. But the sight of both Sphinx and warrior made him decide not to press his luck. When he was beyond the light of the torches and Gabrielle's fire, he turned and fled. Coarse laughter followed him.

Gabrielle came up to begin working the knots free. The Sphinx watched in silence, but as Xena shook out her right hand and scooped up her sword, the creature rose and stretched massively. Great wings unfurled briefly, then folded back to her tawny sides. "Most amusing," she repeated. She looked beyond Xena to Gabrielle, who was coiling the length of rope. "I hope tomorrow's contest is half so amusing. Don't forget—sunrise, three from you two, three from me, best two of three. And one of you returns to Athens to tell the story. My—ah—choice," she added, and bared very white teeth.

Gabrielle swallowed, then put on a smile. "How could I possibly forget? I'm looking forward to this—what a terrific contest it's gonna be!" Xena was eyeing her curiously; she kept her eyes on the Sphinx as the creature turned and sauntered up the road. Her guard backed partway up the road, then turned and followed her. Silence. The Sphinx reached the crest of the road and vanished from sight.

"I'm almost afraid to ask what she meant by that," Xena said finally. Gabrielle started, blinked, and smiled at her.

"Oh, nothing much, really. Maybe I can tell you about it later. After you eat. Soup's probably ready."

Xena's smile didn't reach her eyes. "Maybe you can tell me *while* I eat. I'd like to know what I'm facing tomorrow, if you don't mind."

"Facing—well, sure. Thing is, I'm absolutely starving, and I wager you worked up quite an appetite. The soup's hot, but it won't be that good once it cools off, or if it overcooks—"

Xena sighed loudly, silencing her. "Tell me after we eat. Make it good, too," she added, as she shoved her sword into its sheath, and headed toward the fire.

10

The soup was hot and just cooked, but it wasn't that good. Gabrielle apologized several times until Xena finally cleared her throat ominously. "It's better than mine would be," the warrior said, then drained her bowl with one long swallow. Ixos followed her example.

"Fills the empty spot and it's warm; good enough for me."

Homer dropped his empty wooden bowl on the heated rocks surrounding the fire. "Told you I wasn't fussy," he said with a faint smile. "No anchovies, and better than anything my father ever cooked."

Atalanta, who had been picking at hers, shoved the bowl aside with a little smile. "It's—it's fine, honest. I'm just not—not very hungry." She jumped to her feet, swayed, and sat again, rather suddenly, her face paler than normal. Ixos sighed and edged next to her. He put the bowl back in her hands, and said, "Come on, now, you eat. Just a little more. You haven't had anything all day, have you? Don't bother to lie to old Papa, I know how you are." His voice faded to a whisper. Atalanta eyed the bowl with misgivings and Ixos with irritation, but she finally nodded and began to drink the broth. "Vegetables, too," he said quietly. "A few of them, at least."

Xena looked away from the pair. Her eyes met Gabrielle's; her mouth quirked. "You had a story for me—if that's all the soup there is."

Gabrielle gave a nervous little smile and turned away to check the pot. "Actually, there's a little broth left, and a couple bits of that hard bread." For answer, the warrior held out her bowl. Gabrielle emptied the pot into it, then dropped three pieces of dark bread on top of the watery meal. "Sorry it's so tasteless," she added. Xena chopped a hand in her direction for silence.

"We did that part already. Several times. You weren't expecting to feed us two nights in a row, but it doesn't matter, you came up with something to fill the need. And the stomach." She fished one of the bits of soggy bread partway out of the liquid; it folded limply, part broke off and dropped into the bowl with a splash. She shrugged, ate the remaining bit and licked her fingers, drained the bowl in one long swallow, then leveled a hand at Gabrielle. "And don't try to distract me," she said as she set the bowl aside and leaned forward to shove sticks into the blaze. "You made a deal with her this afternoon—I know that much. I'd like to know what you set up, since it might affect what I do. And, just possibly, what the rest of us do." Mild reproof was in her voice, but her eyes gave away nothing.

Gabrielle dropped the empty bowls into the empty pot, then spread her arms in a broad shrug. "We didn't really do *that* much; just—well, if it's a riddle contest, then obviously Homer and I are the ones who should be challenging her, right? So since we're the ones on the front line, we should set up the way the contest is run, shouldn't we?

I mean, Atalanta doesn't particularly want to face off with her, Ixos would probably rather pass, *you* keep telling me you don't do riddles—''

"Just tell me, Gabrielle," Xena broke in. Gabrielle sighed, very faintly, and told her, with an occasional prompt from Homer. "Great," the warrior said finally. "Just great. You know, I think I should have a say in whether you get named catch of the day."

"Catch of—hey, that's funny," Gabrielle applauded her. The smile slipped. "Almost funny. Well, under other circumstances, it would be. But I told Homer the same thing; no one's gonna get eaten! Not me, not him." Atalanta made an unhappy little noise and set her soup bowl down with finality, then turned her back on them all. "She especially isn't gonna eat *you*, Atalanta," Gabrielle added soothingly. "She said you're much too thin."

"No, I'm not," the huntress mumbled. Ixos murmured something against her ear; the other three stared at her in astonishment. Gabrielle shook herself, blinked, and went on.

"We worked things out. I've got a stake in all this, too, you know; I'm not gonna make a mistake with *that* as the result if I do."

"Gabrielle," Xena said with hard-held patience, "she eats people. You're standing close enough to exchange riddles with her, she gets mad, you're history. All right?"

"I tried to tell her that," Homer said gloomily. "Who knows, maybe she'll eat me instead."

"You?" Gabrielle asked in surprise. "You didn't see the way she was looking at you while I was talking to her."

"Looking—at me?" His voice soared into descant range. Gabrielle laughed quietly and patted his knee. "It wasn't that kind of hunger, trust me; the body and the appetite might be lion, but the mind—well, I bet she never

185

saw a clean, cute young bard in all her life before now. I mean, usually the kind of travelers you get on a back road like this—''

"We get the idea, Gabrielle," Xena said dryly. Homer had gone red to his ears.

Gabrielle patted Homer's knee again and went on. "Well, she may not normally act like an honorable being, but I appealed to that. Trust me, she's got it in her. An honorable being who helped set the rules of a riddle contest for fame and glory wouldn't ruin things by—''

"Polishing off the competition. I hope you're right," Xena said hurriedly. "So. You have the riddles worked out?" Gabrielle shook her head. "You've got what's left of the night," the warrior reminded her crisply, "and you're gonna need some sleep if you want to be able to answer whatever she throws at you. *If* you can."

"Oh, I'm not worried about *her* riddles," Gabrielle replied cheerfully. "She hasn't got much of an imagination, and she might be an immortal and pretty impressive to look at, but basically, she's just your average local girl. I mean, she obviously knows some of the creation myths fairly well, and some of the stuff about plants and animals, that sort of thing. But she'd never heard of King Theseus, and as far as she knows, Helen's currently redecorating the palace in Sparta for Menelaus and entertaining his guests." Silence. Xena frowned, shook her head. Gabrielle elaborated. "She has absolutely no idea what's going on outside her own little world here."

"I—I didn't realize this afternoon," Homer broke in. "That's—that's inspired, Gabrielle! All that talk, I thought maybe you were just nervous, or maybe trying to impress her, and—and here you were, testing her knowledge and she didn't even realize—!"

"Thank you," Gabrielle said modestly, but she was grinning widely as she glanced at Xena, and her cheeks were turning pink. "Now, what this means is, we can give her one riddle like yours about rain, something to make her feel like we're a couple of prize fools. Lead her on."

Xena eased to her feet and picked up the soup pot. "Go ahead and work things out; as you reminded me, I don't do riddles. This pot needs to soak. Think I'll walk down the road and get some water." She bent down to shove another stick in the fire and put her mouth close to Gabrielle's ear. "Keep talking just like you are, but don't give anything else away. We've got company," she said softly, then stepped out into the darkness.

Behind her, Gabrielle stared blankly at Homer, for one rare moment completely at a loss for words. But he had heard the warrior's warning. He thought fast, then nodded and said, "Fine, that's a good idea, Gabrielle. I think maybe you should ask her the one about the legs: you know, four, then two, then three. And maybe after that—" He chattered on, giving Gabrielle time to recover and help him out. Atalanta was staring at both of them as if they'd gone mad.

Quickly Xena walked toward the small spill of water. Just short of it, she slipped off the road into deep shadow, set the pot down and ran light-footedly into the trees, then worked quickly back toward the fire in a wide half-circle. As she'd suspected, there was someone—two someones, actually—crouched behind an enormous oak not ten paces from the fire. Both were listening so intently to the babbling of Gabrielle and Homer that neither was aware they had company until too late. Xena caught one up by his shirt and the other by the neck of his armor, and slammed them together. Foreheads collided with a nasty crack, and the two men fell unconscious with a loud thump.

Gabrielle was on her feet in an instant; Atalanta scrambled about on her knees, feeling for the weapons that had been taken from her. She swore as she remembered, and watched with anger-black eyes as Xena dragged first one unconscious brute, then the other, into the firelight. One man, a fattish, grimy creature in leather pants and filthy wool shirt, was too dazed to move. The other, the one in armor—a small-boned, dark, seam-faced specimen missing one earlobe—groaned and tried to sit up. Xena gave him a shove, sending him flat once more. "I wonder where *you* came from," she remarked. "And why." As he tried to speak, she shook her head. "Doesn't matter. You're not going anywhere until very late tomorrow. If you're lucky, it won't be across the Styx. Gabrielle, help me bind and gag them and settle them against that tree over there."

"She'll miss us," the little man spat. "And she'll blame you."

"What a shame," Xena replied softly. "And if you feel like it, you can tell her all about how you were stupid enough to get caught eavesdropping—after we're gone tomorrow." She grabbed him by the shoulders, and when he tried to pull away from her, swore and clipped him across the chin. He groaned and slid bonelessly to the ground. "Here, Gabrielle, you take this one," she said, and went for the bulky man in the leather pants and wool shirt. Both women were gone for some time, and when they came back to the fire, Xena scowled at her hands and wiped them on the grass. "All right," she said. "We're clear for the moment. Keep your voices down, though. And don't take all night."

"You said that," Gabrielle reminded her, then turned back to Homer. "So, anyway, what we have to do is lead her on, get her overconfident, then hit her with one she'll never guess. And I'm gonna need help on that." He eased next to her; Gabrielle lowered her voice even more.

• • •

Ixos seemed to be asleep—or at least resting. Atalanta was staring at the bowl of soup; if she'd eaten any more of it, it couldn't have been much. By now it had to be stone cold anyway. Xena sat down next to her, took the bowl from her before it slid from nervous fingers, and quietly said, "It's all right, I just want to talk. They're planning; we need to do some of that, too."

"Plan—you've seen one of *my* plans," the huntress replied bitterly.

"I saw it. It was complex enough to please a maze builder, and it might have come off just the way you intended," Xena told her. "You can plan just fine. Leave a little more room for things to happen that weren't supposed to, and you'll be even better. And stick with plans that don't involve scaring little girls."

"I'm too scared even to think," Atalanta said frankly. "And I'm trying hard not to be, mostly for his sake." Her eyes fixed broodingly on the old hunter, who was breathing heavily, his brow furrowed. "He's not young, and he's not a warrior. And I'm—I'm all he has now. If he thinks he has to worry about me, he won't be watching out for himself. I can't lose both of them—Neneron and Ixos were all I ever had, the only people I could tell anything to. That I could trust." She glanced at the warrior, then away again. "I'm so scared, I don't even care that you know."

"You don't look that frightened. Tell me, though, why are you so—so odd about food and eating?" Atalanta stared at her, her face blank. "I saw him trying to coax you to swallow some of that soup: it was bland; could've used salt and maybe some herb, but it wasn't that bad. You were fighting him every inch of the way, and you looked at it like it was meat gone bad. I've seen people pass out from lack of food before—the way you almost did just now. Same thing with my trail sticks last night; they aren't great, but there's nothing offensive about them.'' Silence. Atalanta wouldn't look at her. "People don't eat, they die," Xena said finally. "I can't imagine why you'd be trying to starve yourself to death. It strikes me as an uncomfortable and slow way to go."

"I eat enough," Atalanta replied resentfully. "And it's not your business."

"It wouldn't be, and I wouldn't ask, if I didn't need your help tomorrow." There was a long silence; Atalanta glanced up at her, then away once again; her shoulders were tense, and she seemed to be waiting for the other woman to give up and go away. Xena simply waited.

Finally the huntress eased away from Ixos a little more and said, "He asks me that, too. It's—it's not a problem. I eat enough. More than I should, probably. Even the goddess can't help me win races if I'm fat."

"You're not fat. I can't imagine how you'd ever become fat. You don't eat enough to keep a butterfly alive. And you're so thin, I can count your ribs right through that chiton, when the wind's right." Silence. "I can't think what good it does you or anyone else, picking at your food that way so you can stay too thin."

"I don't starve myself!" Atalanta snapped. She glanced toward Gabrielle and Homer, then at the sleeping Ixos, who stirred, then was still again. "All right, I'm not—not huge. Like a woman I saw in the Athens market two days ago, sitting outside a tinsmith's—I don't look at myself reflected in a lake and see that. One of the women in my father's village used to nag at me about that, but it's not true! I'm just—when you do what I do, you have to be careful not to let the weight sneak onto you. Suddenly, there you are, the size of that woman outside the tinsmith's, and it's too late."

"Weight couldn't sneak onto you if it had a god's blessing,'' Xena broke in. ''Not the way you eat. Slender isn't so bad if you don't have to fight for it. Thin like you are is—'' She hesitated, looking for the right word. Atalanta snorted inelegantly.

''I'm slender. That means long and lean and lacking in curve, and there's nothing wrong with it! And it's what people expect: I'm a runner, a huntress—a virgin huntress, is the way they put it. Like Artemis and Athena. A chubby huntress—they'd laugh at me. I wouldn't dare show my face *or* my body in public ever again.''

''That's it?'' Xena asked after a moment. Her eyebrows went up. ''Image? You starve yourself—for image?''

''I do not starve myself,'' the huntress said between gritted teeth. ''I just—I just don't *need* to be any bigger than I am. People—''

Xena eyed her own arms, held them out. Smooth muscle rippled under sun-bronzed skin. She shrugged. ''People by and large don't really care that much about anything outside themselves and those closest to them—like family. Most people wouldn't notice if you had two eyes on one side of your nose, if you were saving them from peril or death. They're like that.''

''Maybe that's one of the big differences between us,'' Atalanta mumbled. ''They expect it of *me*.'' Silence. Ixos groaned faintly and rolled onto his side. Atalanta leaned forward to tug his cloak down over his knees and up to his chin.

Xena stirred. ''You don't want to let other people tell you who you are, do you? Besides, you need meat on your bones—muscle. You know—muscle? The stuff you use to draw bows, fight, track game, hunt down frightened, stolen girls. The stuff you need if you want to hunt and run with the big boys.'' Another silence. Atalanta eyed her sidelong, then turned back to gaze broodingly on the sleeping Ixos.

191

Xena continued, "If I ate like you do, that one-armed goon would've made stew meat of me. Not a very heroic way to go, is it?"

"Not really," the huntress admitted. She turned a suspicious look on her companion. "Why are you doing this—talking to me like this? I mean, you don't owe me anything; you don't even like me."

"You're right. Mostly because of what happened the last time we met. We got off on the wrong foot, and besides, we aren't much alike," Xena said. "Probably if we were ordinary people, we wouldn't have cared for each other. But I don't like a lot of people, so you're likely in good company." She considered this a moment, pausing to choose her next words with care. This was the wrong moment to anger the huntress or alienate her by saying the wrong thing. "But those little girls up there on the hill—they like you. A lot. I was watching them at the races: their faces, the way they gazed at you when you first came onto the sand, that short yellow chiton, your hair, everything. They'd been waiting for a golden hero, and you didn't let them down one bit. I watched the way some of them ran after that, just knowing you were there; I saw how gracefully a few of them ran after they'd watched your first race with their young hearts in their eyes. They were copying you, trying to do what you do. That's what you want, isn't it?"

"No. Not just—blind worship, hero worship for no reason," Atalanta said. "That's—it's embarrassing."

Xena cast a swift glance over her shoulder toward Gabrielle and Homer, who sat, heads together, giggling over something. *I know, better than you'll ever suspect, runner. She didn't stay like that very long, but Gabrielle was one of those when I first met her. I thought I was angry at the time, whenever she tried to talk to me. Maybe some of it*

192

was anger, but I wasn't really angry with her—at events around me, sure. Maybe a little at myself, though. Because Atalanta's right, that much blind, mindless adoration is embarrassing. No one could ever be good enough to live up to that. Still— "Blind hero worship goes with the lifestyle," she said finally. "And eventually, some of them will grow out of it; they'll give up on hero worship, or on you, or they'll come to see you for what you really are—what you could become, if you try, I mean—and their love will matter to you more. But that's beside the point. For some of those girls out on that beach, you were more than just a famous face and a short chiton that let you run without obstacle. You were someone who'd beaten tremendous odds to do what you wanted to do with your life. You're a grown young woman, and you still race despite the age rules. You hunt. I heard one or two of the girls arguing with their mothers that there wasn't any good reason they couldn't keep running beyond puberty, and they pointed to you as an example. Ask Nausicaa tomorrow, when we get those girls to safety. She's a genuine princess, daughter to a king; she's half-grown; and she's blind from birth. And she's still running. Because of you. You ought to be proud."

"I'm—" Atalanta stared off into the trees. "I never thought of it that way. Ever. It was—always just for me. What I wanted, needed, had to have. Most of the time, it was nice, it made me feel good to be stared at, to hear strangers whisper my name. But all that, that misty-eyed, mindless adoration— As if I were already a hero, without doing anything." Her voice faded.

"You *are* already a hero to Nausicaa, an example she's proud to try to follow." Xena shrugged. "I'm no hero; I just mend things that need to be fixed. When I can. I don't want that kind of lifestyle, or that title. If you do—well,

193

fine. I don't have the right to tell you what you want. And anyway, people need heroes, someone to look up to, to copy until they can find their own way. If they ever do. At least to make their own lives seem better, or just to give them pleasure, the way you did on that beach when you ran. You can't just take one part of it and reject the rest; you can't fake it. You can't—'' she shrugged. ''I'm not good with words, that's Gabrielle's job. But real heroes don't do what they do for gain, or for glory, or for fame. It's just how they have to be.'' She got to her feet. ''Think about it. Maybe you don't have that in you, and maybe I'm stupid, giving you the chance to find it. It's something you'll have to decide.'' She went over to feed the dying fire, then picked up a bulky bundle next to Gabrielle's bag and brought it back, setting it at the huntress's feet. Her weapons. ''Keep an eye on things here for us; I'm going out to make sure we don't have more company and to get some more wood.''

Atalanta gazed down at the pile of weaponry, then fished out her dagger belt and the two blades. By the time she looked up to thank her the warrior was already striding into the night. The huntress bit her lip, then got to her feet and walked over to the fire. Gabrielle looked up; her eyes fixed on the tall woman's face, then the weapons belt. She smiled and edged closer to Homer to make room for the huntress. Atalanta flushed, smiled back, and sat down. ''I thought maybe I could be—maybe a little use,'' she managed finally. ''I know you've got everything planned out but— just in case the Sphinx doesn't play by the rules or something, if I can be some sort of help—'' Her voice trailed off; she swallowed.

''That's great,'' Gabrielle said warmly. ''If Xena's already approved of you, who'm I to say no?'' A wave of her hand took in the restored daggers. ''And—well, you know," she lowered her voice and glanced carefully around before going on, "I *hate* to admit to Xena that something I work out could have problems; when she plans things, hardly anything ever goes wrong. But, well, this time, there's a lot at stake. And you're right, the Sphinx hasn't got a particularly stable personality, has she?"

"She's not known for it," Atalanta said. The corner of her mouth quirked as Gabrielle laughed and clapped her hands together.

"And for good reason, too. I thought that stupid Cyclops was over the edge the first time I met him. Well, he's a novice in comparison to the Sphinx. But—yeah. Xena may have some other ideas, or something else might come up, but I'd say you should make it your job to keep an eye on those girls."

"What if she doesn't bring them out?"

"Oh, she'll have to," Gabrielle said with assurance. "Or there won't be a contest. Because how could we be sure there was—" She sobered abruptly and bit her lip.

"Was anything to contest for," Homer put in quietly. He turned and smiled so warmly at Atalanta that the huntress blinked, then turned away to hide her sudden confusion and rapidly beating heart. "We'll find a way to make the girls part of the deal, so we can see them at all times. So—"

Atalanta swallowed, then turned back. "So I'll be able to keep a close eye on them. That'll help?"

"Well," Gabrielle said. "Think about it. If the guard decides to move them off somewhere, or if the Sphinx decides she's not gonna play by our rules anymore, you might have a better chance of getting to them and getting them away. I mean, you're fast on your feet and you're good with javelins and arrows, right?" Atalanta nodded. "It shouldn't come to that, but if it does, then—well, we're lucky we've got you along." Atalanta cast her a sidelong, unhappy look, but when she would have said something, Gabrielle shook her head and laid a hand on her arm. "That's behind us, remember? Forget about it; concentrate on getting the girls away from here. Any way we can. But with a little luck, it's all gonna fall on these riddles, and I still say there's no way she can beat *us*." She stifled a yawn with the back of one hand. "We'd probably better plan on taking turns on watch, but I think I'm ready to fall asleep where I sit. Once we work out the last riddle, of course," she added, casting Homer an anxious look.

"You've got my suggestions," he said gloomily.

"Well, they're good ones," Gabrielle said at once. "But just obscure enough that she'd cry foul and we'd have a hard time proving we hadn't tried to trick her." She yawned again, and this time Atalanta yawned in chorus.

"If you tr—if you need me to help with the watches, wake me," she said, and yawned again. "I'm going to go get a little sleep now, while I can."

"Good idea," Gabrielle said. She watched Atalanta wander over next to Ixos, unfurl the boarskin cape and pull it over her shoulders, then drop down next to the old man. "What we *need*," she said finally, "is something everyone knows about—even those brutes up there guarding the pass—so if she tries to cry foul, it won't hold up."

"Hmmm." Homer cast a wary glance toward the dark woods just beyond the firelight and murmured, close to her ear, "Wood gives under me. I eat more than the Sphinx—than the Cyclops." He broke off, then shook his head and resumed, "Lighter than daybreak. Poseidon breaks my spell."

"Ahhhhhh—" Gabrielle closed her eyes and wrinkled her nose in concentration. "Good—maybe better than my choice for the second. And everyone knows the substance. But she'll guess fire pretty quickly, don't you think?"

"*You* did," Homer mumbled. Gabrielle eyed him side-long and smiled.

"I'd say the honors were about even. Something really big," she muttered to herself. "And famous—or at least well-known."

"Got it," came a quiet voice from just behind and above her, Gabrielle jumped, turned, and cast Xena what she hoped was a chill look.

"You're doing it on purpose, I swear," she accused. "I thought I'd apologized for that mess on the wrong side of Athens."

"You did. And I accepted." Xena grinned, then dropped down cross-legged next to her. She leaned over to murmur against her friend's ear. Gabrielle's eyes went wide.

"No! Wait—wait! If we—I mean, if—yes!" she said exultantly. "That's it, exactly!" She cast Xena an accusing look. "And you said you don't do riddles!"

"I don't. I do survival—and this seems to qualify. I certainly don't cast riddles into verse; that's your job, yours and his." She cast a warning glance toward the woods. "Quietly, please," she added in an undertone. "There's no one out there, I've checked; but she might have her own means of eavesdropping. She's immortal, remember."

"Nice," Gabrielle exclaimed sourly. "I'll sleep really well after that."

"Go try," the warrior said. "I'll take first watch." But the girl shook her head; a frazzled braid flopped across her shoulder, and she shoved it impatiently over her back.

"*You* go sleep," Gabrielle said. "And I'll wake you up in an hour. We have to get this done now, or I won't be able to close my eyes." She smiled nervously. "Not that I don't expect everything to go just fine," she added.

Xena tugged at the braid and smiled back. "It will. We'll make sure it does. Every one of us."

11

The morning, when it dawned, was already warm, the wind stilled, the sky a brilliant blue. Sunlight touched the tips of the tallest trees, but shadow still lay dark across the lower road when Gabrielle struggled to her feet and rubbed her eyes. She stretched hard, then stepped into the open; Xena was a motionless figure in the gloom, her gaze fixed on the pass. As her young companion came up, she turned to offer her a smile, then gestured with her head. "Get yourself awake, and wake up the others. I think the party's about to start."

"Huh?" Gabrielle squinted up the road. A handful of men had assembled at the high point, and as the sun slid down long, rough trunks and laid their shadows across the road, the enormous, tawny figure of the Sphinx paced slowly into view. She stood very still for a long moment, staring down the road, then collapsed, catlike, onto her side. Xena glanced over her shoulder once more. Gabrielle was kneeling next to the cold fire pit, shaking Homer's shoulder. Just beyond him, Atalanta was awake and checking her weapons, shoving the case of javelins onto her shoulder and settling the quiver in place. Ixos gazed at her unhappily; by the look of things, he was trying to tell her something, but she wasn't listening. *Typical,* the warrior thought. *Hope she listened to some of what I said last night.*

She turned back to study the road, the trees on either side, the ledge above the Sphinx. No one along the road or on it, save the ragged little company at the top, and no one visible along the ledge. Anyone could be back in the trees, or just down from the crest, out of sight, though. *Play it safe; you don't know how many men the creature actually has.* Might have been better to question one of those men last night. Well, there wasn't time now. It didn't really matter, anyway. A full army would take a lot of feeding and plenty of room; the Sphinx didn't strike her as someone who'd want to be bothered with things like that.

Footsteps on the road brought her around: Gabrielle and Homer came up, Atalanta just behind them with Ixos—a very worried-looking Ixos—at her side. "Well, ready when you are," Gabrielle said brightly, but with worried eyes. Homer merely nodded; he was pale, and the hands he stuffed under his cloak trembled.

"Go on, then," Xena said. "I'll be right behind you. Atalanta, stay farther back with Ixos, just in case they try something like those two did last night. Keep your eyes and ears open." She glanced at the two of them. "Ixos, go take whatever weapons you need from those two men we tied up last night; they won't be needing them. Ixos nodded and went. Xena's eyes moved to Atalanta's face. The huntress loosened both daggers in their sheaths. "All right?" Xena asked finally. "You've got it?"

"Right," Atalanta replied crisply. Xena waited until Ixos came back, a bow in one hand, a fistful of arrows in the other.

"Don't look like a visible threat if you can help it,"

Xena added as the older man knelt to string the bow. "We want her to know we're here, but we don't want to antagonize her. At least not yet."

"Got it." The huntress nodded once, then strode across the road and vanished in the shadows. Ixos scooped up the bow and arrows and followed.

Xena turned back, laid one hand on Gabrielle's shoulder, the other on Homer's. "Be careful."

Gabrielle forced a smile. "I was about to say the same thing to you." She took Homer's hand and started up the road.

The Sphinx was thoughtfully examining the claws on her left paw as they came near. She met Gabrielle's eyes, then Homer's, finally looked beyond them to Xena, who stood twenty or so paces back. "The other two," she rumbled. "Where?"

"Cleaning up camp," Gabrielle said promptly. "We don't want to leave a mess in your neighborhood. I—ah—don't see the girls," she added in a casual voice. "If we're going to do this the right way, you know, we have a right to see them. Make certain they're all right."

"I suppose," the Sphinx replied; she sounded and looked bored. *Playacting,* Gabrielle thought. Not a bad job of it, either. Lots of practice, probably. "Bring!" the Sphinx shouted. Her voice echoed, painfully sharp and loud in the narrow cleft, and Gabrielle clapped her hands to her ears. An answering shout came from high above moments later, and the Sphinx gestured vaguely with one very sharp claw. "There. All right?"

Gabrielle shaded her eyes, staring up the stone wall. Morning sun momentarily defeated her, but Homer pointed to a spot partway down from the crest. Two large men in full armor and closed helmets flanked six girls tied together at the waist. "I see them. Everyone all right, up there?"

she yelled. Someone sobbed, but Mitradia's voice silenced her.

"We're—we're fine!" she shouted back. "Honestly!"

"Great!" Gabrielle yelled. "We're working on getting you out of here!"

"Riddles first," the Sphinx reminded her pointedly, then resumed the scrutiny of her claws.

"Right. But, if you really don't mind, I'd like to run through the rules again, just one more time," Gabrielle said. As the Sphinx glared at her, she stuttered, "I mean, you wouldn't want me—I mean, we've got this all set up. I don't want to make a mistake and invalidate the results."

"Rules." The creature made a curse of the word. "Three riddles, one from me, then from you, then from me, then from—we *set* the rules. You aren't that stupid," she added angrily. "You're stalling! You know I'll beat you!"

"Very likely. But just in case you don't win—in case we get lucky or something—then we win in the girls, alive, whole, and just like they are now. Right?" Gabrielle said firmly. She met the Sphinx's cold gaze, managed a nervous smile. "And if you win—"

"When," the Sphinx interrupted her.

"Whatever! Then you—ah—get your choice of— Well, fine, we did set the rules, didn't we?"

"No backing out," the Sphinx warned. "Or trying to run once you've lost. I don't like it when my lunch runs; in fact, I dislike it enough to eat the feet first."

"I get the idea," Gabrielle broke in. "And we're bards. We have to follow a code of honor, so there's no way we'd do anything like that. Right, Homer?"

He swallowed past a very dry throat, then nodded and managed a small smile for the creature towering above him. To his surprise, the Sphinx's rather pale human face went pink across its vast cheekbones. *Maybe Gabrielle was right.*

Well, can it hurt? "And the code of honor is very strict about breaking your word to the greater immortal beings, especially the ones who're so—well," he eyed her sidelong, "so impressively built." He *wasn't* imagining it; the Sphinx simpered at him, then caught Gabrielle eyeing her speculatively and promptly straightened her face.

"Besides," Gabrielle said, "this kind of thing, it's like swearing a sacred oath, and you know what happens when you break a sacred oath." She spread her arms wide, nearly flattening Homer, let her head fall back, and declaimed in a dramatic and echoing voice: "Oh, holiest of all the Muses, beloved Calliope, let the hair fall from my head, and the fingers drop from my hands—or the claws, of course—let my eyes melt and my tongue—!"

"I get the idea," the Sphinx interrupted her hastily. "Sacred oath—fine. You'll get the girls if you win." A smug smile twisted her generous mouth. "You won't—but it's nice for people to think they have a chance."

"My feeling exactly," Gabrielle assured her.

"It's really very kind of you," Homer said. "Especially since I've never—well, I've led a very sheltered life. I never expected to meet anyone like you."

"Riddles," the Sphinx said, almost purring the word. "Me first," she added, tapping the ground with one claw thoughtfully. "What goes on four legs in the morning—"

"Ah, excuse me," Gabrielle broke in. It was hard indeed to meet the Sphinx's formidable glare. "I don't imagine you like being interrupted, but honestly, it wouldn't be fair of us to let you use that one, because everyone knows it."

"Everyone?"

Gabrielle shrugged. "Oedipus has a big mouth. If you need a few minutes to come up with a new one, I don't want you to feel like you're under any pressure or anything."

"I know *plenty* of riddles," the Sphinx replied haughtily, and went back to tapping the ground with one sharp nail. Gabrielle could feel the road shuddering beneath her feet. "All right.

> I move and yet journey not at all,
> I wear down the mighty,
> Yet a thin disk controls me. What am I?"

Homer stared at her, mouth open in astonishment. Gabrielle eased over to press down on his toe.

"You *are* good," she told the creature, and turned to give Homer a warning look. He mouthed "all right" soundlessly, and she looked up at the Sphinx, who was waiting with ill-concealed impatience. "You don't mind if we talk this one over, do you? I can see it's going to be quite a contest."

"Feel free," the Sphinx replied haughtily, and turned her head to inspect a patch of sun-warmed fur on her right flank. Gabrielle looked swiftly back down the road, gave Xena a quick smile and a thumbs-up; a corner of the warrior's mouth twisted before she sent her eyes back to their study of the men closest to the Sphinx, the woods on either side of the road, the girls on the cliff face.

"We know that one!" Homer breathed against Gabrielle's ear. "It's—"

"I know," Gabrielle murmured in reply. "Stall; make her feel good about herself. She might get angry if we guess too quickly. Look worried," she added, and drew her own brows together. A quick glance to her left showed her the Sphinx was engrossed in whatever she was doing to her flank with one enormous paw. *What flea would have the nerve to land on her?*

A long silence. Only when the Sphinx turned back to

face them and finally cleared her throat did Homer look up, an anxious expression on his face. "Well, I *think*—I don't know, it's only a guess. Is—is it the tide? Ocean tide?"

The Sphinx let her chin down on her forepaws and eyed them broodingly. "Impressive," she said finally. "Ask!"

"All right," Gabrielle said. "Ah—Homer, why don't you put yours to her first?"

"Well—of course. I'd be honored." He drew himself up and went into declamatory mode. The Sphinx's dark, bored gaze had taken on an entirely different appearance as he began to speak. Gabrielle thought, *I knew I was right about her.* But he had barely finished the first verse when the Sphinx interrupted him.

"That's wind, of course," she said casually.

"Excellent." Homer applauded her. He glanced at Gabrielle. "I told you she'd be a wonderful opponent, didn't I? All right—your turn."

"Wait," the Sphinx said. "There's no point for so many men to stand out here with me. It's nearly midday, and if they are to eat tonight, they need to go find plunder."

"Well—you know," Gabrielle said doubtfully, "I hate not to just take your word for something like this, but—I don't suppose you'd care if my warrior back there came up here to watch them go, and—not that *you* would break your word, or anything!" she added hastily. "But you know how it is when you're hiring swordsmen for duty in a place like this. You don't always get good quality."

One of the soldiers swore under his breath and took two steps forward; a look from the Sphinx stopped him in his tracks. "It's a valid point," she said thoughtfully. "Not much choice in the quality of riffraff."

Gabrielle clapped her hands and laughed. "D'you mind if I quote that? Assuming we get out of here alive, of course!"

"Feel free, bard," the Sphinx said, and for the moment, at least, she almost seemed to be in a good mood. *Probably deliriously happy, for a Sphinx.* "All right," the creature added magnanimously. "Let your warrior come up to make certain they hold to our bargain."

"Hey," one of the other men grumbled, "that's Xena! I ain't lettin' her—"

"You do as I say, when I say, and how I say," the Sphinx reminded him, "or you know what you are." Silence. Gabrielle motioned for Xena to join them, and succinctly—for her—explained the latest addition to the bargain. Xena merely nodded and moved up the road, stopping just over the crest so she could watch the rapidly retreating dozen or so men move down the road and across a narrow bridge. After several long moments, she nodded once, then returned.

"Everything all right?" she asked Gabrielle.

"Everything's fine," Gabrielle assured her.

"Good. Then—would any of you mind if I went back down to camp? I haven't finished my breakfast, and I'd like a drink of water."

The Sphinx dismissed her with an impatient wave of her paw. "My turn," she said as Xena strode off.

"Concealed from stars, my heart of stone
Will echo your loudest cry."

"Ah—ah—" Gabrielle ran a hand through her hair. "You know, you really *are* good! Same thing as last time, all right?"

"Take your time," the Sphinx purred. A glance overhead assured her the girls were still in place: the guards sat now, the girls sitting or sprawled out between them. The warrior was well down the road, near the spot they'd cho-

206

sen for camping. The other two: well, one was old enough to be no threat to anyone, and as for that skinny virgin huntress—the smallest of her men could break the shameless creature in half without much effort. *Haven't seen so much bare skin since I asked a riddle of that armsman bathing in the stream back yonder.*

It probably didn't matter much to the outcome, but it was nice to know where people were.

Xena gestured, just a small jerk of her arm in front of her body, where it would be shielded from the Sphinx's gaze; Atalanta came into the road to join her. "Don't look like we're talking about anything but what's for breakfast. She's probably watching us, and she's got good eyes."

"All right." The huntress set one hand on her hip, ran the other through her hair as though untangling the previous night's snarls.

"Good. She's sent most of her men down the road to forage—or pillage, more likely. There are only two I can see up there with the girls."

"There *are* only two," Atalanta said. "Ixos and I went up that side of the road. The ledge is a little higher over there, so we could look right down on the girls and all the way down the back slope to their camp."

"Good. What's the ground like over there?"

"Not very many trees, but a lot of big stones and boulders. Some brush." She sent her gaze casually across the road, across the riddlers, and then, very briefly, above them. "It's not that steep."

"Fine."

"You think—?"

"I'd prefer to have the girls in *our* hands while all this is going on," Xena said evenly. "Even if the Sphinx is honorable about this contest, I wouldn't trust those men as far as I could spit them.''

"Got it—I think," Homer said. "Could it be—a cave?" The Sphinx snorted inelegantly, finally nodded. "I can't believe what a pleasure this is," Homer went on. "Having a real opponent, I mean. If—I only hope I live to tell the story of this day. It'll be such a challenge to get it all right. The combination of strength, glorious golden fur, such beauty." At his side, Gabrielle held her breath. *Don't lay it on so thick, you fool!* she thought. A low, throaty chuckle was the Sphinx's only response.

"All right," Xena said. "I'm gonna do like last night— take the pot, go for water. I told her I was thirsty, after all. Then we can—" She stiffened as one of the men she'd flattened the night before yelled and charged out of the woods, sword upraised. "Great," she mumbled, snapping the chakram free and sending it into flight. The morning sun lapsed into flashes of golden light as the ancient weapon slashed its way through the air. The man seemed barely to feel the deadly, furtive touch of the disk on his neck before he fell, and the chakram returned easily to her hand.

"Nice," Atalanta said mildly. She swore under her breath and leaped the bank, then darted into the woods. A deep curse and then a yelp of pain, followed by a solid, meaty thump as the second man fell, hard. The huntress went to one knee to check the pulse in his throat, then got up again. Xena shoved the chakram back into place and beckoned to Ixos to follow her into the camp.

Back up the road, it was Gabrielle's turn to shift into bardic voice:

"A bird swoops by in hurried flight
And steals the sun's eternal light.
Beware this brazen fire thief
(round as an egg, thin as a leaf).
Don't get too near, or she will bite!"

The Sphinx was quiet for some moments, her eyes idly resting on the road and the two conversing in the distance. She stiffened as Xena turned and threw her weapon; her eyes narrowed as it came back into the warrior's hand. "Mmmmm. Of course. That round throwing thing." Gabrielle blinked up at her; the girl's mouth hung open in blank astonishment. "That—*her* round throwing thing," the Sphinx added, gesturing down the road. Gabrielle turned to look, watched Xena fix the lethal little device in place and sighed. "A chakram," she said, with another little sigh.

Homer looked puzzled at the Sphinx, momentarily; he patted her shoulder, then, and gravely said, "Bless you."

Back down the road, in the woods beyond the rough camp, Xena stood and brushed dirt from her knees; the two unconscious thugs were tied to separate trees, well apart. "They won't get loose *this* time," she said grimly.

"You can't think of everything," Ixos said quietly.

"Maybe not. All right," she added briskly, turning to face Atalanta, who was testing her arrow shafts and dropping them one at a time back into the quiver. "You ready?"

The huntress shoved the last of them in place, pulled the strung bow over her shoulder, and got to her feet. "Ready," she said, then turned to point into the woods, at a narrow opening between two huge oaks. "They came that way. Their trace leads back in the direction we want to go, and it's not a trail. Good enough?''

''Good enough,'' Xena said tersely. ''Remember, we keep this *quiet*.''

''Just like those two,'' Atalanta replied, and gestured toward the unconscious men with her chin; her hands were full of javelins. She bundled them together, then fitted them into the case hanging from her belt. ''You leading, or am I?''

''You're the tracker,'' Xena said softly. Atalanta glanced sharply in her direction, but there was no malice in the warrior's face. ''You lead.''

''Right. Papa, come help me,'' Atalanta said. ''You still see things I don't.'' The older man patted her shoulder awkwardly as he moved to join her, then stepped aside to let her pass through the oaks. Xena gave the two unconscious men one last hard look, then checked the clearing for shadows. Late enough. Even Gabrielle might not be able to stall the third riddle much longer.

High on the pass, the sun shone almost straight down. Gabrielle blotted her forehead and cleared her throat. ''Boy, all this contest stuff sure does work up an appetite. I don't suppose you'd want to—'' At her side, Homer hissed something urgently. The Sphinx smiled; it wasn't a pleasant smile. ''Ah—right. Sorry for asking!''

''We can—*some* of us can eat after the contest is finished,'' the creature told her ominously.

''Sure. In all the excitement, I just plain forgot.'' She blotted damp palms on her skirt. ''So—you have your final riddle for us?''

''Oh,'' the Sphinx purred. ''I certainly have.

> When olden days were not yet old,
> The goddess raised her sword of gold.

Full many men have met that blade
With weapons sharp, of iron made,
To earn their keep. But none has e'er
Defeated yet that goddess fair.
For iron is hard and gold is soft,
And still she holds her blade aloft
Each year, and comes again to wield
Her sword on last year's battlefield.''

"Oh, good one!" Homer applauded. To Gabrielle, he looked honestly pleased by it. *I might be pleased with it, too—later, once we figure out the answer,* she thought gloomily. The Sphinx dimpled at him and waved a paw.

"Take your time," she said. Homer nodded and turned his back, gesturing urgently to Gabrielle.

"So?" she whispered. "You've got it, right?"

"Are you kidding?" he demanded under his breath. "It's a multiparter—those are *terrible* unless you can find the key to some bit of it. Wait—let me think." He buried his face in his hands, fingers tapping nervously against his brow. "Wait." He looked at her again, and his eyes were alight. "Sword of gold. Holds her blade aloft—it's grass—*no!*—wheat!"

"Of course," Gabrielle hissed. "There's a scroll I saw somewhere, I forget, Demeter was called the goddess with the golden blade! Battlefield—''

"Wheat field," Homer replied at once. "And men harvest the wheat each year, but it comes back the next. Ah—you want to give her some more time on this?"

"As much as we can," Gabrielle whispered. "Don't look now, but there's no one on the road down there. Xena's up to something, and it's up to us to keep *her* amused in the meantime."

"Great," Homer mumbled. He cast a wary eye at the

Sphinx, who was picking at her teeth with one claw. "Ah—we need a little more time, if you don't mind, my lady!"

"Take what you need," the Sphinx told him with a warm smile.

She wasn't smiling some time later when Homer finally laid their answer out; shadows were starting to crawl down the road, and the air was still and thick. "All right," she said at last. "Your final riddle. And if I guess it—?"

"Well!" Gabrielle managed. "I guess we have to have one more each, to break the tie. That's the way it's usually done," she added.

"More riddles," the Sphinx said thoughtfully. "It's been an entertaining day, better than most I can recall. I will almost regret eating one of you."

"Well, that makes us even, I guess," Gabrielle said. "Because one of us will most certainly regret being eaten. Homer, why don't you give the lady our last?"

But before he could speak, one of the Sphinx's guards—the captain, by the badges on his shoulder and on his hat, though he wasn't any cleaner or better clad than the others who'd blocked the road earlier—arrived. "Begging your pardon, ma'am," he said with a low bow. "They've got a meal going down there, want to know if you'll want your share set aside as usual, and if they should make something special for the little girls, like last night?"

"It may not be needed," the Sphinx replied grandly. "Wait here. It shouldn't take long, and you can carry my answer back." She turned a warm eye on Homer, who managed a warm smile in reply. "Go ahead," she ordered.

Homer squeezed Gabrielle's fingers, swallowed hard, then shifted into bardic voice:

> "The ancient giant from the East
> Was slain by man, and slain by beast,

And laid to rest upon his pyre.
To feed a ravenous desire,
He'd swallowed a woman whole (a thing
that pleased a prince, but not a king).
Then, feeling hungry still, he tried
To swallow a horse—and thus he died.''

He bowed low, and when he straightened again, the
Sphinx was staring at him, wide-eyed. "I had a more simple riddle planned," he said modestly. "But after the wonder you presented us, I would have been shamed to give
you any less than the greatest riddle I know."

"Mmmmm." The Sphinx's eyes closed, and her chin
dropped to her paws. The grubby, ill-attired captain at her
side rolled his eyes and sighed—very quietly. He took a
step back, a second, and moved his hands. Gabrielle looked
up in time to see one of the soldiers guarding the girls
repeat the gesture. Swords out, the two pulled the girls to
their feet and began a slow retreat up the ledge, back out
of sight over the crest.

Well up the slope above the pass, Atalanta lay stomach-
down between two black boulders, hidden in deep, dry
grass, eyes fixed on the two armsmen holding the girls. As
she watched, one of them stood and gazed down to the road
below, then moved his hands in a quick pattern—not hunters' pattern, nothing she could translate, but there was no
need. The two men were pulling the girls back from the
edge, moving toward their camp, perhaps. She turned to let
Ixos know—two swift movements of fingers and hands suf-
ficed for that—before locating Xena so she could edge back
and tell her what was happening. But the warrior was nowhere in sight.

• • •

"Got it!" the Sphinx shouted. "I—wait. No." She mumbled to herself and sank into thought once more. Not too deeply, however; as the captain at her side began to move cautiously away from her, she came alert and glared down at him. "I said you were to wait," she said sternly. "You know the penalty for disobedience." The man went white to his lips; he nodded. The Sphinx turned away from him, let her eyes close, and started mumbling to herself again. Homer's face was slick with perspiration, his eyes worried. *Probably the mirror of my own*, Gabrielle thought tiredly.

No Xena anywhere. *She has no business*—Atalanta thought angrily, then shook her head, hauled bow and quiver from her shoulder, and leaped to her feet. Nothing mattered but getting control of those girls before those men could get any farther away with them. Already they were below the ledge that overlooked the road. *Sound won't carry that way—not very well,* she realized, and charged between the tall boulders, deftly snagging two blue-shafted and fletched arrows from the quiver as she ran. One of the girls saw her first; she gasped, and both men guarding them turned, a girl in front of each, a sword to her throat. Mitradia was one of them. Atalanta skidded to a halt, her hands a blur as she fitted the specially cut arrows to the string, sighted swiftly, and let fly one and then the other. Mitradia tugged free of the startled man holding her and threw herself flat, but there was no need: the arrow would have missed the top of her head by at least a hand's width. It buried itself in the throat of the Sphinx's guard; less than a startled breath later, the second man fell, mortally wounded in exactly the same place.

Mitradia snatched at the fallen guard's dagger and cut herself and Nausicaa free of the others, handed the blade to the girl beyond Nausicaa, and, drawing the princess with her, ran to the huntress. "We knew you would come," she said, and her eyes were shining. "We knew you would do it somehow."

"Thank you." Nausicaa's voice was very soft; her eyes fixed vacantly on a spot just beyond the huntress's left ear. "My father will be grateful; I'm sure he will reward you."

"Please," Atalanta said quietly, "I don't want any reward. Just—finding you alive and well is reward enough." *It's true,* she realized with something of a shock. *How— how odd.* She let her bow and quiver fall, and wrapped an arm around each of the girls. "Let's go help your companions, and get out of here, shall we?"

Behind her, Ixos came forward to gather up his ward's bow and quiver. He turned; Xena had stepped into the open, and her eyes were warm as six young girls enveloped the kneeling Atalanta, who was trying to cut the rope from the last of them. "Warrior," he said softly, "thank you."

Xena shook her head. "Thank *her*. She's the hero." A faint smile touched her mouth. "Now she knows how to do it."

"I have it," the Sphinx announced suddenly. Gabrielle eyed her narrowly.

"You're sure? I mean—an answer's an answer, right? You've had two tries at it and called both hints, and that's fair, but the third time—well, this is either it or it isn't."

"I have it," the Sphinx said firmly. Silence. She drew herself up, wrapped the long lion's tail around her legs, and announced, "Bellerophon!" Gabrielle stared at her open-mouthed. "Well, of course it's Bellerophon," the creature purred. "He was a hero, so they could call him giant; he— well, anyway, it's Bellerophon. You know," she added helpfully, "the one who found Pegasus and fought the Chimera, and—"

"It's a nice answer," Gabrielle said. "But—um—it's not the right one."

"Not? *Not?*" the Sphinx roared. "It has to be! I—all right, what is your answer? And the explanation had better be good," she said ominously.

Homer smiled. "It's Troy." The Sphinx scowled at him. "Troy—Ilios. Where the Trojan War was fought over Queen Helen?"

"Trojan—Troy?" the Sphinx began. Homer waved her to silence, and to Gabrielle's astonishment, the creature sank on her haunches and prepared to listen.

"Troy. Golden Ilios of the straits, across the sea. Once a Hittite colony. Well, I'm sure you aren't interested in history," he added hastily as the creature snorted. "Right on the isthmus, vital trade center. Lots of wealth at stake. I see you aren't much interested in economics, either. All right, King Menelaus went to his grandpa's funeral, and young Prince Paris of Troy took advantage of his guest rights to convince Queen Helen to run away with him. He was small and had a nice smile and pretty curls, and he also had a reputation as someone no girl could say no to. She was bored, her husband was more interested in drinking and hunting and showing her off at parties than in learning anything about her as a person. Menelaus comes home, sees his wife—his property—is gone and puts together an army to flatten Troy's walls. One battle after another, no one makes any headway, and then all at once, the Greeks pull out and leave a huge wooden horse at the gates. The Trojans decide it's a blessing from the gods, pull it in, start partying—and once most of the soldiers are sleeping off the wine and mead, Greek soldiers jump down out of the horse and kill everyone in sight. Troy fell that night."

216

Silence. A long, chill silence. The Sphinx glared down at him; Homer gazed up at her, his face expressionless. "You're—it's an impressive story, but there can't be a word of truth to it," she snarled finally. "The riddle is invalid."

"Beg your pardon, ma'am," the captain at her side mumbled, "but—ah, it's very much true. I was there. I know." The Sphinx transferred her glare to the captain, who shrank back from her. "Swear it is, sure's my name's Patroclus! I wasn't in the horse—I have this horror of enclosed places—but I was outside the gates, one of those ready to charge in and kill as many Trojans as I could once I got inside. And find Helen for the king." He scowled at the Sphinx. "Shows you how *some* treat their armed," he mumbled resentfully. "King sent most of us away once he got home. All those years of fighting, everything, he *still* didn't get her back, and he took out his spleen on us. Not like you, ma'am." Patroclus glanced at the silent, motionless Homer and Gabrielle, then back at the Sphinx. "We got four sheep and a goat down there, and Mannius just sent word that he and his charge got a spare stag. We'll share, happily."

"It wasn't a fair contest," the Sphinx growled. She glared down at Gabrielle, then her gaze shifted farther down the road. "You cheated!" she shouted. In the distance, Atalanta and Ixos urged six frightened girls to greater speed, while Xena drew her sword and her chakram and took up rear guard in the center of the road. "I could just—I'll fly down there. They won't stand a chance!"

"No, you won't," Homer said softly. The Sphinx stuttered to a halt, stared down at him, confused.

"I won't?"

"Of course not. You swore a great oath, and from the first moment I saw you, I knew you were a being of your

217

word. Such a beautiful creature," he added softly, and stepped forward, one hand outheld. "May—may I?" The Sphinx stared at him in confusion; he stroked her nearest paw, then the fur of her shoulder. "No man would ever suspect such soft fur," he whispered. "Such beauty, intelligence—so much honor. You won't break your word. For what?" he added as she shifted; his hand lay against her throat. "Six small, frightened children?"

"Think of it," Gabrielle urged her. "You lost the contest, but only just by a thread. And now you have two bards—the great Homer and myself—to spread the tale of your beauty and your talent. I can't bear to think of you immortalized by Oedipus as a grim, fierce, ugly creature who knows only one stupid riddle and who kills herself in a fury when it's answered."

"He says that of me?" the Sphinx demanded quietly. Her eyes were wide with shock.

"He says it," Homer replied as his fingers kneaded the long tendons on either side of her throat. "But with me and Gabrielle to make him out a liar—"

"Two bards against one adventurer who couldn't tell his mother from a bad dream," Gabrielle assured her. "We can tell the world the truth. And those girls? They're babies. Let them go home and tell the world, with us, how generous the great, immortal Sphinx is."

Silence. The children and the three guarding them were nearly out of sight. The Sphinx turned her head to let her lips brush Homer's fingers. "All right. Go in peace—both of you." Homer bowed low to kiss the Sphinx's near paw, then took Gabrielle's hand and turned to start down the road.

"Show trust," he murmured. Behind them, he could hear rustling noises as the Sphinx levered herself upright, and his back ached with the certainty of his immediate death. But her voice came, then.

"A stag, Patroclus? You know—I find, these days, I like the taste of stag better than human."

"All to yourself, ma'am," the guard replied grandly. "All to yourself."

Epilogue

Midafternoon. A strong breeze came from the sea, blowing dust across the square before the Athens Academy for Performing Bards. Gabrielle sat on the edge of the dressed stone pool, anxious eyes fixed on the gates. They opened, and Homer came out, looked around, and moved to sit next to her. An embarrassed silence held for some moments.

Gabrielle tugged at blue-green cloth finally. "Changed your tunic, I see," she said.

He smiled. "I can't believe how wonderful it is to be clean again. I—just want you to know, a part of me will always envy you, Gabrielle. Living your tales as you compose them. I—guess I'm better suited to finding them and finding a way to retell them."

"There's nothing wrong with that," Gabrielle protested. "Maybe I live a story—like the last battle for Troy—but then someone else comes along—like you—and finds a way to make it *matter* to people. To lots of people. That's at least as important as sleeping in the mud and expecting to die at any moment. All right?"

He gazed down at her, finally smiled, a playful gleam in

his eye. "All right. I guess Docenios thinks the same way, because he said he wasn't going to report me to my father as a truant. He's going to call it fieldwork, even though I'm not supposed to be doing fieldwork for another two years."

"Oh, Homer," Gabrielle murmured; one hand cupped his beardless cheek. "I'm going to miss you."

"I'll miss you, too," he said very softly. Silence. They gazed at each other, and finally he set one hand under her chin and bent down to lay a gentle kiss on her mouth.

"I wish," she began, then shook her head. "It just wouldn't work, would it? I—Xena means so much to me. You do, too, but it's different. And I tried, once, for the Academy. I couldn't give up the traveling, the hardships— whatever it is, I have to be *out* there, learning things first-hand."

"That's good," he said quietly. "And I'm happiest here—I know that now; I tried your way, and it isn't for me. What I do best is take the stories others bring me and make them real in a way that—that maybe you wouldn't have seen at the time."

She smiled, then set her lips against his for a very long moment. "Good-bye, Homer. I'll see you again. Soon, I hope." She blinked as Vision suddenly reasserted itself. "Don't forget, I think it's important. Catalog of ships."

"I won't forget. Good-bye, Gabrielle." He stood to watch her go: a slender, golden-haired, almost childlike figure—incongruous in Amazon brown. *Who would think it?* Behind him the Academy loomed, its stone walls familiar— a haven—a home.

Down at the Athens docks, Atalanta turned to extend a hand; the fingers trembled. Xena shrugged, took the hand, and held it firmly. "You'll be fine. Trust me, you're doing the right thing. Just like you've done since you pulled those girls from that ledge.

"You tricked me, vanishing like that," Atalanta complained, but her eyes were warm.

"It had to matter to you; you had to see what counted. I was there, close enough to fix things if you couldn't handle the pressure," Xena said. "You did fine."

"Those poor children," Atalanta whispered. "I—if their parents don't understand, don't help them—"

"Most of them do. Gabrielle talked to the girls last night, after you fell asleep." She raised an eyebrow; the huntress grinned abashedly.

"I was tired," she said. "And sending Ixos back to his cabin—I didn't think I'd ever convince him. But he'd be lost on a ship, and I really don't think he'd like Colchis. He's not fond of mutton, you know."

"Go," Xena said, and gripped the other woman's fingers, hard. "Don't forget to eat occasionally," she added dryly. Atalanta shook her head.

"That's not an easy promise to keep. I'll—try." She looked beyond the warrior, and Xena turned. Arachne stood, her color high and a green-covered bundle between her outstretched hands. Though it had been only a few days, it seemed like months ago that they had all met on the beach for a simple footrace.

"I—Gabrielle said you'd be here on the docks. I—I brought you this, the work of my hands, to honor what you do with yours," she said shyly. Atalanta took the bundle, and shook it out. Her eyes widened, sought Xena's. The warrior shook her head very slightly. The huntress squared her shoulders, brought her chin up, and gave the weaver a very warm smile.

"How beautiful this is. I'm honored, and blessed, that you should think me worthy. Tell me your name, so when

223

anyone asks whose work this is, I can tell them."

"I—honored huntress, I'm Arachne," the weaver whispered, her eyes wide and adoring. The huntress slipped the cloth over her shoulders, then took the weaver's hands between her own.

"Arachne. If I have any say, your name will be revered for always. Thank you so much."

Moments later, the ship eased away from the docks. Xena offered one final wave, then turned and glanced at the sky. Getting late. Athens would be warming up for the late hours. Time to find Gabrielle, and go.

Very late evening. A sickle of a moon rose over the eastern sea; Xena strode down a broad avenue, Argo's head on her shoulder, Gabrielle prattling happily beside her and skipping occasionally to keep up.

"So," Gabrielle finished, "what's next?"

Xena shrugged. "I don't have anything in mind."

"Me either. Well, except finding something to eat. Do you know," she added indignantly, "I never *did* get any of the meat from that stand on the shoreline?"

"Maybe just as well," Xena murmured. "Someone said this afternoon that half the people who ate there while they were at the races got sick."

Gabrielle snorted. "Wonderful. If you can't trust your nose, what can you trust? Anyway, if you owed me for that boat trip to Ithaca, I don't want to think what I owe you! So what's next?"

"Getting out of Athens," Xena said. "Without getting arrested for some stupid breach of law that wasn't a breach last time I was here. Too many ridiculous, hair-paring rules, and more coming every day. Let's go."

Gabrielle glanced over her shoulder; in the crowded market behind them, someone was yelling furiously about his pilfered purse. "Fine with me."

Summer passed; heat faded, and leaves turned from green to brown. They fell. Spring came to the island kingdom of Phaecia at long last, and Nausicaa, who had grown several fingers' worth, came down to the shore in a splendid car drawn by two high-stepping horses. Her best friend, Mitradia, rode with her, Mitradia directing her hands so the horses went the right way, Mitradia describing the sights. Half a dozen servants and young friends of both girls followed with a cartload of clothing and draperies.

Laundry, Nausicaa thought gloomily. Still—her father was becoming insistent on the proper forms of behavior for maidens, as well as the duties of a princess; he wasn't forbidding her her own ways of carrying out those duties. She pulled back on the reins when Mitradia told her the stream was at hand; the surf in her left ear bore the right pitch and strength of sound to agree with what Mitradia said. Four steps ahead, one short pace to the side. Water within reach, and within hearing. She directed the girls and servants with her to deposit the soiled cloth on the shore, then to take all the cars but her own away. Easier for her and her friends to have fun if they weren't being watched so closely by a bunch of—of dull grown-ups.

The afternoon passed pleasantly; the air was warm, the horrors of a year before—hard hands on her arms; hard, chill, implacable voices against her ear—dissolved in this moment of languid, spicy heat. *There is only the moment,* she told herself. Gabrielle had said that to her. Only the moment. Take the moment, and enjoy it, or learn from it. But don't try to trade it for another moment.

Squeals from those around her. "Mitradia?" she demanded. Of all her friends and servants, only Mitradia had common sense to match her own.

"Oh!" Mitradia's voice was too high, her intonation astonished.

"Tell me," Nausicaa demanded.

"He's—he's unclad!" Well, that would account for the babble of frightened girl voices all around them. "And he's—he's—" Mitradia's voice was no less astonished.

Water splashed not far from her feet. Nausicaa swallowed and stepped forward; warm salt water sloshed around her toes and receded. "Sir, as the only child of King Alcinus, and his heir, I bid you welcome. Whatever travails have held you in the past, there is no trouble here awaiting you. I am Nausicaa."

"Nausicaa," a rough voice whispered. "Nausicaa? Dear child, I do humbly claim the sanctuary you offer in this hour of need. I am your father's friend, home at last after so long a time. I am—Odysseus."